AFTER ALL

EVER AFTER IN SAPPHIRE FALLS

ERIN NICHOLAS

ABOUT AFTER ALL

Big, hot Sapphire Falls cop Scott Hansen, the source of Peyton Wells' dirtiest daydreams, has only one fault...he's crazy about her.

She'll do absolutely anything Scott asks if he obeys three simple rules: they're both naked; there are lots of hands and lips involved; and they absolutely do not call it a relationship. The R word gives her hives. Why can't the guy just be happy with no-strings sex?

Scott knows Peyton didn't exactly grow up with the best role models for strong, healthy relationships. Her dad gave up everything for his mentally-ill wife, including being a real father to his daughter. Now in charge of her own life, Peyton wants a good time devoid of any responsibility for someone else's happiness. But Scott's determined to be the one person in her life to show her that she's worth an effort—even if it means staying out of her bed until she's ready to commit to something as simple as a damned movie date.

But, when Scott's injured on the job, Peyton can't stand the idea of anyone but her playing nurse—and Scott sees the perfect opportunity to show her that a relationship with him can be the best time she's ever had.

But nothing with Peyton is ever easy. After all, he doesn't call her Trouble for nothing...

Copyright 2017 by Erin Nicholas

All Rights Reserved.

No part of this book, with the exception of brief quotations for book reviews or critical articles, may be reproduced or transmitted in any form or by an means, electronic or mechanical, including photocopying, recording, or by any information storage and retrieval system without express written permission from the author.

This is a work of fiction. Names, characters, places, and incidents are the product of the author's imagination or are used fictitiously, and any resemblance to actual persons, living or dead, business establishments, events, or locales is entirely coincidental.

ISBN: 978-0-9988946-9-0

Editors: Kelli Collins

Line Editor: Nanette Sipe

Cover artist: Dana Leah, *Designs by Dana*

First, always, to the Sapphire Falls fans. You're the reason I get to keep coming back to this town! Thank you, thank you!

Also to my family who has fully embraced this crazy life that we have now where I spend as much (or sometimes more) time with imaginary people and the voices in my head. I love you from the bottom of my heart. You really know how to make dreams come true!

And to my team who makes this all happen book after book... in spite of me. Kelli, Nan, Kim, Crystal. Don't know what I'd do without you girls around me!!

1

The lifted hot-pink Chevy with black flames painted on the truck bed rounded the corner a block ahead, and Scott's heart actually thumped a little harder on the next beat. Like a freaking Pavlovian dog.

He was thoroughly and completely screwed.

He'd actually accepted that some time ago. But every once in a while, the realization rose up and hit him right between the eyes. Or right in the chest.

Peyton Wells had him wrapped around her little finger. And she knew it.

He should hate it, he knew. Being enamored with a trouble-maker wasn't a great thing for a cop to be. But this wasn't just any troublemaker. This was Peyton. And frankly, he'd been done from the moment she'd told him to kiss her lily-white ass—which he had already been a little obsessed with—two years ago.

Besides, most of her troublemaking was B.S.

Scott pulled into the parking lot of the Stop, the gas station/convenience store/pizza place/ice cream shop on Main and First. He parked his patrol car and headed inside.

A minute later, from behind his back, he heard, "He must not know."

"That's what I'm thinking."

He turned from the coffee dispenser and his half-full cup to see two of his best friends, Kyle Ames and Derek Wright, watching him from next to the chip display. They'd clearly meant for him to overhear them, based on the huge grins they were wearing.

Those were let's-give-him-hell grins.

"What are you two talkin' about?"

"You just must not have heard the news," Kyle said.

It wasn't uncommon for the town doctor and the main bartender at the only bar in town to know things before Scott did. He might be one of only two cops, but when it came to town gossip, the bar was second only to the Bang and Blow, the hair and nail salon. The third best place in town to get news would be Dottie's Diner. But Kyle's medical clinic waiting room worked too. As far as secrets in this town—well, there weren't any.

"Why do you assume I don't know whatever this is?" he asked, topping off his cup and grabbing four little creamer tubs from the bowl on top of the microwave.

"Because you're in a good mood," Kyle said.

"How do you know?" Scott asked.

"You're whistling and smiling and putting vanilla creamer in your coffee."

Scott tossed the empty creamer tubs into the trash. "Vanilla creamer means a good mood?" Scott asked, amused. "I didn't realize you'd been paying such close attention to me. That's kind of sweet." He took a sip and watched Kyle roll his eyes.

Derek looked from one to the other. "Seriously? He uses vanilla when he's in a good mood?"

"I use vanilla when the hazelnut is out," Scott said. He leaned back on the counter behind him. "What?" he asked when he caught the look Derek was giving him.

"Seems like you should be a black coffee kind of guy," Derek said.

Scott cocked an eyebrow. "You have an issue with how I take my coffee?"

Derek seemed to be thinking about that. "Maybe."

Scott gave a short bark of laughter. "Why?"

"Just seems less tough—our town cop drinking coffee with flavored creamer," Derek said with a shrug. "I might feel less safe now."

"You *should* feel less safe now," Scott agreed. "Disparaging my coffee means a slower response time when you hit 9-1-1." He sipped again.

"You would never do that," Derek said.

Of course not. "Why don't you just shut up about my coffee and you don't have to find out?" Scott asked.

"Lauren Bennett drinks hazelnut in her coffee," Kyle said to Derek. "And I think she could kick your ass. With heels on."

Scott nodded. "That's a good point. I wouldn't base toughness on creamer preference."

Derek glanced around, as if making sure no girls had overheard him. He located the security camera over the ATM and said loudly, "I apologize. That was a stupid thing to say."

Kyle and Scott laughed.

"So what is this big news that I don't know?" Scott asked. Hell, he had time. Until his radio squawked, he didn't have anywhere specific to be. If Kyle didn't have patients waiting and Derek didn't have to be at the bar, it was fine with him if they shot the shit for a while.

"Peyton's fancy girls' weekend," Kyle said, suddenly looking very smug and nearly giddy with being able to tell what he knew.

Scott frowned. Peyton had a girls' weekend almost every

weekend. The girl simply didn't know how to stay home. Of course, he suspected that she pretty much hated being alone. She usually had someone to lay low with—her half-sister Hope, her friend Heather, her friend Tess, her friend Lucy, her friend Brooke. Peyton had a lot of friends. Nearly every woman her age —and even a few several years older—were drawn to her fun, what-the-hell attitude and her penchant for turning anything into a party.

Then again, Hope, Tess and Brooke all had their guys now and probably liked to stay in a lot more—without Peyton—than before. That left Heather.

But at least it was a *girls'* weekend. The ones that involved guys meant Scott had to buy more Rolaids. And beer.

"And her blind date," Derek added.

And Rolaids and beer it was. *Fuck.*

Peyton didn't want a relationship with Scott. She didn't want a relationship with anyone. She did, however, want sex with Scott. And since he wasn't putting out—in a gut-wrenching, dick-torturing effort to show her that he was willing to wait for more— she went out with other guys.

Not as much as she had when he'd first moved back to town. But also more than never.

Scott took another swallow of coffee and tried to decide how to react to this. Kyle and Derek knew how he felt about her, so it wasn't like it would shock them if he reacted badly. Like throwing hot coffee across the Stop, for instance. But since he, Kyle and Derek weren't the only people in the shop, that would also get spread around town like dried-up leaves in the wind, and there was no need for the good people of Sapphire Falls to think their cop had anger issues.

Because he didn't. He had frustration issues.

He had Peyton issues.

"How do you know this?" he asked Kyle.

"She and Heather were in here just a few minutes ago. They were stocking up on road-trip food and talking about it," Kyle said.

"Road-trip food?" Scott asked.

Derek grinned. "That's probably the best part of the story."

Scott straightened. "Tell. It." He used his best don't-fuck-with-me voice. Of course, the three people it did *not* work on were these two, and the woman they were discussing.

"Girls' weekend is in—"

"Oh, let me tell it," Kyle interrupted. "You get ready to catch the brain tissue that comes exploding out of his head."

"No fucking way," Derek said. "You're the doctor, *you* do the brain tissue clean up."

"But I think—"

Scott threw his cup into the wastebasket as he stalked up to the counter. "Gus, where are Peyton and Heather heading?" he asked the eighty-something, best hot-fudge-sundae maker in town behind the counter.

"Baltimore," the older man said.

Scott started to turn to his friends to point out how easy that had been when the word actually fully sank in. He twisted back to Gus. "*Baltimore?*"

Gus nodded.

"Is there a Baltimore, Nebraska, that I don't know about?" Scott asked, already feeling the pounding between his eyes. Peyton caused the blood to pound in his skull as easily as she caused the pounding of blood behind his zipper.

"Nope," Gus said simply. "Maryland."

Scott really did appreciate a man who got to the fucking point. Even if he really hated the fucking point he was getting to.

"Why?" he asked. But this was directed at his friends.

"Wedding. Friend of Heather's needed a date. And then his friend needed a date," Kyle reported dutifully.

"They'll be back Sunday," Derek supplied.

Scott turned and headed for the parking lot. His hand hit the door harder than necessary, but he didn't slow. He yanked his car door open and got behind the wheel. Then he turned on his sirens and headed for the highway.

It wasn't *exactly* an abuse of power to go after Peyton with his lights on. He knew for a fact she'd be speeding. Peyton Wells didn't do anything slow or by the book.

Baltimore? She was going to *Baltimore*? On a blind date? For the weekend? What the ever-living *hell*?

Of course, he couldn't stop her. He wasn't her dad—not that her actual dad had much say in the things she did—or her boyfriend. And not that he'd try to tell her what to do if he *was* her boyfriend. Though she sure as fuck wouldn't be going on a blind date.

But Peyton had never been on a plane. She didn't know her way around a big city like Baltimore. And the last time she'd gone somewhere with Heather, they'd ended up in a Vegas police station being questioned about a jewel theft.

He pressed the pedal harder.

Of course, Peyton hadn't been involved in the jewel theft, but she'd been flirting with the thief all night and he'd used her as a cover. And if she hadn't thrown Scott's name at the cops in Vegas as a character witness, and they hadn't called him, Scott might have never known about all of that. But she *had* given his name, and he had immediately gotten on a plane to Vegas. Or as immediate as anyone could get on a plane from Sapphire Falls. Unless you were in local millionaire Levi Spencer's inner circle, you had to drive to Omaha, get through security and wait the obligatory hour plus to board a plane.

Scott inched the speedometer up a little further. She'd been on the highway for about fifteen minutes, unless they'd stopped somewhere else after the gas station before hitting the road. It would take him a little bit to get to her. Still, it was a long way to Omaha. He'd catch her before she got there.

He radioed Ed, the other cop in Sapphire Falls, and let him know he was taking care of a personal matter and that Ed would have to cover things for a while.

Finally, Scott saw the rear end of that hot-pink trunk that always made his heart stutter. It happened again, but this time because that truck really was heading in the direction of the airport...where Peyton would be flying out to be some other guy's date for the weekend. A blind date. Someone she didn't even know. In a city hundreds of miles away. And Scott didn't really want to go to Baltimore when she called to say she was in trouble. He would, of course, but he didn't want to.

As Peyton's brake lights flashed, he knew she'd be pissed he was pulling her over. But he didn't care. He'd clocked her at sixty-five on the fifty-five-mile-per-hour highway, for one thing. And for another—*what the hell*?

"Well, of course." Peyton scowled at the rearview mirror where red and blue lights flashed.

"Were you speeding?" asked Heather, her best friend and the reason for this last-minute trip to the airport.

"I wasn't going fast *enough* apparently," Peyton muttered as she made sure to signal—because Scott would give her hell for that too—and pulled onto the side of the road. Yeah, she knew exactly who was behind her. In spite of being outside of his jurisdiction. He'd give her some explanation about how, as a police officer, everywhere was his jurisdiction if someone was breaking the law.

"What?" Heather asked. "What's going on?"

"You can't get new shoelaces in Sapphire Falls without

everyone knowing what color they are," Peyton said. "You really think you and I are heading to *Baltimore* without anyone knowing?" And, as the town cop, Scott was always only about five minutes away from knowing all of her business.

The last man she wanted to see at the moment appeared at the driver's side window.

Good lord, the man was gorgeous. And his ticked-off, you're-pushing-me face always made her tingle. He was most definitely wearing that now.

Peyton rolled down her window and made sure to sigh heavily. She hadn't actually expected him to chase her down, but she wasn't exactly shocked either.

"Miss Wells, I need to have a word with you."

Oh yeah, and then there was the deep, firm voice. She was sure there was some complicated psychological reason why Scott using that tone gave her goose bumps, but all she knew for sure was that it most definitely did.

"I'm sorry, Officer Hansen," Peyton said, "but we're on our way to the airport. Don't want to miss our flight."

"So I hear." Scott reached for the door handle, pulled it open, and gestured for Peyton to get out.

"You know that I could turn you in for abuse of power," Peyton said, but she slid off the seat to the ground.

"I'll give you my supervisor's number after we talk," Scott told her, slamming the door behind her.

Yeah, Scott didn't have a supervisor. Well, maybe the mayor. But that was TJ Bennett. Peyton's brother-in-law. And no way would he take her side over Scott's. TJ was a great guy. He really cared about her and would always have her back. But he also thought Scott was "good for her". Which meant he appreciated and encouraged Scott's always-there-for-her-no-matter-what thing.

Always there for her no matter what. Well, Scott was definitely that. And after twenty years of being more or less left alone—even more than she wanted to be—she thought it was probably normal to oscillate between loving it and getting the heebie-jeebies when it reminded her of her father's unwavering-devotion-to-the-point-of-crazy to her mother.

Scott escorted Peyton to the back of her truck with his big, hot hand around her upper arm.

She worked on hanging on to her annoyance. He was so damned bossy. She wasn't used to being bossed. She was shocked that she liked it. Sometimes.

He stopped in the space between the front of his car and the back of her truck. He planted his hands on his hips and Peyton took a second, as she always did, to appreciate the view.

He was so hot in that uniform. She didn't know if it was the badge or the gun or just the way the whole thing fit... Yes, she did. She'd known cops before Scott. She knew firefighters and guys in the military too. And while she admired them, she didn't find any of them hot the way she found Scott Hansen hot. And that had been *before* he'd pulled his handcuffs out on St. Patrick's Day.

"Knock it off," he told her firmly.

She put her hands on her hips too. "Really? I can't look at you now?"

"Could you put just a tiny bit of contrition in your expression at least?" he asked, with the very familiar you're-trying-my-patience-Peyton tone in his voice.

"Now *there's* a Scrabble-winning word," she said dryly. "What am I supposed to be feeling contrite about?"

"Speeding?"

"You didn't pull me over because I was speeding. That's your excuse for pulling me over. But only because it won't read well on your report that you pulled me over because you think I should have told you about Baltimore but didn't."

She could practically hear his teeth grinding.

"*Baltimore*? Really?"

"Heather needs me."

"And there's a blind date?"

She watched him closely. Ah. This was partly about the trip. Her last trip out of town had ended with Scott coming to her rescue. But this was also about the other guy.

"There's a blind date," she confirmed. Would he tell her not to go? It wouldn't change her plans, but it really might cure her of some of her Scott fever she was suffering from. She was not going to hang out with a guy who thought he could be jealous and controlling. "A friend of a friend," she added. "A wedding. Last-minute change of plans on that end. Heather doing him a favor and I'm doing *her* a favor."

"Do you have your mace?"

She widened her eyes. "My mace? We're going to a wedding."

He handed over a canister of mace he must have been holding all this time. Peyton fought a little grin. It wasn't exactly funny. Scott absolutely meant for her to mace first and ask questions later. But she couldn't help but appreciate that he gave her mace instead of a lecture.

"The big city is different than Sapphire Falls. Even than Vegas," he said.

Okay, so they weren't skipping the lecture entirely. "I know. I'll be with Heather and her friends the whole time. She's *from* there."

"Just be aware of your surroundings. And keep your purse close. And the mace in hand."

"Yes, sir."

For a second his eyes narrowed, and she knew he was trying to figure out if she was being serious or if she was messing with him. She knew he liked when she let him boss her around. But she'd been clear about the fact that that would be a bedroom-only kind of situation.

"What's the guy's name?"

"What guy?"

His frown deepened. "The one with the wedding."

"Oh, Greg. His friend is Seth."

"Last name?" he asked.

"Anderson."

"Is that Greg or Seth?"

"Greg."

"What's Seth's last name?"

She thought. Did she know this answer? She wasn't so sure she did. "Not sure."

"What does Greg do?"

"Lawyer."

"What firm?"

"No idea."

Scott sighed. "And Seth?"

"Oh, he's a cop," she said with a smile. That would have to make him happy.

Scott scowled. "He's a cop?"

"Yeah." Okay, so he didn't look happy.

"I need his last name."

"I don't know it."

Scott gave a low growl and Peyton felt her good places tingle. She loved that growly thing.

"Have Heather text it to me."

"So you can check up on him?" Peyton asked.

"Yes." He didn't even blink.

"Why?"

"So I know where to start the investigation if you end up dead."

Wow. Okay. "Fine."

Scott took a breath through his nose and then let it out. He even unclenched his jaw. "I'm sure you'll be fine. You're smart.

You'll be with people Heather knows. Just...put my number into your phone as ICE."

Oh, crap. She bit her bottom lip. "ICE?" she asked, playing dumb.

"In Case of Emergency. Then, if anything happens, they'll call me first."

"Okay, I'll do that."

"Do it now."

"I'll do it as soon as I'm in the truck."

"Peyton, do it now."

He reached for her—or rather, her back pocket, where she always tucked her phone. She carried a purse, but it was a big bag with only one center pocket, and she was always digging around to find things. He'd lectured her about that before, claiming that while she was rummaging in her bag, someone could come up and grab her. She knew he was being overprotective and she hadn't changed bags, but she *had* taken to putting her phone in her pocket.

Scott's fingers slid into her back pocket and pulled her phone out, while she tried to pretend to be annoyed...instead of on the verge of sighing. She loved his hands on her and loved when he got close enough she could smell him. "Hey," she protested. Kind of.

He swiped his thumb over the screen and pulled up her contacts. "Nice password," he muttered. "Maybe you should do something other than your birthday?"

"How's some strange guy in a dark alley in Baltimore gonna know my birthday?" she asked. And loving that Scott did know her birthday. And then trying not to love that quite so much. So what? He knew her birthday. He probably just remembered from those few months when he'd busted up parties before she'd turned twenty-one.

Scott scowled at her. "Maybe from the driver's license in the purse he stole from you first or that he pulls off of your shoulder while he has you at gunpoint?"

Well...shit.

"You already have an ICE in here," he said a moment later.

"Yeah, I know." She crossed her arms.

"Hope?" he asked, but then he must have opened it, because he lifted his head. "Me?"

Yeah, so he was already her ICE. Big deal. She sighed. "Hope's got TJ, and is going to have the baby. She doesn't need anyone else putting her down as her contact person."

Scott cleared his throat, but Peyton couldn't look at him directly. Fuck, she really would have preferred to have him find that out when she was unconscious in a ditch somewhere or something.

But yes, Scott was her emergency contact in her phone. And on her employment paperwork at the bakery. Not that she thought anything bad was going to happen there, but there had been a blank line that needed a name and phone number.

He'd given her his personal cell number the first time he'd been called to intervene in a "Peyton issue" as David Stuart, the high school principal, had referred to the situation. She'd been twenty and drunk off her ass and had punched Jeff Little in the face in the high school parking lot after a football game because he'd called her friend Jen a slut. Scott had been the one to pull her off of Jeff. When he'd dropped her off at home, he'd told her to call him anytime she needed something.

So, as she'd done with everything interesting at that age, she'd tested it out. Or rather, she'd tested Scott. Over and over. Of course she had. No one had ever said to call anytime, and actually meant it, in her life. Her friends said they'd be there for her, but their parents sometimes had something to say about that. She'd had teachers say she could depend on them, but her English teacher with a husband and four kids wasn't going to get out of bed at three a.m. and come untangle whatever Peyton had gotten into.

She knew that. She knew that everyone else had families and things to do that had nothing to do with Peyton, and that she shouldn't interrupt or mess up. Hell, her own parents had things they didn't want her to interrupt or mess up.

But Scott—he didn't have a wife and kids, he lived to work, hell, he got *paid* to come bail her out. She'd figured she was making his job in quiet little Sapphire Falls interesting. She was doing *him* a favor. And yeah, okay, it had felt nice to have someone show up again and again and again.

Sure, some of the time he was pissed at her, and sure, a few times he'd taken her down to the jail and made her sit in a cell until she'd calmed down. But he was always there. No matter what she'd done, what time it was, where she was, or who she was with.

And now, a few years, some insight, and a bit of maturity later, and she was torn between the soft, warm, fuzzy feelings that still gave her...and regretting all of it. Because this pattern was exactly the reason why they couldn't be more than what they were right now—two people who wanted to tear each other's clothes off, who got off on challenging each other, who could make the other fume or laugh with only a few carefully chosen words. And who could never be more than that. The pattern was set. The habit was established. The imbalance was deeply ingrained. Scott gave. And Peyton took.

And even as she recognized, and hated, that she was a taker, she couldn't quite break herself of it entirely with Scott. Because if she did, they wouldn't have anything at all. And she wasn't quite mature and insightful enough to let him go completely.

At least not yet.

So she kept writing his name and number down and just

prayed no one would ever need to use them so he wouldn't find out.

Well, now he knew.

Suddenly he stepped forward and grabbed her by the wrist, jerking her forward.

She knew what he was doing. He was testing her self-defense moves. That he'd taught her. He did this stupid thing periodically. She grabbed his thumb and pulled back on it, stepping close. "Don't make me knee you in the balls or head butt you," she said.

"But that's what you would do," he said firmly.

"Yes." Damn right she'd knee a guy in the balls if he grabbed her like that. Except Scott.

"Don't forget it," he said.

"I won't." They were practically nose to nose.

"And don't forget to let me know when you get there. And when you're home."

"Okay." She stared into his deep green eyes, swirling with emotions.

Damn, this guy. He was something. When she was trying to have a good time, he was a real pain. But when she was alone at night, or feeling unwanted or unsure, she thought of Scott and how much he seemed to like her in spite of all the shit she'd done. The hard time she'd given him. The stupid decisions she'd made. Her pathetic attempts to get her dad's attention with her stunts.

Scott still claimed to want her—not for sex, but for more. Whatever that entailed.

"And just—" His voice was low and gruff. "—don't forget this either."

He cupped the back of her head and pulled her in for a kiss. A *kiss*. The kind she'd been craving since St. Patrick's Day.

He kissed her, lips only, like he was drinking her in. Then he deepened it, his tongue stroking hot and bold against hers. Then he pulled her fully up against his body, his fingers tightening in her hair, the kiss taking on an urgency.

Finally he pulled back, his eyes dark.

Her entire body hummed with want and an aching need that she knew could only be relieved by this man. The one who wouldn't touch her breast if she *begged* him. Unless she went to the movies with him and let him tell everyone she was his girlfriend.

Peyton covered her face with her hands and gave a loud, "Argh!"

"And slow the hell down the rest of the way to Omaha," he said, stepping back, seemingly unaffected by her frustration.

She took a deep breath and held out her hand. He put her phone in it and she tucked it into her back pocket. Then she turned and headed for her truck.

"I want to know when you get there," he called after her.

She lifted a hand in acknowledgement but didn't look back. Because then he'd see that she was still feeling that kiss.

"I mean it, Peyton."

She waved again.

"And no jail cells this trip, okay?" He paused. "And *no* handcuffs."

She almost laughed at that. Scott knew she had a thing about his handcuffs. So Seth being a cop was getting to him.

Good.

2

I t wasn't as if he wasn't often grateful to be the cop in a quiet little town where not much exciting happened, but on the day that Peyton decided to fly off to Baltimore with Heather for an impromptu girls' weekend/blind date, he would have been happy to have little more to do than cruise the streets, stop in at the businesses, and do paperwork.

He was finally winding up his shift, looking forward to stopping in at the Come Again with Kyle and Derek for an hour or so, and wondering why in the fuck Peyton hadn't texted to tell him she was safely on the ground in Baltimore. He was also going through all of the things he was going to do if he didn't hear from her in the next thirty minutes, including calling the Baltimore PD and getting on a plane himself. He turned the corner at Main and First, headed for the bar, but noticed Hope Bennett's car at the pump at the gas station. He pulled in.

"Hey, Hope." Scott took the gas nozzle from her and inserted it into her gas tank.

"Hi, Scott." She grinned up at him. Her blonde hair was so

light that the pink tips she put in showed up vividly under the fluorescent lights overhead. "Thanks."

"Where's your big, strapping husband? Shouldn't he be filling your car?"

"He's in the field," she said. "And I've been putting gas in my own car for a long time now." But her smile assured him she knew he was kidding.

TJ Bennett was not only Sapphire Fall's mayor, but he was also a local farmer with several hundred acres who worked his ass off. As did all of the farmers here. Scott had grown up here in farm country, but he hadn't really appreciated the hours and the work it took until he'd gotten older. He knew that was one of the reasons he loved it here—hard-working, honest people who did the right thing and helped each other out deserved to have their peaceful, friendly way of life protected. Hell, the rest of the world could take some love-your-neighbor-as-yourself lessons from Sapphire Falls.

"How are you feeling?" he asked.

"Big as a barn and excited and terrified," Hope said with a light laugh.

Scott smiled back and was hit by a streak of jealousy for TJ. Not because Scott wanted Hope, but because Scott wanted what Hope had given TJ—and vice versa. Hope had come to town, essentially a gypsy. She'd been intent on seeing the country from the seat of a tiny yellow Fiat, pulling a tiny one-person camper behind. She'd lost her mother and had decided to live one summer the way her mother had—with her whole heart, open to new experiences and people, with no rules.

She'd ended up in Sapphire Falls—one of her mother's old haunts and favorite places—met TJ Bennett her first day, and the rest was history. And a really great love story.

And while here, she'd met Peyton, the half-sister she hadn't even known she'd had.

"Soon right?" Scott asked.

Hope ran a hand over her belly. "Very soon."

"And you don't know if it's a boy or a girl?" Scott asked.

"Nope. Total surprise."

"How about names?" Scott asked, as the pump clicked off, indicating the tank was full. "Anything picked out."

Hope gave him a smile. "You can just ask me about Peyton, Scott."

Well, so much for being interested in something other than his own concerns. Scott ran a hand through his hair. "Have you heard from her?"

"Since she texted me that she was on her way to Baltimore with Heather a few hours ago?" Hope asked. "No."

"She should have landed over an hour ago," he said.

Hope nodded. "Probably."

"That doesn't concern you?"

Hope laughed. "No. But then I didn't tell her to check in."

"Why not?"

Hope lifted a brow. "Because she's a grown woman and I don't need to know where she is every second of the day."

Scott blew out a breath. Yeah, okay. "What if there was a problem?"

"Scott," Hope said, patiently. "In the past three years, when has Peyton ever had a problem that you *didn't* get called about?"

Well, there might have been two or three but...yeah, she had a point. "So you think she'll call if there's an issue rather than calling because things are fine."

"I think that she's in a big city with her girlfriend and they're probably having fun, and yes, I know she'll call you if there are any issues."

Hope was right. He was overreacting. But what was fucking new about that when it came to Peyton?

You know," Hope went on. "It's possible she's not calling you on purpose."

"To drive me crazy?" Scott asked.

Hope laughed. "Actually no. She's trying to...not just need you."

Scott frowned. "Not *just* need me?"

"I think she'd rather not need you at all, actually," Hope told him.

He felt his frown deepen. "Why not?" Peyton needing him was one of the things he most looked forward to. The woman could handle herself. She could deal with anything. She was fierce and strong and loyal and just about everyone in town owed her a favor. That she called him...yeah, pathetically, it made him feel important. "Because of Dan and Jo?"

Hope opened her mouth, then shut it.

Scott nodded. "She says I remind her of Dan sometimes." He kept his tone devoid of his dislike for the other man. Dan was Hope's father too, after all.

It didn't look like him reminding Peyton of Dan was news to Hope, judging by her expression.

"She's told you this?" he asked.

"Peyton doesn't have many thoughts and feelings she doesn't express," Hope said, almost apologetically.

Well, he couldn't disagree with that. When Peyton was pissed, you knew it. When she was hurt by her dad, you knew it. When she thought you were smothering her, you knew it.

"And she thinks she's like JoEllen," Hope added. "And there is nothing that Peyton wants to avoid more than being like her mother."

Peyton's mom was sick. She had, evidently, been diagnosed as bipolar when Peyton was very young. But it wasn't her mental illness that Peyton hated, Scott knew. It was the way that JoEllen used it to control her husband. And how Dan used it as an excuse to focus everything in his life on Jo. She was a manipulator and Dan was an enabler. Everyone in town knew it. Everyone in town *saw* it. It was no big secret. But it had kept them both from being parents to Peyton. She'd been Sapphire Falls' charity case as a little girl, and then on her own as soon as she was old enough to be. Or as soon as she was old enough to no longer want to be pitied.

The whole thing made it very difficult for Scott to be nice to her parents when he ran into them around town. And he didn't think he was the only one who felt that way.

"Peyton's nothing like Jo," he said. "She's strong and independent and totally focused on her friends and the people she cares about."

Hope nodded. "I think so too. But when she was a kid, Peyton saw Jo's manipulations and problems as a way of getting Dan's attention. So Peyton used the same tactics. She got into trouble, caused problems, *needed* Dan to come get her and clean up her messes. It's an old, bad habit, and she was using it when she met you too. She pushed her boundaries with you over and over for a long time."

Scott couldn't deny any of that. "But she's grown up."

Hope shrugged. "I'm not the one who has to believe that. She is."

"And she thinks me being there for her is similar to how Dan's made JoEllen the center of his entire universe at the expense of everything else?"

But even as he said it out loud, Scott groaned internally. Peyton was *not* his whole life. But okay, she did take up a lot of his time and energy and thoughts and...

"Fuck," he muttered.

Hope laughed lightly. "Listen, personally, I love having someone so enamored with her."

"Don't use words like enamored," he said. "I have a feeling that would make her break out in hives."

Hope looked vastly amused. "I think you're right."

"And you think that's why she's not calling or texting? Because she doesn't want to be needy?"

Hope nodded. "I do. And maybe in an attempt to not be on your mind all the time."

"It doesn't work that way," he said. "It's not like I only feel that way when I hear her name or see her."

"I know."

"And she'll never understand that? Or understand that it's okay?" he asked, feeling a stupid sense of desperation and wishing like hell he could hold it back. But there was something about Hope Bennett that made a person feel comfortable being totally open. Even about things they hadn't been totally open about with anyone else. Even themselves. But yeah, he was fucking *afraid* that Peyton would never come around.

Hope gave him a sympathetic look and reached out to squeeze his arm. "Maybe you need to need *her* a little bit too."

"Need her?" Hell, he could make a very long list of things he needed from Peyton. And they didn't even all involve her being naked. He needed her to laugh, he needed her to feel safe, he needed her to know she was amazing. He took a deep breath. Okay, not what Hope meant. He knew that. But he wasn't great at needing things for himself.

"Yes," Hope said thoughtfully. "She needs to be needed. She comes to her friends' defenses all the time when someone does something shitty to them, but it's always..."

"Crazy? Over-the-top? More than necessary? Stuff they don't even ask for some of the time?" Scott filled in, some of his frustration bleeding into his words. Peyton was loyal and tough. But it was almost as if she was channeling a shit-ton of rage into standing up for her friends when they'd been slighted.

Huh, Scott thought as that idea went through his head. That was pretty much exactly what she was doing. Like jumping on a plane to Baltimore with Heather at the last minute with very few details. She was doing stuff for people that no one had ever done for her. And then some.

Hope nodded. "I just really think she needs to be needed for more...normal stuff. Everyday stuff."

Everyday stuff. That was what he was fricking trying to do. The woman wouldn't even agree to go to a movie with him. He huffed out a breath. "And I shouldn't be there every time she calls?" Scott asked.

"I think it's great that you're there when she calls," Hope said, shaking her head. "I just don't think that you need to go hunt her down in Baltimore when she *doesn't* call."

"Yeah, okay." That would mean squelching several of his instincts regarding Peyton, but yeah, okay.

Just then, something caught his eye over Hope's shoulder. A group of kids had just entered the square. Which wasn't unusual, exactly. But it was just after seven on a Friday night and those kids were only in sixth grade. And they were huddled around something that they seemed very excited about—and very interested in hiding.

Yep, that was his cue.

Hope noticed his attention had shifted and turned. "What's going on?"

"Need to check on something," he said, nodding in the kids' direction. "Thanks for the talk. And advice."

"Anytime. One last word?"

"Okay."

"Don't give up on her. No one needs to be loved more than Peyton. And no one's going to be tougher to love. But she's also going to be totally worth it."

And that right there grabbed him by the heart and squeezed.

Because Hope was right. And Scott was the man to do it. "I can't promise to walk on eggshells about it," he said.

Hope gave him a bright smile, and Scott figured that right there was how TJ Bennett had fallen ass over boots for her. "Eggshells is the *last* way to be with her."

Yeah, then he had this covered. He absolutely felt like *stomping* into Peyton's life—and heart. No tiptoeing, no being careful. Stubborn, no-nonsense, all-in—that was more his style.

He gave Hope a little hug and then started across the street to the town square.

There was no reason for the kids *not* to be in the square this time of night. It was April, so daylight savings time had kicked in and it was lighter later; it was Friday, so there was no school tomorrow; and hey, hanging out with friends in the heart of Sapphire Falls was the best, at any age. But it didn't hurt to check up on eight eleven and twelve-year-olds oohing and awing over something. If it was a new video game or some great YouTube video, that was one thing. If it was pictures of naked women, alcohol or smokes, he'd have to intervene.

"Hey guys," he called as he hit the grass. He supposed if they ran, he'd also know something was up. All he really needed was to snag Chase Walker. It appeared he was the center of attention. The kid's back was to Scott, but he was wearing his hoodie sweatshirt with WALKER across the back.

"It's *Scott*," he heard one kid whisper loudly.

"Crap, the cop!" said another.

"My dad will *kill* me!" was another response.

Oh, yeah, Scott needed to see whatever this was. "What are you guys—"

Chase swung around just then. He was holding a gun.

Scott stopped. Chase looked scared. Really scared. And a gun in the hands of someone who didn't know how to use it, and was scared, was almost as bad as someone who was aiming it on purpose.

"Chase," Scott said firmly and calmly. "Put it down."

"We're not doin' anything," Chase said quickly, shaking his head back and forth. "I'm just showing them."

"Okay." Scott nodded. Hopefully the damned thing wasn't loaded. "Is it yours?"

Chase nodded. "Got it for my birthday. I'm gonna take classes with MacKenzie and then Dad's going to take me target shooting."

Scott nodded again. MacKenzie Cruise had a shooting range and obstacle course out on her land. She taught shooting with all types of guns, as well as archery. She was even talking with Tucker Bennett about bringing in some competitions and using his dirt bike track and arena as a site.

"And you wanted to show it off to your friends," Scott said. "I get it. But we can't have guns in the square."

Chase looked even more nervous now.

"Does your dad know you took it out?"

Chase shook his head. Yeah, that's what Scott had figured. "Okay, well, you give it to me and I'll take care of it until we can get it back to your dad. You shouldn't have this out without him around. Got it?"

"You can't tell him!" Chase said.

"I have to," Scott said in a tone that left no room for argument. "Bring it over here to me."

Chase glanced back at his friends. The move shifted the gun higher and suddenly there was a loud crack—and then Scott felt a white-hot pain stabbing him in the thigh.

He went to his knees. Son of a bitch, he'd been shot.

"Shit!"

"Oh my God!"

"Did you kill him?"

Those were the shouts he heard first. He gritted his teeth and pressed his hand against the painful spot in his thigh. His hand came away with a lot of blood. It was pulsing under his hand, the blood bright red, and Scott swore. He'd nicked an artery or something. He focused on the kids. He had to get the gun away from Chase before he accidentally shot someone else.

"Chase," he said tightly. "Don't drop it. But set the gun on the ground. Carefully." Of course the fucking thing had been loaded. Of course the safety had been off. *Son of a bitch.* At least the bullet had come for Scott and not one of the kids.

Chase did as he was told, quickly, and then backed away. His face was pale and tears were streaming down his cheeks.

"I'm going to be okay," Scott told him. But he felt like his head was spinning. Shock possibly. Or loss of blood. Fuck.

He fumbled in his pocket and pulled out his phone. He heard Hope's voice next.

"Oh my God, Scott!"

She must have seen what happened or heard the gunshot from across the street.

She knelt beside him, and even with the pain in his leg and the dizziness washing over his mind, he had to wonder how she was going to get back up.

"Don't put yourself into labor," Scott said, trying for lighthearted. But he thought he sounded more like he was trying to talk through a lot of pain.

"If I go now, it's fine. Baby is almost full-term," she told him, clearly also trying for levity. It didn't sound much better from her.

"Call Kyle," Scott said, handing her his phone. Then he lay back on the grass and pressed his hand against his wound. It hurt like a mother, but he had to try to stop some of the bleeding.

The sound of other people thundering toward him registered as he listened to Hope talk to Kyle.

"Scott's been shot. In the thigh. Town square. Just a minute ago."

Short and sweet. That's all Kyle would need. He was at the Come Again with Derek. Literally two blocks away. That was as good as calling 9-1-1. Kyle would get here and the ambulance would be two minutes away. It was parked just on the other side of the square and Derek was one of the EMTs.

Then Hope shifted in beside him. She'd pulled her T-shirt off, leaving her in a silky tank, and was pushing his hand out of the way.

"We need something more than your hand," she told him.

He nodded. She was probably right. She was a nurse. She also did yoga and was into essential oils and herbs and stuff.

"You got any potions on you for this?" he asked.

Did his voice sound funny to everyone else like it did to him?

"To magically heal a gunshot wound?" she asked with a smile. "Sorry."

"How about to kill the pain? I don't want Kyle and Derek to give me shit about being a wuss."

Hope was leaning most of her weight on his leg. It burned, but he knew that whatever was bleeding was going to need a lot of force to stem it. "Well, they'll have to deal with me if they give you any shit," she said. "And remember, I help Kyle out in the clinic. If he gets mouthy with you, I'll book him with patients through lunch for the next week."

Scott laughed. But that also sounded, and felt, weak.

Kyle was kneeling over him a minute later. "Jesus, Scott, you just have to make things dramatic, don't you?" he asked, examining the wound. "*Fuck*," was his assessment a moment later.

Yeah, that wasn't good. But Kyle and Hope and Derek were there. So he was going to be fine.

With that thought, Scott let the darkness that had been threatening at the edges of his consciousness wash over him.

S o, he'd finally figured out how to get Peyton Wells to come to him.

He just had to get shot.

Scott tried to lift a hand to drag it over his face, but found he was pulling a long tube attached to a needle in the back of his hand as he did it. IV. Right.

He used his other hand, scrubbing it over his stubbled jaw and through his hair. He felt like hell. He wasn't in pain—the IV was helping with that—but he was groggy and he fucking hated that.

Especially when he was going to have to deal with Peyton. The woman could make a saint lose his shit. And Scott was no saint. Especially considering how much he was enjoying her being bent over, stowing something in the drawer in the cabinets across from his hospital bed.

But the fact that she was here at all made his pulse pound harder than the sweet curve of her ass in those jeans. She'd come back from Baltimore—fucking Baltimore—because of him.

"Hey, Trouble."

She gasped and whirled, clutching something to her chest. Her brows almost immediately slammed together over the blue eyes that shot sparks that always went straight to Scott's heart. And other places. Lower. Much lower.

"Damn," she muttered.

"Whatteryoudoin'?" Fuck. He was slurring. It was the damned pain meds. And the anesthesia that should be wearing off any damned minute. He hated both.

"Honestly? Wishing you were still unconscious." She tucked her hands behind her back.

Yeah, he had to see what she was holding. "Sorry." He worked on sitting up more fully in the bed. The head of the bed was propped slightly, but he definitely couldn't get a good look at her in his position.

He sucked in a quick breath as his leg moved. *Fuck.* He gritted his teeth and reached for his thigh, moving it with his hand instead of the muscles that had been pierced by the bullet.

"Oh, for God's sake." Peyton was at his side a moment later. "Lie still."

"Wanna siddup." Scott closed his eyes as his tongue refused to articulate his words again.

"Why?"

"So I can see you."

He heard her sigh and felt her move in closer. He opened his eyes and found her leaning on the railing by his arm.

"Here. I'm here."

Her voice was softer now, and Scott wondered if it was the meds that were making her eyes look as if she was actually concerned. Truth be told, there were a few times in the past three years that she probably would have gladly shot him herself. In the leg. Nothing fatal. But still.

"Whaday issit?" he asked.

"Saturday."

"You were in Baltimore," he said, grateful that it at least came out as four separate words this time.

"Yeah. I was."

"When did you come back?"

She sighed. "Last night."

"Right away?"

"Yes. This is a pretty elaborate way to keep me from going on that date," she said.

It was almost as if she was teasing him.

He felt one side of his mouth curl up. "Not sorry."

She gave a soft laugh. "Yeah, well, now that I see you're going to live through this, maybe I'll head back out there. Seth was cute."

The pain meds didn't slow him down a bit when he grabbed her wrist. "No."

She was clearly surprised by his touch too, but she didn't pull away. "I gave a couple bags of blood, brought you more clothes and..." She coughed. "What more do you want?"

"You." That was always the answer.

Peyton shook her head. "Still pushing with a bullet in your leg and major doses of morphine pumping through you?"

"They took the bullet out," he said. "And yeah. Always." So he was feeling a little sappy. It was the drugs. And the fact that she'd flown back from Baltimore. And that she was here. So what? He still meant every word.

Emotion flickered in her eyes at his answer. "The morphine is making you loopy," she said.

He glanced up at the plastic bag dripping overhead. "It's morphine?"

"Yeah. That's what the nurse said when I asked."

Scott focused on her again. "You asked?"

Peyton frowned, as if he'd caught her doing something she didn't want him to know about. "I needed to know how goofy you might be when you woke up."

"Why?"

"Maybe I need to borrow some money."

He shifted on the mattress. He didn't like this position at all. He loved her concern, but he felt pretty damned vulnerable right now. He felt as if his thoughts were slogging through thick mud to get to his mouth. He couldn't move without his leg protesting, and he was in only a hospital gown. As he became more coherent, he also became more and more aware that he was definitely not at his best or strongest. Best and strongest were required for handling Peyton Wells.

"You can have as much as you want," he told her.

She frowned. "Maybe I need to borrow your car."

"Take it."

"Maybe I want to take advantage of you."

She leaned closer and Scott took a big breath of her sweet-and-spicy scent. His body stirred, as usual, and then he shook his head, as usual. "You wouldn't."

"Wouldn't I?" she asked, that not-quite-teasing gleam in her eye. "You know better."

Scott knew that Peyton wanted him. Everyone knew that. Peyton wasn't great at hiding her feelings—good, bad, and everything in between. And she hadn't done one thing to hide how she felt about Scott, from him or anyone else.

But she didn't want dinners and movies and holding hands at hometown football games and parties with their friends at the river, and all of the other things couples did together. And that's why he kept turning her down for the hot sex she offered on a regular basis. And he might be the only person on the planet as stubborn as she was.

Except of course for St. Patrick's Day. But that had been a huge mistake. He never should have given in. For one thing, Peyton thought she'd won. For another, he hadn't been...his best. Jesus, he hated thinking about St. Patrick's Day.

"Of course, I really do like it when you can fully participate," she said.

He saw the heat in her eyes and knew that she was remembering the times that she'd worn him down. St. Patrick's Day might have been the first and only actual sex they'd had, but she'd gotten some kissing and some well-placed stroking over the years in some of his weaker moments.

Yeah, so, he hadn't been able to completely keep her at arm's length. She was persistent. And sexy as hell. And the woman he wanted more than he'd ever wanted anyone else in his life.

"So, fine. I don't need anything," she said. "I just came to check on you."

He still held her wrist, so when she tried to straighten, she couldn't get too far away. He tugged and she leaned in again. "You came to check on me from Baltimore?"

She nodded.

"You left that poor blind date sad and alone?"

"Well, he was with Heather."

"But he got a good look at you? Talked to you for a little bit?" Scott asked.

"Yeah."

"And he knows that you came rushing back here for me?" Okay, so he apparently had the capacity to be a jealous ass when it came to Peyton.

She lifted a brow but said, "Yes, he knows I came back here because you got yourself shot."

"So he got to see and talk to this sexy, sassy, funny girl who then turned around and rushed to the airport to come home to another guy?" Scott summarized. He grinned. He shouldn't feel smug about that. But he definitely felt smug. "That's awesome."

Peyton rolled her eyes, but didn't say anything.

"And you brought me more clothes?"

"I did. Hope said you were in uniform and they had to cut your pants up anyway. And for the record, the town cop not locking his back door is kind of stupid."

"It's Sapphire Falls." He didn't need to lock his door. No one else did.

And he made sure that was okay. Nobody messed with his town.

He loved the place. He'd grown up there. He'd left for college and the academy and he'd worked in Omaha for a while, but he'd always wanted to come back. Especially after being a part of a multistate sex trafficking task force. He'd been gung-ho to get in there and bust up some bad guys and do the hero thing. He'd seen some shit and done the good-guy thing. And then when given the chance to settle down in his hometown and jump in on the task force only as needed for special operations along I-80, he'd taken it.

He was home now. He was taking care of his family, friends and neighbors.

And there was Peyton.

"What else did you bring me?" he asked.

She still had one hand behind her back, he noted. Holding something she didn't want him to see.

"Nothing." She frowned. "I came to check on you, I brought you clothes, and I gave blood."

He wouldn't have any of her blood. She hadn't been here when he'd been hooked up to the pints to replace what he'd lost in the town square. But the fact that she'd shown up and donated, because of him, made him happy. It was a big deal that Peyton was here, bringing him things. Even if they were his own clothes. He wasn't sure she'd ever given him anything before. Other than her sweet body and a few secrets...

He shut that down. He couldn't get all stirred up here. St. Patrick's Day had been a mistake and he wasn't repeating that. He was not sleeping with Peyton again. Not unless she agreed they should have more than sex.

But this was the kind of everyday stuff he needed. Maybe this was a step in the direction he and Hope had talked about. Not the getting-shot part. But the part where he needed Peyton to help him out.

"You're hiding something behind your back," he said. "What is it?"

"None of your business."

He wasn't buying it. "You brought me something else but you

were planning to stash it in the drawer with my clothes and have me never find out who it was really from."

He saw the flicker in her eyes that said he was dead-on. He grinned. "What is it?"

"Naked photos of me."

Scott's hand tightened around her wrist. "Don't mess with me."

She would absolutely give him naked pictures of herself. That was exactly the kind of thing she'd do to tempt him.

Scott completely believed that he was stronger and truer and more fucking noble than any other guy he knew because he'd been resisting *this* for the past almost two years.

Twenty months ago—not that he was keeping track— Peyton had started messing with him. He knew it had begun as a game to get the big, tough do-gooder cop to crack. Men always cracked when Peyton turned on her special smile, shortened her skirt, and batted her big blue eyes. But not Scott. By then, he knew her. She had plenty of attention, plenty of adoring male fans, plenty of fun. What she didn't have were many people who really knew her and cared about her and wanted to protect her.

"Show me what you brought me," he said in his best cop-in-charge voice.

Not that that voice ever worked with Peyton.

"You're a pain in the ass, you know that?" she asked.

Which is what she always asked when she realized that he knew her better than she thought he did.

"Show. Me."

With a heavy, mostly fake, put-upon sigh, she pulled her hand from behind her back.

It was a bouquet. Kind of. It was three bags of Corn Nuts stuck to three pencils and tied with a bow. It was a bouquet of Corn Nuts. His all-time favorite snack. She'd even included nacho cheese, barbecue, *and* ranch.

He looked up at her. "If I wasn't crazy about you before, now I am."

She rolled her eyes as she laid them on the bed. And that was something he was going to change eventually too. She *was* going to believe him when he said that stuff.

"They're just Corn Nuts. You know how I feel about them."

He did. She felt they were one of the most overrated snacks. But her favorite thing was popcorn balls, so he couldn't trust her taste. He definitely went for salty over sweet. Spicy was even better. And he loved that she'd brought these.

"You made them into a bouquet," he said with a grin. Peyton was hardly the whimsical type. Or the crafty type.

"I was stuck in the Atlanta airport with nothing to do," she said with a shrug. "In one shop, they had bouquets with candy bars and I thought...never mind. It's dumb. Exactly why I was trying to hide them."

Yeah, Peyton didn't show her soft side much, but it was there. And he fucking loved it. Especially the idea that it might be directed at him. He tugged her down and as she leaned in, he knew that she knew exactly what he intended to do. She kept coming anyway.

"Not dumb," he said gruffly against her mouth.

When her lips met his, a definite shot of *hell, yeah* went through him. But he kept it sweet.

Then she gripped the front of his gown in her fist and kissed him harder, deeper. Her other hand cupped his cheek, ran over his face, and down his neck and over his shoulder. Almost as if she needed to reassure herself that he was there and okay.

He wanted to grab her and hug her and comfort her. Even though he was the one hooked up to tubes and monitors. But that was a normal state for him with Peyton. Something about this woman made the protective, fighter-of-good-versus-evil inside of him swell to gargantuan proportions. Always had.

"Mr. Hansen."

Peyton straightened quickly as the nurse came into the room.

Crap. That was horrible timing. Or maybe it was perfect timing. He cleared his throat. Peyton looked at him and he looked down at his lap. She followed his gaze and then grabbed the blankets and bunched them up over the erection she'd caused.

Scott grinned. The girl got him, even if she didn't want to. She moved to block the nurse's view of his happy-to-be-alive body part while he fought to get his desire under control.

But he didn't miss that Peyton ran the pads of two fingers over her lips. Men didn't kiss Peyton sweetly. Men didn't make Peyton go soft. Except for him. He was different, and one of these days she was going to understand that.

3

Peyton was sure her cheeks were pink as she moved to block the nurse's view of Scott's hard-on. And that was ridiculous. She'd been in all kinds of scandalous situations that were perfect for blushing. But she never did.

One sweet kiss from this guy though and she felt flustered. And then he had to be all obvious about how he felt about her. Resisting this guy tried every ounce of her patience.

Dammit. It was always like this with Scott.

Worse this time because yeah, she'd been worried. Really worried.

He'd been *shot*, for fuck's sake.

And now the panty-melting grins and smartass remarks were making her feel *comforted*. Because they meant he was fine. And she'd realized that she *really* needed him to be fine.

She swallowed and moved back as the nurse approached the bed. She was going to chalk her rattled emotions and reactions up to seeing Scott in a hospital bed. Big, tough, smart-ass, fix-everything, always-there Scott. In a hospital bed.

Peyton pulled in a breath and told herself that if she cried right now she was *not* getting French fries on her way home. She'd already cried—in the cab in Baltimore on her way to the airport after getting the call about the shooting, in the airport bathroom after she'd made it through security and realized she had an hour to kill, in the Atlanta airport bathroom when she'd realized she was still four hours away from him and that a lot could happen in four hours.

That was more crying than she'd done in a year.

"How are you feeling?" the nurse asked Scott, giving Peyton a smile. Her name tag said Angie.

"Groggy," he said.

Peyton smiled slightly. She kind of liked groggy Scott. He was usually so on and intense. Nothing ever missed his notice, especially about her. Sometimes she thought he could read her thoughts. She didn't mind having a break from feeling constantly exposed around him.

But, if this was as groggy as he got, there was no relaxing. He'd known she was hiding something. Even if they'd only been Corn Nuts.

"I can turn the drip down," Angie said.

Scott nodded, but Peyton asked, "Is that a good idea?"

She was as surprised as they were that she'd spoken up. This was Scott. He always knew what he was doing.

"That's controlling the pain, right?" she asked anyway.

The nurse looked back at Scott. "It *is* important to stay on top of your pain at this point," she said.

"I don't like the groggy feeling," Scott said, looking at Peyton. "I'm fine with a little pain."

Peyton frowned at him. He was such a stubborn ass sometimes. All the time. "It's stupid to hurt if you don't have to."

"I'm fine."

"I have to agree with your girlfriend," Angie said. "There's—"

"I'm not his girlfriend," Peyton broke in.

Scott gave her a scowl. Well, she wasn't.

"Oh." Angie looked back and forth between them. "Okay."

"Peyton is my..."

Peyton lifted a brow at him. How was he going to finish that sentence?

"Personal nurse," he said. "She's here to learn everything she needs to know about what I'll need when I go home."

"Oh," Angie said again.

Peyton felt her eyebrows shoot up. She gave him a frown. Okay, so he was on morphine, but personal nurse? Really?

"You're a nurse?" Angie asked.

"No. He's loopy. He's having flashbacks to my Halloween costume."

"Well, she's in nursing school," Scott said.

She'd taken two nursing *classes*. Not even nursing classes, actually. Prerequisites. And she hadn't even finished those. Nursing was very...*caring*. Not really her style.

On the other hand, her work at the bakery in Sapphire Falls was perfect. It was straightforward work—mix, pour, bake, frost. She could, and had, screwed even that up from time to time, but that was fixable. You could scrape icing off and start over. You could toss it all in the trash and start fresh. And people were *happy* about what she gave them at the bakery. Cookies, cupcakes, pie. Yeah, that was definitely better than shots and medicine and bad news. Definitely.

"She's always wanted to be a nurse," Scott said.

Peyton looked at him. She'd told him that once. A month ago. He'd remembered that? And more, he'd taken her seriously?

There was something funny in his voice when he said that. Pride? No way. She stared at him. Yes, that was freaking *pride* on his face when he talked about her being in school. Which she no longer was.

He gave her a smile that was a bit goofy and a lot adorable.

And she knew that no one used the word "adorable" with Scott Hansen much. Or ever.

They could maybe turn the drug drip down *a little*, Peyton thought. "The kind of care I want to give you is probably not the kind the doctor is going to prescribe," Peyton told him. "In fact, it might be on the list of things *not* to do for a little while."

"Well, Kyle is a really good friend. I don't think he'd put that on the list," Scott said.

Yeah, he was definitely drugged, because Scott never went along with her teasing about sex.

"I definitely think that you should move in and nurse me back to health," Scott said, just before yawning big.

Peyton narrowed her eyes. Wait a second. Scott *never* went along with her teasing about sex. Suddenly she wasn't so sure he was as hopped up on morphine as she'd thought. He was being all sweet and kind of off-kilter, and he'd sensed she'd been worried. Hell, the way she'd gripped his hospital gown when he'd kissed her, as if she'd needed to hold on tight for fear of losing him? Yeah, that was one thing. But then she'd brought him Corn Nuts? That had been a stupid move. Like flying back here because all she'd been able to think about since the second Hope had said, "Scott's in the hospital," was that she could *not* lose him, couldn't *not* be there.

Crap.

All stupid. Because *all* of this—from his goofy smile and big fake yawn and "she's in nursing school" bullshit—added up to one thing. He wanted to play house. He thought this was the perfect chance to show her how a "real" relationship could be between them. The thing he'd been pushing for over a year now.

Yeah, he was stone-cold sober. And conniving. And nuts.

Well, he wasn't the only one. On all of those counts.

"I guess you *will* need help bathing, won't you?" she asked, running her hand up and down his lower leg. "Wouldn't want Kyle or your mom or a total stranger doing that."

Scott suddenly not only looked sober, but a little concerned. As he should be.

"I'm not going to need help bathing," he said.

"And you won't be able to get up in the middle of the night for a glass of water or anything without help, so it's probably best if someone sleeps over—right next to you," she said, still stroking his leg.

He tried to shift away from her touch, but he couldn't do it without using his hand and being completely obvious about it. It was not a nice thing, but Peyton gave herself points. She also gave him a two-can-play-this-game smile. He wanted her around, fussing over him and spending extra time with him, just the two of them? Well, his left thigh was the *only* thing not working properly on him. He had to know that if she was taking care of that leg, she'd want to take care of the rest of him too.

"I think I can handle pissing in the middle of night," he said with a frown. "Maybe if you could just bring over a casserole or two..."

Peyton flat-out laughed at that. Scott had no idea if she could cook. At all. The most he'd ever seen her eat was pizza at the Stop or a burger at the Come Again. He might be a little woozy if he thought he could have her at his house, hanging out, being together in every way *except* naked in bed. It seemed he was now realizing he'd made a mistake. Thinking Peyton would be sweet and concerned about his leg and *not* make any other moves on him? Yeah, big mistake.

He'd started this and she was so finishing it.

Peyton looked at Angie. "I definitely want to see him naked. And that's a lot of what goes on with home health, right?" She had friends who worked as nurse's aides in the local nursing home and for home health. There was a lot of bathing, dressing and undressing that went on in home health.

"Um, well, that would probably work," Angie said slowly. She was clearly a little surprised by the blunt naked comment.

Though she shouldn't be. Scott Hansen was gorgeous and strong and a freaking knight in shining armor with a dry sense of humor and a quick mind and an alpha streak that made Peyton weak in the knees. *Of course* she wanted to get him naked.

She just didn't want to marry him.

"That's great," she told the nurse enthusiastically. "Just tell me what to do. I mean, *Scott* loves to tell me what to do..." She winked at Angie and squeezed Scott's leg at the same time. "But I mean medically."

She didn't need to glance at Scott to know that he was part ticked off and part turned-on. Because St. Patrick's Day had proven that he was every bit the bossy, demanding dirty talker she'd pegged him for early on. He loved the idea of her letting him boss her around. As much as *she* loved the idea. In the bedroom only, of course. Or on the hood of his squad car...

"Well, he will need dressing changes, and it's much easier if someone else does those initially," Angie said, pulling Peyton back to the present. "And he won't be able to drive with the pain meds. Not until we can get him on something milder. And he'll be on crutches for a time."

"Crutches?" Peyton and Scott said at the same time.

"Yes. The gunshot tore some muscle. Until that heals, the doctor will want you resting that leg." She looked at Peyton. "Simple things like getting up for a glass of water become a lot more difficult. You don't have to be a nurse to help him with those things."

Well, that was a good thing, because her two classes didn't even qualify her to do CPR. "Great. I'm in."

"And she's right about the bathing," Angie said to Scott. "That can be uncomfortable for friends and family. We do have home health available and many patients take advantage of that for those more personal things."

Scott frowned. "I can handle that myself."

"You won't be able to shower or get into the tub without protecting the wound," Angie said. "So it's easier if you have someone else to help."

Scott seemed to think about that. Then his gaze slid to Peyton. And for some reason she suddenly got suspicious.

"So a nurse's aide could come over and help me though?" Scott asked.

"Right," Angie confirmed.

Suddenly Peyton knew *exactly* what he was doing. One of the girls she'd gone to high school with, Sydney, was a nurse's aide. Who did home health. And she was really cute. And she had a thing for Scott.

The jealousy card? Really? Well, okay then. He wanted her jealous? She could so do jealous.

She pulled herself up to her full height, put on her bitch-with-an-attitude and said, "If *any* other woman gets within twenty feet of your front door and she's not your mother, your sister, or *my* sister, I'm turning the hose on her," Peyton told him. "There's only one girl in Sapphire Falls who's gonna be soaping your junk, and you're looking at her."

Angie looked as if she wasn't sure she wanted to be here for this conversation, but Scott's eyes narrowed. And Peyton realized she'd done exactly what he'd wanted her to do.

"You soap me, you eat dinner across the table from me," Scott said.

She narrowed her eyes right back at him. "Meatloaf for the chance to put my hands all over that big, hard body? Fine." If he hadn't been shot and she wasn't still a little shaken about that, she might have held on to her resolution that sex without meatloaf was better. But fine, she'd try the meatloaf angle. Whatever.

"Fine," he agreed. If he was surprised by her acquiescence, he didn't show it.

"And in exchange for taking sweet, gentle care of your dressings, I get a shoulder massage after each dressing change." Her hands on him? Yes, please. His hands on her? Oh, yeah.

Scott clenched his jaw. Then said, "Fine."

She grinned.

"But," he added, "I want to go out to dinner once a week. With you. The two of us, together."

Negotiating. Interesting. Getting naked with Scott wasn't a problem at all. She'd been trying to do that for over a year now. It was the other stuff—the hanging out and being "normal" stuff that tripped her up. Because there was no "normal". People were crazy and relationships were hard and it hurt when people disappointed you. And she'd be damned if *she* would be the one to disappoint Scott Hansen.

She'd made it very clear what he could expect from her and that was what she was sticking with. Come hell or high water, as her grandpa would say. But if he thought eating meatloaf at home and going on a date once in a while would actually change anything, she supposed she would have to *show* him versus *tell* him.

She shrugged. "Then I get to sleep in your bed every night. I'm not sleeping on the couch, and you shouldn't either, so don't be thinking that you'll just give the bed to me."

He dragged air in through his nose, then let it out slowly. Finally, he said, "You have to wear pajamas."

"Deal." Like pajamas would matter. They could be taken off.

The sound of someone clearing their throat interrupted. But it wasn't Angie.

Dr. Kyle Ames was standing inside the door. Grinning like an idiot. "Hey, everybody."

"Hi, Kyle," Peyton said with a smile.

"Hey," Scott greeted. Without a smile.

"How's everything in here?" Kyle asked, crossing to the bedside. He'd directed the question to Angie.

"Just trying to...get everyone on the same page," she said.

Kyle laughed. "That's virtually impossible with these two, but I appreciate the effort. And that no one's yelling."

"Oh, no yelling," Peyton said. "I'm going to be Scott's primary caregiver."

Kyle lifted a brow and looked at Scott. "You okay with that?"

"Why wouldn't I be?"

"Because *she* seems happy about it. She's never happy when *you* get your way about something."

Scott sighed. "We've...come to an agreement."

"We understand that there will be a lot of naked time on Scott's part over the next few days. And we all know how I feel about Scott and naked time," Peyton said.

Kyle nodded. "That we do." He glanced at Scott again. "But we also know how Scott feels about naked time."

"Well, I figure if she gets me naked, the chances of her killing me are lessened," Scott said dryly.

Peyton grinned. Love-sick puppy impression or not, the guy amused her, and she appreciated that. No one did sarcasm quite like Scott Hansen. "That is a very good point. And don't forget—it's not just seeing. There will be soap and rubbing too."

Scott shifted on the bed and Peyton laughed. She did love having the upper hand. She really did *not* feel that very often with him.

Angie spoke up then. "Let me show you the dressing change."

Peyton moved back to let the other woman next to the bed.

"Okay." She could change a Band-Aid and reapply ointment to the guy's thigh. That was no big deal.

But when Angie pulled the sheet back, Peyton's first word was "whoa".

Angie looked up. "What?"

"That's...a lot higher on his leg than I thought it was."

"Yes, the bullet nicked part of his femoral artery," Kyle said. "If I hadn't been there, he could have died."

Scott rolled his eyes.

Peyton frowned. "What?" she asked him. "Is that not true?"

"It's the seventeenth time he's said it since I checked in," Scott said.

Kyle shrugged. "It's true."

"Please, go on," Scott said. "Having someone digging around in my groin is preferable to listening to Dr. Ames pat himself on the back."

Angie gave a little laugh, but she proceeded to pull on gloves and then lift the dressings from his leg.

Peyton had a strong stomach. And she really had no trouble being this close to this part of Scott's body. But damn—that looked horrible.

"Dude, I might change my mind about the naked thing," she said.

"Is that right?"

She looked up at him. He didn't look concerned. "I'm afraid every time you uncover that," she waved in the general direction of his cock, "I'll flash back to this." She waved at his wound.

He chuckled. "You still promised meatloaf," he said.

Peyton shook her head. "Raw hamburger—not a good mental image right now either."

"Suck it up, buttercup," he told her. "You signed on. You can handle this."

Suddenly he looked cocky again. Could she handle this?

The blood? Absolutely. Being around Scott twenty-four-seven? Not so sure.

She watched the rest of the dressing change and then crossed to the desk and grabbed her bag, pulling it up on her shoulder. "Okay, I'm gonna head home. Lots to get ready for."

"Ready?" Scott asked.

"Well, I have to pack to move in with you for the next week," she said. "Need to buy new batteries—don't want to run out. Find my nurse's uniform. Dig out my handcuffs." She turned back and gave him a smile. "But I guess I don't need to bring those, do I?"

"Your nurse's uniform?" Scott croaked out.

"The one you wore for Halloween?" Kyle asked, a huge grin on his face.

"Yeah, I think that will definitely get me in the right mindset." The "uniform" was really more of a costume. A tiny, tight, short-skirted naughty nurse costume. If she remembered correctly, Scott had really liked it.

"Not fair," he told her, his eyes flashing.

"See you soon."

"I'll bring him home tomorrow," Kyle said.

"Doctors give their patients rides home?" Peyton asked.

"When their primary caregivers are going to be wearing the uniform that you wore on Halloween?" Kyle asked. "Hell, yes."

Peyton laughed and reached for the door.

"Oh, but, Peyton?" Kyle called.

She turned back. "Yeah?"

"Be sure you bring enough batteries for *two* weeks."

She frowned. "Two?"

"At least," Kyle confirmed.

Two weeks living with Scott? Shit. But she gave them a huge smile. "Good to know, Doc. Thanks." Her eyes found Scott again. Even lying in a hospital bed, he looked like everything she wanted and wished she could have. But couldn't. "See you at home," she said brightly.

She made it to the hallway before she blew out a breath and leaned back against the wall.

She was going to need more than her nurse's uniform. A lot more.

H e was going to need more than meatloaf. A lot more. Looking back, Scott wasn't sure how that entire negotiation and plan had actually gone down. He'd really felt like he'd been ahead. But now, Peyton was going to be helping him shower and sleeping with him in his bed? And wearing her naughty nurse costume? How the hell had that happened?

He'd like to blame it on the morphine, but he knew the truth. Peyton. She could always get her way with him.

In the past, being in public together had kept things from getting too out of hand. But behind closed doors? In his *bed*?

He was definitely screwed. Literally.

"Man, you are so screwed," Kyle said. For what seemed like the hundredth time since Peyton had sashayed her cute butt out of his hospital room with a smile that said *I've so got you.*

"Don't know what you mean," Scott lied.

"That itch you can't quite seem to scratch?" Kyle asked. "Yeah, it's going to be *living* with you for the next two weeks."

"By the way, thanks for that," Scott said, ignoring the itch thing. Everyone knew it. There was no use rehashing it. *Again.*

"Hey, man, I don't make the rules about muscles and shit healing," Kyle said, typing something into the computer by Scott's bed.

"Muscles and shit? Stop with all the technical talk, Doc," Scott said dryly.

"You want me to go over all the anatomy that you ripped up?" Kyle asked. "Sure thing. But I kind of thought the important part here was how long Nurse Sassy Pants was going to be *living* with you."

Nurse Sassy Pants. That was about right. "Just don't tell Derek," Scott said. "I don't need you both thinking this is hilarious."

"Oh, it's *fucking* hilarious."

Scott sat up quickly as Derek's voice filled his room. His gaze narrowed in on Kyle's phone propped up on the bedside table. And on speaker.

"You fuckers. Isn't that some kind of HIPAA violation or something?" he asked, slumping back against the pillows.

Kyle nodded. "Which is why we should discuss your love life instead of your health."

"Remind us again why you won't just sleep with her?" Derek asked. Then added, "Again."

Because, of course, they loved the fact that he'd fallen off the wagon on St. Pat's Day. Because, of course, he'd made a big deal out of being so strong and focused that he could resist her.

That had been stupid.

"Every guy in the county wants to sleep with her," Scott said. "And given half the chance, they would."

Kyle nodded, and Scott knew Derek was in agreement as well. They both admitted that Peyton was stunningly beautiful, and that her smart mouth and spunk were a turn-on. Though they also both admitted that they wouldn't want to be the one having to deal with a pissed-off Peyton on any kind of regular basis. Peyton could be sweet as candy. She could be funny as hell. She was a ton of fun and always up for anything. But she had a temper, and she didn't even try to dial it back.

It almost always came out when someone she cared about had been wronged or someone had done something stupid or cruel to someone else. The guys who dated Peyton's girlfriends knew that if they fucked up, their headlights and windshields were at risk, not to mention their noses and other body parts. Scott had taken a baseball bat out of her hands mid-swing, twice —once the guy's truck had been the victim, and once the guy's barbecue grill. Scott had also hauled her off a guy who was twice her size because he'd shoved her friend up against the outside wall of the Come Again and threatened her.

That time, Scott had let her get a few good swings and kicks in before he'd pulled her off.

Peyton was a little bottled-up and pressurized can of emotions, and you just never knew when she was going to erupt.

Her riled-up, passionate, defend-everyone side got him going. He'd admit that. He wanted to kiss the hell out of her every time and then throw her over his shoulder, carry her home, and unleash some of that passion without any clothes on.

But it was her sweet side that got him right in the gut. And that was how he'd ended up losing his mind a month ago. She hadn't been pissed off that night. She hadn't been spoiling for a fight. She'd been sweet and mellow.

"And you want to show her that she can be wanted for more than all of that," Kyle said, completing Scott's thought about why he had been avoiding sleeping with her.

Okay, he was going to blame this on the drugs later too, but he said, "Everyone just sees what's on the surface. Her friends look at her and see a good time. Her sister looks at her and sees a girl who's trying but just can't quite get her shit together. Her parents look at her and see her independent streak and just feel relieved because they don't have to do anything for her. Guys look at her and see a hot body and an adventurous streak and think 'hell yeah' for a weekend. And it's all...not enough," he said. "She's more than all of that, but she's comfortable with people just seeing these parts of her."

Kyle was watching him, a slight frown on his face. "If she's comfortable, why are you trying to get more out of her?"

"Because comfortable and happy aren't the same thing," Scott said.

"And you're going to *make* her be happy?" Derek asked from the phone. "You can't force someone to be happy."

"But I can *show* her," Scott insisted. "To her, letting someone close means being vulnerable. Like her parents. Neither of them could live without the other. Particularly her mother—there have been suicide threats, even an attempt or two." Kyle and Derek both knew this. Everyone did. "She's worried about turning out like her mom. And making someone miserable, like her dad."

"Dan doesn't seem miserable," Derek said.

But Kyle was nodding. "They have a tough relationship. Dan doesn't seem miserable, but he's given his whole life to Jo. Maybe he doesn't let himself think about being miserable. He convinces himself that he likes how things are."

Scott nodded. "I think he gets off on being the only person Jo wants or needs."

Kyle agreed. "So Peyton thinks being in a relationship, letting someone too close, makes you crazy."

It sounded funny, but it wasn't. "That, or she's afraid she's already crazy and letting someone too close will make them unhappy."

Neither of his friends said anything for a moment. Scott appreciated these guys. They gave each other a lot of shit, and had a lot of fun, but he could be serious with them too. Kyle was an excellent physician. There was no one better to be standing beside Scott, taking care of the town they both loved. And Derek was an EMT, a volunteer firefighter, and a general go-to guy around town, along with helping Bryan Murray run the social spot in town.

The Come Again was a bar, and some could argue that a bar

caused more problems than it solved. But Scott wasn't convinced. The Come Again was a meeting spot, a place to kick back and relax, a place to laugh with people who had known you your entire life. There was something about stepping through the doors to that place that made everything feel better. Having a place to go, where everyone was welcomed and where you could always find a smile, to spend time with people you genuinely liked and enjoyed was, in Scott's experience, incredibly important.

"I can see why she's nervous about being with you," Kyle finally said.

Scott looked up at him. "What?"

"I do," his friend said with a nod. "She's got some wild swing, you gotta admit. She can be sweet and happy, but she can also be a damned hellion. I can see her being worried about being with a guy she likes and cares about. You're an all-in guy, Hansen. If you really start something with her, you're not the type to bail when things get tough. So she figures if she gives in, *you're* stuck. And she cares about you enough to not want to make you miserable."

Scott scowled. Mostly because he knew Kyle had a point. Dan was all-in with Jo. He was sticking through everything the woman threw at him—sometimes literally. Peyton saw her dad in Scott. Not the whipped, clingy enabler, but the guy who wouldn't leave even if he wanted to.

Dammit.

He shoved his hand through his hair. "When are you letting me out of here?" he asked.

"Tomorrow morning," Kyle told him. "If your numbers stay good."

"And you're taking me home?"

"Sure thing. I have clinic hours in Sapphire Falls tomorrow. I'll spring you from here around seven a.m."

"Great." The sooner he got home, the better. Before Peyton

decided to put a sex swing in his bedroom. Or get on another plane out of town. He knew she was a flight risk at the moment.

"Oh, and Derek will come along," Kyle added.

"He will?" Scott asked.

"I will?" Derek asked at the same time.

Kyle grinned and reached for his phone. "Let me give you a rundown of the things Peyton went home to pack and the uniform she's going to be wearing when we get to Scott's. You'll definitely want to come along."

Scott refused to give Kyle a reaction as his friend headed out of his room. Then he flopped back in the bed and threw his arm over his face.

The next couple of weeks were going to be tough.

And recovering from being shot was going to be the easy part.

4

P eyton knew exactly how things were going to go down at Scott's.

She threw her bag behind the seat of her truck and climbed in. He was going to try to be sweet and romantic and flirty and "couply". Her only hope was to distract him. As a cop, Scott was not easily distracted. She knew that well. Which meant, she was going to have to blow his mind and keep him constantly sexed up if she was going to survive.

She had fit two weeks of clothing in her smallest duffel. Because it was all *tiny* clothing. And yes, she fully intended to greet him at the door in her nurse's costume.

But she needed to swing by the grocery store on her way over to his place, and she didn't want to risk giving anyone a heart attack by wearing it up and down the aisles at Conrad's.

She was in and out of the store in ten minutes and on her way to Scott's. At some point, she would cook for him, of course. But she didn't really want him getting too comfortable in a "regular couple" routine right away.

This whole situation was about sex.

And okay, him getting better.

But she was *not* making him meatloaf.

She was at the stop sign in front of the diner when she happened to glance over. And noticed Reed Walker's truck parked in front.

Peyton slammed on her brakes, scowling at the black and silver Ford. Looked like she had one more stop to make. She pulled into a spot across the street and then headed for Dottie's. It was just before eight, so the place was packed. The group of older guys in the middle, with the three tables pulled together and a jillion coffee cups in front of them, would be there for the next couple of hours. And had already been there for a couple. There wasn't a guy in the group under the age of sixty, and who hadn't lived in Sapphire Falls for at least fifty of those years. They held court every weekday morning and every other Saturday. And they knew more gossip than the ladies at the Bang and Blow Salon.

But the rest of the place was full of farmers and the people who ran the businesses that sat around the square. Everything opened at eight-thirty in Sapphire Falls, after everyone filled up on pancakes, eggs, and coffee and strolled to their shop doors.

It was nice. Because if you needed to find someone between the hours of six a.m. and six p.m. in this town, the chance was great that they were somewhere within two hundred yards of the gazebo in the center of the square.

And sure enough, Reed Walker was sitting in a booth by the window with two of his friends.

Peyton stomped to the table. "*Seriously?*" She planted her hands on her hips and gave Reed a glare. "Your kid got a *gun* and you didn't lock the fucking thing up?"

Reed didn't glare back. He actually had the good sense to look sorry.

"It was locked up," he said.

"He's *eleven*, Reed!" Peyton said. "He got it unlocked, loaded and into the town square!"

"I know." He nodded. "I know."

"Scott could have *died!*" Peyton exclaimed. "Or Chase could have shot one of the other kids!"

"It was an *accident.*" But Reed looked miserable.

Good. "It was a *preventable* accident!"

"I know. We've had a long talk with him—"

"You *talked* to him?" Peyton demanded. "That's it? You *talked*? How about grounding his ass? How about taking the *gun* away from him until he's older and more responsible? How about *watching your kid*?"

"Hey!"

But it wasn't Reed who was suddenly in her face. It was Travis Bennett. One of TJ's brothers.

"Let's take it down a notch, okay?" he said to Peyton, his voice calm but firm.

She glanced at Reed. "Anybody else gets hurt because *you* didn't take care of your shit, and I'll kick your ass." Reed was several years older than her and probably outweighed her by a hundred pounds, but she had a lot of pent-up rage. That was dangerous. He should watch it.

"Peyton," Travis said. "Let's go outside."

"You're taking me outside?" she asked with a laugh. "For yelling at a guy whose kid almost killed my—Scott." Dammit. That wasn't a great slip. In the middle of Dottie's at one of the busiest times of day? She needed to be careful.

"But Scott's okay and it was an accident and he feels terrible about it," Travis said.

"He *should* feel terrible about it. Guns aren't toys!" She glared at Reed. "You've been around guns all your life. How can you not be more careful?"

With that, Travis turned her and started nudging her toward the door.

"But he—"

"You know, if you don't want the whole town to know how you really feel about Scott, you might want to *not* go stomping around and fighting everyone on his behalf," Travis said by her ear.

She deflated a bit with that. She'd done the same in Baltimore. Seth had made a crack about the tough guys being cops in Baltimore and she'd gotten right up in his face and defended Scott and the important things he did in Sapphire Falls.

Damn.

She let Travis steer her out onto the sidewalk in front of Dottie's. He let go of her and she turned to face him. She crossed her arms. "I'm right." She felt the need to point that out.

"You are," Travis said with a nod. "And Reed knows it. Calling him out in public isn't going to fix anything though."

She took a deep breath and blew it out. "Yeah, okay. I just..."

"Couldn't help it," Travis supplied.

She nodded.

"I know how that goes."

"You do?"

"Sure. I'd take anyone on over anything for my wife or one of my girls."

Travis was madly in love with his wife Lauren and his two daughters. Everyone in town thought it was hilarious that Travis, one of Sapphire Falls' best-known flirts, was raising girls. Peyton thought it was great. Men who were awesome dads were her personal heroes. Every little girl deserved a dad who would kick ass for her.

But that didn't explain *her* reaction to this whole thing with Scott. "It's not love," she said. "I would have felt this way no matter who Chase had shot. An eleven-year-old shouldn't be around guns."

Travis nodded. "You might have felt the same way. And knowing you, if you ran into him somewhere, you would have said something. But you wouldn't have seen his truck and come stomping in to confront him in front of half the town."

Peyton opened her mouth to say she most definitely would have...but she wouldn't have. Probably.

Just then, Reed came through Dottie's door.

"I want to tell you that Chase was scared to death about what happened," Reed started before anyone else could say a thing. "He doesn't even want to learn to shoot now. But MacKenzie convinced him to try it out. He's not even going to look at a gun until we get out there for lessons."

Peyton thought about the little boy, and the fact that seeing a grown man bleeding from a gunshot right in front of him would have been scary—and way worse, knowing he'd caused it.

The rest of her temper dissipated. "I'm sorry, Reed. I might have overreacted a little."

Reed gave her a small smile. "It's okay. I would have done the same thing if something like that happened to someone I love."

Again, she opened her mouth to protest, but she caught Travis's eye over Reed's shoulder. He gave her a small grin with one eyebrow up, and she realized that protesting she wasn't in love with Scott might make it even more obvious that she was. Or, at least, that she wanted to be.

Yeah, that was it. She might *want* to be in love with him. A little. Maybe. If things were different. If *she* was different. But she was also a hothead who often spoke before she thought things out, and who really did think that an eleven-year-old should *never* have access to a gun he didn't know how to use.

"Well, tell Chase that Scott's going to be fine," Peyton said to Reed. "In fact, maybe in a few days, Chase could come over and do a little yard work or something and see for himself."

Reed brightened at that. "That would be great. It would make him feel like he was doing something to help Scott out. Wonderful. I'll give Scott a call."

"Oh, call me. I'll be staying over there, helping Scott for a while. I can let you know when would be a good time to visit."

Too late—way too late—she realized what she'd said. And given away.

Both men's eyes widened, but, to their credit, neither of them said anything directly about that.

"Okay, I'll do that." Reed pulled his phone out and Peyton inputted her number.

"See you later," she told him as he turned to go back into the diner.

"Let us know if you need anything," Travis said. "Casseroles or help around your—Scott's—house or anything."

Peyton could tell he was fishing a little, and gauging her reaction. And what was with the clear assumption that she couldn't cook or manage the house? She'd managed to get almost to twenty-four years old without dying, and Lord knew it wasn't because her mom and dad were super doting. "Lauren doesn't cook," Peyton pointed out.

Travis grinned. "No, but my mom does."

That was actually an understatement. Kathy Bennett was one of the best cooks in the county—if not the state.

"Well, in that case..." Peyton could absolutely fake not being able to cook if it meant Kathy might bring something over to Scott.

Travis laughed. "I'll stop over in a couple of days. Let you guys get...settled."

Yeah, "settled" sounded very much like an innuendo right there. Peyton shook her head. "I'm not telling you anything."

"You're going to make me go back into *Dottie's* with no juicy gossip for us all to speculate about?" Travis asked. "Come on."

She pretended to consider that. Then she said, "Okay, I heard a rumor that Scott's home health aide has a huge crush on him."

With that, she headed across the street to her truck, grateful that Scott wouldn't be getting out and about for a while. Hopefully the gossip about her confronting Reed would have died down by the time he was.

Of course, there was also the possibility that the tale would have grown *bigger* by then.

S cott steeled himself as he mounted his front steps with one crutch under his right arm. And it wasn't even about the nursing costume he was sure Peyton was wearing. It was just the fact that she was there. In his house. Waiting for him to come home.

Kyle got the door for him. Derek carried the other crutch that the therapist at the hospital had said he wouldn't probably need to use, and the bag of wound-care supplies he'd need.

"Hey, honey, we're home!" Kyle called into the house.

"Be right there!" was Peyton's reply from what sounded like his bedroom.

Scott squeezed the handrest on the crutch. Damn, this was so not how he'd envisioned having Peyton in his bedroom for the first time.

The three men were all in the front door when Peyton came around the corner.

And even knowing she'd be wearing it, and remembering what it looked like from Halloween, Scott was not prepared for the sight of her in the tiny, tight nurse's costume. In his living room. Welcoming him home.

It wasn't just the white fishnet stockings and bright red fuck-me heels that matched the red cross on the right breast of the top.

It was the smile she wore. She looked like she was up to something. She also looked happy to see him.

But damn, her short skirts and high heels had a way of making her legs look even longer and, in spite of himself, he couldn't keep from thinking about how they'd feel wrapped around his waist every. Damned. Time.

No one could *really* blame him for what had happened on St. Patrick's Day. Her little leprechaun costume had been, essentially, just a green version of this. And he was only human.

Derek coughed. "I might be coming down with something and need some nursing too."

Scott didn't even look away from Peyton as he told his friend, "Get out. Now."

Chuckling, Derek tossed the bag of supplies to Peyton.

Kyle gave her a once-over. Again. And said, "Be gentle with our boy here. He's in a weakened state, remember."

Then they both, thankfully, got lost.

For now. Scott knew he hadn't seen or heard the last of them. Which, normally, he was grateful for. Not so much right now. He needed *lots* of alone time with Nurse Sassy Pants.

"How are you feeling?" she asked.

"Feverish."

She grinned. "Want a sponge bath?"

"I want you to put more clothes on." He knew he sounded grumpy. And that wasn't exactly how he was feeling. Though cheerful was definitely not right either. He was—frustrated.

Frustrated that she was here, finally, and *none* of this was the way he wanted it to be. Frustrated that her being here, in her mind, needed to include a sexy nurse's costume. Frustrated that he wanted to stalk over to her, sweep her up into his arms and take her into his bedroom and do all of the things that costume made him think about doing. And that he couldn't.

She tipped her head, studying him. They were standing about

twenty feet apart, but Scott had a feeling she was reading all of those thoughts on his face.

"Sit down before you fall over," she finally said, moving toward him.

He assumed that she meant to help him to the couch, but he couldn't handle having her in reach. "I've got it." He moved swiftly toward the sofa, ignoring the twinge in his leg that said he'd gone too fast.

Of course, once he was down with his leg on the coffee table and the crutch propped next to him, it was a lot harder to move fast. Which was how he found himself with Peyton sitting right next to him, looking like a goddess and smelling like everything he wanted all rolled into one delicious, lick-able package.

He closed his eyes and leaned his head back on the cushion behind him. "Fuck."

He felt her shift on the cushion beside him.

"So, we pretty much laid out how this was going to go at the hospital, right?" she asked.

"What do you mean?" Keeping his eyes closed was kind of working. He couldn't see all that gorgeous skin and those tempting curves. But he could *feel* her. And smell her. And his whole body hardened anyway. He heard her drop her shoes one by one onto the floor and imagined her with her legs curled under her, sitting sideways facing him. That meant her bare legs with those stockings were right *there*...

He wasn't going to survive two weeks.

Not without throwing her down and taking her over and over and—

"You want to play house, right? Take this chance to show me how wonderful a relationship could be. Tempt me to make it real and long-term."

He rolled his head and opened his eyes. Yeah, she'd caught on to that at the hospital all right. It had seemed like a great plan. He wanted to date her. Hell, he wanted to live with her. So why not force her into it?

He gave a little laugh at that thought. Very romantic. "Yeah, okay, I thought this would give you a taste of what you're missing."

She nodded. "And you figured out that I also intend to use these two weeks to seduce you, right?"

He took a deep breath. Yeah, of course she did. Hell, she used every minute they were together to try to do that. "And how would that be different than every other time we're within ten feet of one another?"

She smiled. "Oh, you'll see how it's different."

Yeah, he was a dead man. He was either going to die of lack of blood to his brain, or because he took Peyton to bed and couldn't move for food or water afterward.

"So this is a game of chicken—we both bring it on and see who gets their way?" he asked.

She smiled. "Pretty much. I mean, if you're not smart enough to avoid playing chicken or truth-or-dare with me, then you deserve the consequences."

Well, she had a point.

"Think you're a tough girl, huh?" She was. On the surface. He was sure that there had never been a dare Peyton hadn't taken with a big old loud "hell yeah". But she wasn't totally tough. There were moments when he caught glimpses of what he could have sworn was wistfulness—like she wanted so much more than she was letting herself want. "You think you can be with me for two weeks and then want things to go back to how they were?"

She wet her lips and shrugged. "I think that the sex is going to be so good that *you* won't be able to go back to how things were."

He focused on her mouth. Her sassy, sexy mouth that he wanted to see smiling, wanted to hear saying things like "you make me so happy", and that he wanted to *feel* doing...

"For two weeks, I'm going to sell the relationship idea, you're going to sell the sex idea, and we're going to see who caves first?" he asked.

She nodded her head slowly, her long black hair falling forward and brushing against the upper curve of her breasts, half of which were peeking out of the deep V in the front of the dress. "May the best man, or woman, win."

He studied her. Her cheeks were a little pink, her pupils were wide. She was excited.

Hell, he was too.

He knew he had no prayer of resisting a Peyton seduction for two weeks. But he thought maybe she didn't have a chance of resisting the things he wanted either. Not with a constant, steady application of things like simple fun and sweetness. Normalcy. Comfort. Typical couple stuff. Typical *outside of the bedroom* couple stuff. He knew that she worried about him being overprotective and demanding of her time and attention. So, this was the perfect chance to show her that they could both have their own space, their own interests, time apart—and yet still be crazy about each other.

No, he thought a second later—crazy was not a good word to use.

Her mother's mental illness was no joking matter. He didn't make light of it, and knew when Peyton did, it was a defense mechanism. But still, he needed to not do anything that would call to mind her mom and dad.

Sweet and fun and comfortable and normal, he reminded himself. That's what he was concentrating on. Even as he was all too aware of the perfect pair of breasts only a few inches below his mouth.

God, he was going to be so easy for her.

"Okay, but you have to actually *try*," he said. "Every time you do something sexy, I do something normal and you have to go with it."

She laughed. "Normal?"

"Sweet, romantic, regular couple stuff," Scott said firmly.

"Regular couples don't do sexy?" Peyton asked. "No wonder I've never wanted to be one."

"You know what I mean."

For a moment, he thought she was going to tease him further, but instead, she nodded. "Okay, fine. But if you do something regular, then I get to do something sexy," she said. "It's only fair we keep this balanced and get an equal chance to make our case."

This was hardly going to be balanced or equal. It wasn't as if she needed to talk him into wanting the sexy stuff. But he *did* need a chance to make his case for more, and this was the best shot he had. "Fine."

She straightened one leg, stretching the limb across his uninjured thigh. "So should we lay down some definitions and rules?" she asked.

"Definitions and rules?" he repeated, trying to ignore the smooth, toned thigh on his lap and the silky stocking covering that thigh. "That hardly sounds like you."

"Yeah, well, neither does playing nursemaid or letting a guy romance me on purpose, but here I am."

Damn, he liked that. He liked her doing new things with him —*for* him. He liked getting her outside of her comfort zone. He loved the idea of romancing her...and her having to take it. Again, that didn't sound all that romantic and sweet, he knew, but he couldn't help it.

Even as his hand settled on her thigh, Scott knew he was making a mistake. "Give me a for instance," he told her.

She thought about it for a second, and Scott ran his palm over a few inches of the silky stocking under his hand. Just a few inches. Just for a second.

"Okay, if you send me a sweet text that says 'thinking of you' or something, then I get to send you a text back. That's not sweet."

Scott had about a million things he could text that would fit that bill. And, yeah, a few dirty texts in return would be only fair, he supposed. He also supposed he was full of shit when he said that he didn't want that stuff. He did. He just wanted it *too*. Along with the rest.

"Okay. But if you greet me at the door in a skimpy costume that makes me instantly hard, then you have to sit down at the table with me for dinner and have an actual conversation," he told her, running his hand over the stocking again. Just once. Or twice.

She nodded seriously, as if they were negotiating a multi-million-dollar business merger. "Right. The meatloaf thing. Fine. Then if you want to cuddle on the couch," she said, reaching up and running her fingers up the back of his neck and into his hair, "I get to touch you the entire time."

No woman's hands had ever felt as good on him. He simply couldn't find it within himself, even knowing that he was staring at a huge Peyton victory by the end of their two weeks, to say no to that. "Okay. But if I call you during the day, you can't turn it into phone sex."

There was a tiny quiver at the corner of her mouth, indicating that maybe she was fighting a smile. "Okay, but if I call you during the day for phone sex, you can't turn it into a real conversation."

God, he liked her. He wasn't sure they'd ever teased quite like this before. And even if they were technically in a battle of wills, he couldn't help but think they were playing for the same final outcome. More time together. More to what was between them. Just more.

And he was going to be easy for her. So very fucking easy.

But he didn't have to admit it. He could put up a small fight. At least initially.

"Fine. And no worries about couch cuddling tonight," he said. "Think I'll head to Kyle's to watch the game," he said.

She lifted both brows. "Okay."

She was surprised. She hid it quickly, but he saw it. He fought a grin. That would also be key here—keep her on her toes and off-kilter.

"Then I can run home and get some things done then," she said.

"Sounds good." He paused. Then, knowing he probably shouldn't, said, "But you'll come back over later?"

She smiled. "I'll be cuddled up right next to you all night."

Right. Like he'd forgotten for one second that she was going to be sleeping in his bed. He wouldn't last one night. As it was, he was about five seconds away from tipping her back, covering her with his body, and reaching under that skirt.

Before he could reach for anything, though, she swung her leg off of his lap and unfolded from the couch. "So how about some lunch?" she asked.

"Um..." Scott couldn't help but watch her move. "Isn't that kind of a normal couple thing to do?" he asked, more than a little distracted by all of that skin.

"Well, I figure it will balance this out," she said.

"Balance what—" But he froze as she bent over to pick up her shoes.

Because of course he'd been looking at her ass. He looked at her ass every chance he got. And it was right there. And that skirt was so nice and short. Okay, he'd been hoping for a glimpse of cherry-red panties. Or really any color panties.

But he didn't see panties. Because she wasn't wearing any.

What he did see, however, was a whole lot of pink. That was not satin or cotton or silk.

"Jesus, Peyton," he growled.

She straightened and looked back at him over her shoulder. "You okay?"

He looked up to meet her eyes. "You're not going to even pretend to play fair, are you?"

"What's not fair about this?" she asked, turning to face him.

"Really? You walking around here and *bending over* without underwear on is *fair*?" he asked, his heart still hammering.

She shrugged, totally unconcerned. "No underwear is sexy. And now I'm going to make you lunch. That's normal. Something normal for each something sexy. That's fair."

Scott scrubbed a hand over his face. What had he gotten himself into?

After a moment, she gave a light laugh. "I think what you're missing here is that you're kind of full of shit, and I know it."

Scott dropped his hand and focused on her. "What?"

She nodded. "There is such a thing as being with someone for sex only, but you're saying that you want a normal relationship. Well, that's fine, but you're ignoring the fact that a normal relationship includes sex," she told him.

Scott frowned. "I'm not ignoring that. I want to add the other stuff in."

She shrugged. "Okay. But even if we're a 'regular couple'," she said, using her fingers to make the air quotes, "and having lunch together and phone conversations that don't include the words 'wrap your hand around your cock and imagine it's my mouth', and even if we go to the movies, and get each other silly gifts just because, I would still absolutely dress up in costumes and role-play nurse and patient—or any other damn thing you wanted. I would absolutely walk around this house with no panties on and bend over in front of you with the hopes that you'll pull me down on your lap and push up my skirt and make me come so loud you hope that your windows are shut. And there would absolutely be a time when the windows *aren't* shut and your neighbors get to hear just how fucking awesome our sex life is."

She put a hand on her hip. "So yeah, I'll make you a freaking meatloaf and watch TV with you and spoon with you all night. But if you think that this is going to be all how-was-your-day and let's-have-everyone-over-for-a-barbecue-this-weekend   and pancakes in bed without me ever pouring maple syrup on your cock and sucking it clean and getting the sheets all sticky, then you're *way* off."

Scott had never been so turned on in his life.

Sure, the maple syrup blowjob thing helped, but that combination she'd just described? Neither of them would get over that.

"Fine," he finally said. "When you bring my lunch in, you bend over all you want."

Her eyes flashed for a moment, but then she took a deep breath. "I hope this goes without saying, but the only reason I'm making you lunch is because you were shot. *That* won't be a typical thing either. You're a big boy."

Yeah, he was. He nodded. "Noted."

And he definitely watched her ass as she headed for the kitchen.

The next two weeks were looking better and better. In spite of the hole in his leg.

5

———

Peyton only got about five minutes to compose herself before Scott hobbled into the kitchen and took a seat at the table.

She didn't say anything. If he could get this far, he could make his own damned sandwich. And the fact that he was in the mood for a sandwich after she'd bent over in front of him with no panties on was more than a little annoying. But she'd signed up for taking care of him. Soaping him up in the shower sounded like all she really wanted to do, but of course she needed to help him with things like lunch. She supposed, on the first day anyway, that balancing on a crutch while putting ham and cheese on bread might be a challenge.

A few minutes later, he chuckled and she turned, ready to demand to know what was so funny about her making a sandwich.

"Did you see the skit Fallon did last night?" he asked.

Peyton frowned at what had to be one of the last things she'd expected him to say. "What?"

He held up his phone. It was open to a video clip from *The Tonight Show*.

She carried a sandwich, chips, sliced apple, and glass of milk to him and took the phone. "No. I didn't watch last night and I haven't been on Facebook today."

"Watch it," he said. He picked up the sandwich and bit into it.

Whatever. She pressed the arrow to start the clip. A minute later, she was grinning. She looked up. Scott was watching her, munching away on his chips.

"You like Fallon?" he asked.

Yeah, this felt like a regular couple thing. But yes, she liked Fallon. "I do."

"You watch?"

"Sometimes."

Scott nodded and popped an apple slice into his mouth. "I love him."

It was definitely a point in Scott's favor that he was a Fallon fan. Not that he needed anymore points in his favor, really. She was, admittedly, a pretty big fan of Scott's too.

She put the phone back on the table as Scott reached for his napkin. He picked it up, his eyes on her, then dropped it. It fluttered to the floor.

"You wouldn't mind bending over and picking that up for me, would you?" he asked.

Peyton's heart kicked against her rib cage. That smile, that look in his eyes, that gruffness in his voice... She'd do anything he asked if he asked it like that.

And yeah, this plan to balance the normal-couple, regular-relationship, kind-of-fucking-scary stuff he wanted with the sexy, his-hands-all-over-her stuff she wanted, was not *all* bad.

She licked her lips. "I can do that." She started to bend but he stopped her with a hand on her hip.

"I think you know where this is going. Turn around."

Her heart thumped as electricity shot through her limbs. Followed by a dose of skepticism. If he was just messing with her, turning her on, getting her riled up... "Keep in mind that if your hands do not make it under this skirt, there are all kinds of things I can put in your next meal."

"Turn around."

Low, gravelly, firm. All the things she liked best. Peyton turned slowly, feeling his hand slide from her hip to her butt cheek. Big and hot. Like all of him.

The costume was hardly made of high-quality material, so it was thin, making every inch he touched tingle and heat.

"Like this?" she asked, jutting her butt more firmly into his hand.

He squeezed. "Yep. Now pick it up."

She did, slowly, her heart hammering. His hand stayed on her and as she bent forward, it slid from her butt to the back of her thigh.

She'd gone with the no-panties thing to tease him and turn him on, yes. She'd made sure he caught a glimpse. And yeah, she had big hopes for what came after the glimpse. But being right *here*, his hand on her, his eyes on her, feeling like he was a lot more in control at the moment than she was, made everything in her body go hot and liquefy.

She wanted Scott more than she'd ever wanted another guy. Even him looking at her a certain way could set her on fire. But the one time she'd actually gotten into his pants, it had been fast and hard and hot—three of her favorites words—on the hood of his car.

This felt different. Very different. Deliberate. And she wasn't so sure she was going to end up with one bit of her dignity left. Because if Scott Hansen wanted her to beg, she'd beg.

"Damn, that's a gorgeous sight," he said gruffly.

His hand hadn't moved, but she could feel his eyes on her. Like, really *on her*. On all of her good parts. That were completely on display, right there, only inches from his hand. And mouth.

Butterflies swooped through her belly at that thought. Oh, yeah, she'd beg him alright. If that's what it took to get his mouth on her—

Then she felt the stroke of his finger and her knees wobbled.

"So fucking pretty," he said, his voice gravelly as his finger stroked over her folds.

She gasped and pressed back, needing more.

His other hand slid over her cheek, bare now that she was bent and the skirt had pulled up. That hand also served to hold her in place. He wasn't letting her move back, or forward away from his touch either—not that she would think of moving *away*. He ran his finger over her again and again, but the pressure wasn't hard, it wasn't quite in the right place, it wasn't *enough*.

"Scott," she said. "Stop playing."

"Oh, hell no. I'm definitely playing. And you're not going to rush me this time."

This time? She'd rushed him last time because they'd been outside, screwing around—literally—on the hood of his car, and she'd been afraid he was going to come to his senses and change his mind. She had to admit being worried about that a little here too.

"Sco—"

Then he turned his hand and his middle finger pressed against her clit.

His name turned into a moan and she shifted against his finger, needing more friction. He let her move for a moment, then pulled his hand away.

"Hey, I—"

She felt the hot press of his mouth against her butt cheek. He kissed, then licked, then bit gently. "There, I've kissed your ass," he said. "Now turn around."

She straightened, her head feeling a little dizzy as she did it, but she wasn't sure it was from the movement. Guys said their blood all went from their brains to their cocks. Well, the same could be said of girls. Her pulse was pounding through her whole body, she was achy and hot and wet between her legs, her nipples tingled—but she didn't think she had any blood circulating in her brain. Because she was ready to do *anything* Scott asked her to do. And she didn't generally take orders very well.

She turned and was stunned by the heat in his gaze. She'd seen him worked up and turned on before, but this was next-level hot.

"I know you said you wanted to be pulled into my lap," he said, his eyes tracking up her body, from the strip of bare skin below the top to the valley of her breasts, then up to her face. "But I'm not sure that's gonna work at the moment."

His leg. Right. Peyton wet her lips and prepared to respond...

But he said, "I think we can make do though."

Well, hallelujah.

He moved her to straddle his left, uninjured thigh.

"Pull your skirt up and open your top."

The firm, commanding tone was familiar. The words were not. And she *really* liked both. Peyton opened the top first, just because she couldn't be *completely* compliant, undoing the three snaps that held it together, barely, over her breasts. For Halloween, she'd worn a red bra underneath that had shown through the white material faintly and had played peek-a-boo at the V in front. Today, she hadn't. She parted the top, baring her breasts.

Scott sucked in a breath through his nose, his eyes darkening. But he said nothing.

Leaving the top on but open, she lifted the hem of the skirt. Not that she had to go far to show him everything. The skirt was ridiculously short and had definitely required a good wax job.

Shirt open, skirt lifted, stockings and heels on, she felt

naughty and turned on, powerful and yet completely ready to submit to anything he asked. Her effect on him was heady. At the same time, she wasn't sure she'd ever *needed* someone the way she needed Scott.

She was used to affecting men. She knew that it went back to the days when she hadn't felt wanted, and needed to know that someone wanted her for something. She'd grown past using her body and sexuality to get her way—well, unless she was teasing and tormenting Scott, of course. But that was just because he did the same thing to her. Even if it was unintentional some of the time. She still liked to flirt and she loved sex, but if she was completely honest with herself—something she wasn't all that good at, actually—she hadn't really been into anyone since she'd realized how she felt about Scott.

She wet her lips, watching him look at her. He seemed to just be drinking in the sight. She wanted to tell him that he could see her like this every day. Hell, all day long if he wanted to. He could also see her completely naked. And spread out on his bed. Or his kitchen table. But for some reason, she wanted to let him talk here. Tell her what he wanted. What he needed.

Finally, he blew out a breath. "Damn, you really are trouble, you know that?"

She smiled. Trouble had always sounded like an endearment to her.

He lifted a hand and cupped her breast, running his thumb over the tip. She moaned and he smiled.

"Love that sound."

When had a man's *voice* turned her on so much? It was crazy the way his voice and that husky tone made heat swirl through her belly and shoot straight to her clit.

He played with her nipple, his eyes locked on hers, and Peyton was also struck by the fact that she wasn't sure having a hand on her breast had ever felt this intimate. That sounded stupid—people touching each other's naked body parts should always feel intimate. But with him watching her, as if wanting to read every response to every touch, it felt like *more*.

Of course it did. This was Scott.

He circled her nipple with just the tip of his thumb, the nail lightly scraping and tightening the tip further, making everything else in her tighten as well. She let her head fall back, arching closer, silently begging him to take her in his mouth.

But he didn't. Not right away. He took her nipple between his thumb and finger and squeezed gently. Peyton gasped and tried to press her legs together as the ache in her core intensified, but she couldn't with her knees on either side of his thigh.

"Scott," she panted.

Then he tugged harder and she cried out.

"Fuck," he muttered. He brought her forward and fastened his hot mouth on her nipple, sucking hard.

Her hand flew to the back of his head as pleasure pulsed through her.

His hand cupped her between her legs and she instinctively moved against it, seeking pressure on her clit. And deeper. He sucked harder on her nipple as she ground into his hand, and she felt her orgasm building quickly.

But then he lifted his head, staring up at her as he moved to slip one big, thick finger into her.

She couldn't look away from him as she grabbed for his shoulder, her knees threatening to buckle. She gripped his shirt, loving the feel of his muscles lightly bunching as his finger moved in her.

"Ham sandwiches and finger fucking the hottest girl I've ever known?" he said as his thumb circled her clit. "Definitely something I could get used to."

She felt her inner muscles tighten at the "finger fucking"

thing. By-the-book, rule-following hot cop Scott Hansen, talking dirty, was one of the best things in her life.

"If this is what happens for sandwiches, I'm going to have to make you a meatloaf after all."

He moved his finger deeper and faster and she gripped his shirt harder. "You make me meatloaf and I might just set you up on that counter and start with dessert."

Her inner muscles reacted, happily, to that as well. "See? This arrangement is going to work out great." A few "normal" things balanced with some holy-crap-hot things? Yeah, she could do normal for two weeks. Or she could sure as hell fake it.

"You riding my finger like you need it more than air? Yeah, definitely something I could get used to."

She felt the release winding tighter and tighter. "Why don't you open your pants and I'll show you exactly how and what I like to ride."

"Not this time."

Had his finger been anywhere else, doing almost anything else, she would have protested that, but as it was, the rough pad of his thumb against her clit, with a startling knowledge, or instinct, or whatever, for the pressure and speed to apply, was about to send her into orbit. And she figured the take-your-pants-off conversation would come up again later.

His other hand gripped her ass, pressing her more firmly against the hand between her legs. He added a second finger, thrusting deep and hard and fast, and in less than a minute, she was flying.

She cried out his name as her orgasm crashed over her, and as soon as the ripples faded, he brought her down onto his leg, his hand in her hair, his mouth devouring hers.

When he finally let her up for air, she felt boneless and breathless and better than she had in... Since St. Patrick's Day.

"There," he said against her mouth. "Now we're evened up."

She pulled back to look at him. "Evened up?"

He rested his forehead against hers. "You didn't come on St. Patrick's Day, Peyton. I know it."

She hadn't. But she'd had a hell of a good time. It had been hard and fast and hot, and the source of much inspiration with her vibrator since.

"You didn't have to—" she started.

"Yeah, I did."

Right. Of course he did. Not giving her everything he thought she needed and wanted would have made him crazy. She shook her head. "So instead of thinking about how hot and awesome that was, instead of thinking about the handcuffs and the hood of your car and how *naughty* that all was, you've been thinking about how I didn't come? And you just needed to even things up?" She pushed off his lap and pushed her skirt down and re-snapped her shirt.

He took a deep breath, then nodded. "It *was* hotter than hell, and I still can't believe I did that."

"Because you really thought you could out-stubborn me?" She propped a hand on her hip.

"Because it was on my *squad car* behind your house, and I was still in uniform."

Yeah, he had been. That had added to all the heat. "You were off-duty," she said with a little smile she couldn't hide.

He narrowed his eyes. "Trouble. Capital T."

"Who is making you meatloaf for dinner."

Those narrowed eyes went dark again. "Is that right?"

"I'll meet you on..." She looked around and pointed at the counter next to his fridge. "That counter, at six p.m. Bring your appetite." Then she winked and headed into the living room.

"You're not going to help me back to the couch?" he called after her.

"You made it in there just fine on your own," she called back.

She looked around the living room. She didn't know what exactly she was going to do now. Her body was still humming from the orgasm, but it seemed clear she was the only one who was going to be getting that special treatment at the moment. Until tonight. He wasn't leaving that kitchen twice in one day without taking his pants off. She giggled at that. If "normal" couples got busy in the kitchen fifty percent of the time they went in there, she could maybe be more normal than she thought.

Scott followed her a moment later and she turned. But before she could say something smart-ass or flirtatious—like "thanks for the orgasm"—she got a good look at his face. He was in pain.

She frowned, moving across the room. "You need to rest."

He shot her a grin. "Trust me, I feel like my time's been well spent."

That grin. Almost made her forget what they'd been talking about. But she couldn't help replaying what had gone down in the kitchen. He hadn't used his leg, so...this had to be just general healing pain. Right? But probably a good thing she hadn't gotten his pants off.

She put his free arm around her shoulder, helping him to the couch. Or pretending to. No way could she actually help this big guy move around. But it made her feel better to try. "So that's really why you wouldn't go all the way with me," she said. "Your leg."

She knew that wasn't it. Scott would absolutely want to "make up for" her not having an orgasm the first time they'd been together.

"Go all the way?" he repeated as he lowered himself, with Peyton's pretend help, onto the couch. "Is this seventh grade?"

She smiled. "So that's why you didn't *fuck me* right then and there?"

He groaned. "You're right. Let's use 'go all the way'. Or we could just not talk about it at all."

She laughed. "Me saying 'fuck' bothers you?"

He shifted to get comfortable on the cushion. "Makes me want to do it, Peyton."

She froze for a second. Him using her name like that always did it to her. "Is that right?" she said, resuming her sassy attitude rather than letting on that she wanted to hear him saying her name like that, over and over again, every day.

He gave her a lazy look. "It's not the only thing that makes me want to do it, of course. But yeah, hearing you say 'fuck me'? Instant hard-on."

She felt her grin break free. This Scott, this teasing-about-sex Scott, definitely did it for her.

But then she again noted the look of fatigue around his eyes and the little grimace when he moved his leg. He was hurt. She was here to help.

She leaned over and helped him rotate so he was lying along the length of the sofa, his leg propped up on the opposite arm. She went to the bedroom for more pillows and got one behind his head and two under his leg. Then she grabbed the bag of supplies from the coffee table, shook out a pain pill and went to grab a glass of water. She handed both over and watched him swallow them without complaint.

"You can ask for the pain pills, you know," she said. "I'll watch the time, but I'm not giving them unless you ask. There's no problem with becoming dependent if you're using the recommended dose as needed, but if you think you can get by with just ibuprofen, that's probably a better way to go."

He looked up at her with surprise. "How do you know all of that?"

Crap. She could lie. Say she got it from her nursing classes. Or even from watching *Grey's Anatomy* or *ER*, her two favorite shows in the universe. But she sighed and confessed, "I looked it up last night when I got home. I also watched a couple of YouTube videos about dressing changes. Just so you know."

He coughed, but if he felt like smiling, he hid it. "YouTube videos?"

She crossed her arms, knowing she looked defensive. And feeling defensive. "I want to be sure I do it right."

"You probably haven't covered all of that in school yet, hu—" His question was cut off by a big yawn.

She nodded. "Nope, haven't covered that yet." True enough. Though if she'd stayed in school, she might have. Hopefully Scott knew nothing about nursing school curriculum.

"Proud of you," he said, his eyes sliding shut.

She stared at him. "What?" she asked.

"Proud of you. And school."

Ah, shit. Why'd he have to say that?

"I love that you want to take care of other people, even though people have kind of sucked about taking care of you. You haven't let that make you hard."

Her heart slammed against her chest and she couldn't breathe for a second. The hell if she hadn't. She had definitely let her lack of caregivers make her hard and cynical. The meds were making him a little goofy. Maybe. Or he was just super tired. Possibly. But that had sounded really sincere. And exactly like the kind of thing Scott would think.

"Yeah, well," she managed, looking for a way to distract him. "Don't know how well I'm doing here. I wasn't as focused on her instructions yesterday as I should have been."

"Oh?" His eyes hadn't opened again.

That could work in her favor too. He couldn't concentrate on the ins and outs of her nursing program if he was sleepy.

"Your wound is really close to a part of your body I'm *very* interested in," she said. "My gaze might have wandered."

His eyebrows pulled together even though his eyes stayed

shut. "I need to rest. Talking about my cock, and your interest in it, isn't very relaxing."

She laughed and dropped her arms. He was distracted now. "Okay, we'll talk about it after your nap. Do you need anything?"

"You."

Her heart skipped.

"In normal clothes."

Oh. She sighed.

"Can't fall asleep if I know you're sitting over there with your wet, bare pussy on my chair."

Geez, even if he'd partially slurred some of those words, they worked to make her body pulse with desire.

"Fine. But if I can't talk about your cock and say things like 'fuck me', you can't say pussy," she told him.

That stirred him a bit and he shifted again. "Hey."

"What?"

"You can't say 'pussy' either."

She smiled. "You like that?"

"Yeah."

"Noted."

"Trouble," he murmured.

But a moment later, he was asleep.

Peyton stood looking at him—or rather, staring at him like a needy little girl with a gigantic crush—for just long enough to feel creepy. But man, he was gorgeous. Big, strong, confident. And for some reason, he really liked her.

Of course, living with her for two weeks might cure him of some of that.

Five minutes later, she was dressed in a black tee, hot-pink leggings with black trucks on them, and she had her feet propped on Scott's coffee table with her computer open on her lap.

She went through her emails, checked Facebook, even

checked Tumblr. But in the end, she couldn't keep herself from clicking onto the website she'd been avoiding for months.

The next round of nursing classes started in six weeks. Just enough time to get her prerequisites finished. If she started right now.

6

_____

S cott awoke stiff, sore, and feeling slightly disoriented.
    It was his couch, his house—he knew all of that
instantly. But there was a woman in it. Singing.

And that had never happened before.

He pushed himself up to sitting, his leg protesting, though not
as much as he would have expected.

He peered over the back of his couch where the sound was
coming from.

And was treated to quite a sight. Peyton was bending over, in
tight, hot-pink pants.

Damn, if that woman's sweet ass was right in front of him
every time he woke up, he could get used to that _quick_.

And her singing Miranda Lambert a cappella? That was
almost as good as the view.

"Hey, Trouble," he said, greeting her as he had at the hospital.

This time she didn't gasp though. She turned with a bright
smile that slammed into Scott's chest.

"You're awake."

He scrubbed a hand over his face. "Yeah."

"You've been asleep for three hours."

Yeah, he felt like it. He just wasn't sure if that was a good or bad thing. Then he took in the sight around her. She had all six of his kitchen chairs, the coffee table, and the rolling chair from his desk in the guest room gathered in a cluster. Each thing was draped with a number of articles of clothing. Mostly shirts and leggings. Very bright shirts and leggings. In fact, it took him a minute to even find something that was a solid color rather than a multicolored design of some kind. "What are you doing?"

"Photographing some of my new stuff for Facebook." She held her phone up. "I was going to do it when I got home, but then I moved in here, so I had to bring it with me."

Scott sat up farther and ran a hand over his jaw. It was scratchy from two days of no shaving. "I don't understand what you just said."

She laughed. "I sell this stuff online. Every time I get a shipment, I take pictures to post on Facebook, so people know what I've got."

"Ah."

Then he took a closer inventory of what *she* was wearing. It was better than the nurse's uniform. Kind of. It was a very fitted pair of soft-looking leggings that had his palms itching to touch.

Of course, she could have been wearing a potato sack and he'd want to touch.

"You changed clothes."

"You asked me to."

"You never do what I ask you to do."

She turned fully. "Not true. You told me to bend over earlier and I bent over."

Okay, now he was fully awake.

And he needed to get out of this house.

Sexy nurse costumes and bending over without panties were a problem. But not, interestingly enough, as big of a problem as her making sandwiches and wearing normal clothes and doing normal things in his house as if she was perfectly comfortable here and ready to stay for the long haul. She'd been here for—he glanced at the clock—for less than six hours. She hadn't even put in the equivalent of a full workday. And she'd already gotten an orgasm. Not that he minded giving that to her. At all. In fact...

Scott made himself focus. He had no problem touching her. Giving her pleasure. Enjoying the body that had been making him ache for far too long. But the next two weeks were about trying a real relationship. Sex *and* the other stuff. So far, she'd made him a sandwich and put on a pair of leggings. Normal, but that shouldn't be enough to break down his walls. He wanted more and he needed to be strong.

And he needed to get out of the house tonight before he just said *to hell with it* and gave in to every one of her wishes.

"I, uh, am going to head to Kyle's for the game." He pushed himself up off the couch.

The couch—where neither of them were going to be sleeping, according to their agreement.

"Oh, yeah, that's right," she said. "You did mention that."

"Yeah, he's going to grill some burgers and we'll just hang out." Scott had no idea if Kyle would grill him a burger, but his friend would come pick him up and let him hang out at his place for a few hours. Scott might have to beg, and he'd certainly have to put up with some shit, but Kyle would do it.

"Great," Peyton said, but she'd turned back to her leggings and shirt display.

"I mean, if that's cool with you?" he felt compelled to say.

She glanced over. "Of course. Once you're fed and medicated and you're in between dressing changes and showers, I don't really need to be here, right? It's not like we're just going to sit around and watch TV or something."

Right. That would be too *normal.* "I guess. What are you going to do tonight?"

"I'll stop by home and take care of some stuff. And then I'll head into the bakery. I told Adrianne I could get some stuff started for tomorrow."

He frowned. "You go into the bakery at night?"

She shrugged. "Sometimes. I'm kind of a night owl." She said it with an eye roll that said Scott, of all people, should know that. "And so it works for me to go in late and get things prepped for the morning. That way she doesn't have to get in so early."

Adrianne was a wife and mom of three—two boys and a girl, all very close in age—whose husband, Mason, often traveled to Washington, D.C., and even internationally with his company, IAS. Scott had no doubt that Adrianne could use all the help and extra hours at home that she could get. And it didn't surprise him at all that Peyton saw that and pitched in. She might be Trouble with a capital T, but she had a big heart and saw people and what they needed. Even if she would hate knowing that he'd noticed.

"Okay." Scott hadn't known that Peyton went in late at the bakery sometimes. Not that he should have known that. But it felt weird that he didn't. "You'll come back over later?"

She gave him one of her mischievous grins. "Can't cuddle up with you from clear across town."

She didn't live "clear across town" from him, but that wasn't the point. She was coming back tonight. That was really all he needed to know.

"Okay, then I'll see you later." He started for the kitchen.

"Wait! What are you doing?" She was around in front of him before he'd taken more than three steps.

"Going to the kitchen."

"Why?"

"For water."

"I'll get it for you."

"Peyton, I'm—" But she was already around the corner. A few seconds later she was handing him a glass of water. "Uh, thanks."

What he really needed was to get into another room so he could text Kyle and tell him the plans for the evening. He already knew he'd be springing for some beer. And any groceries Kyle didn't already have.

"Take it easy tonight, okay?" she asked, looking up at him.

"I will."

"If you start to get tired or sore or anything, just call me."

He wanted to grin at the idea of Peyton coming to pick *him* up for a change, but he fought it. "Okay."

"And don't forget your meds at eight. That's the next time you can take them."

Yeah, okay, this was a normal couple kind of thing, and he liked it. Her taking care of him. It was nice.

He went with his instinct and leaned in, giving her a soft kiss. "Thanks. I'll see you later."

She looked a little stunned as he turned and headed for the bedroom.

He liked that look on her.

Thirty minutes later, he was on Kyle's couch, wondering why he was friends with the two guys sitting in the recliners in the living room with him.

"So you're pushing the normal-couple-relationship thing and she's pushing the sexy, let's-play-nurse-and-patient stuff, and you're pretty sure you're losing?" Derek summarized.

"Yep."

"That sounds about right," Derek said with a nod, tipping back the can of beer he was holding.

"That she's winning and I'm losing?"

"Yep. I mean, you're offering something she doesn't want. She's offering something you both want. Of course you're losing."

Damn.

"So I have no hope."

"Of tying Peyton Wells down in a relationship if she doesn't want it?" Derek asked with a laugh.

"Remember, we talked about how to be supportive?" Kyle asked, throwing a French fry at Derek. He hadn't agreed to grill, but he'd agreed to go pick up burgers from the Come Again.

"I just don't get why everything has to be so *official* with him," Derek said with a shrug. "I mean, she's crazy about him. Everyone knows it. Why can't he just be happy with that?"

"I'm a bad guy for wanting more than sex?" Scott asked. He was beginning to think that given one single, simple excuse to just take Peyton to bed and never let her out, he'd go for it. There was more to life than sex. But really, really, really good sex could make up for a lot.

"You've already got more than sex," Derek said, rolling his eyes.

Scott scowled at him. "Really? Like what?"

"Let's see," Derek said dryly. "She hasn't been with anyone else in a year. You're always her first call, for everything. She can't let you leave a room without talking to you. She rushed back here from Baltimore to be by your side. She's living in your house. And she almost kicked Reed Walker's ass earlier today because of you."

Scott felt his eyebrows pulling tighter and tighter as he thought about Derek's words.

She hadn't been with anyone else in a year? He tried not to keep *too* many tabs on her and other guys. He knew she flirted, danced, when out with other guys. Sometimes. Though, yeah, it did seem like it had been a while. And not letting him leave a room without talking to him? Sure, that might seem true—okay, that *was* true—but it was usually to give him shit or tease him about something. It wasn't like they *talked*. But he did like the way she always found him and made a point of coming up to him, even in a crowded, fun party at the Come Again or down at the river.

"She's *staying* at my house to help me out while I heal," he said.

Derek laughed. "Okay, sure. Because clearly you're on death's doorstep."

Kyle laughed too. "And you have no one else who could have helped you out. No best friend with a medical degree or anything."

Scott rolled his neck. He heard what they were saying. He wanted to believe that Peyton cared about him and wanted to be there. Okay, he knew she cared about him. They were...friends. At least.

"And when she called me on her way to the hospital, she was *all over* my ass," Kyle said.

Scott frowned at him. "She called you?"

"Yeah. TJ picked her up from the airport so Heather would have her truck when she gets back from Baltimore. On the drive back, she called me for a report and to tell me that if I didn't keep you alive, she'd marry me and make me miserable for the rest of my life."

Scott couldn't help the warmth that spread through his chest hearing that. "What's this about Reed Walker?" he asked, thinking back to what Derek had said.

"She marched into Dottie's this morning and chewed his ass for not having the gun locked up, and then lost it when she heard that Reed has only talked to his kid about it."

Scott was torn between feeling damned good that she'd come to his defense and worried about what she'd said to Reed. Walker was a good guy, and Scott knew he had to feel like shit. "Did you see all of this?" he asked his friends.

"We were with you, remember?" Derek asked. "But I heard all about it when Mitch and I stopped in at the hardware store."

Kyle nodded. "My front desk staff was talking about it when I got to the clinic and I heard it from two patients."

"So, the point is," Derek said, pointing a French fry at Scott. "You've already got the girl. Why can't you just be happy with how things are? Don't get so hung up on what you're calling it or whatever."

"I agree," Kyle said. "Peyton's not really the caregiver type, you know? Her being there for you means something, I think."

"It definitely means something," Derek agreed. "But I'm not so sure she's not the caregiver type."

Scott looked over at his friend. Derek was definitely the more laid-back of Scott's friends. Kyle was the perfectionist, the always-had-his-shit-together guy who had blown through high school and college, charged right into medical school, and then moved back to Sapphire Falls immediately. That had always been his plan. He'd put that plan on paper when he was about fifteen and had never veered from the course. Except for the fact that he was supposed to meet his high school love, Hannah, here to build their practice together, put their dream house on the land Kyle still owned outside of town, and make two or three beautiful, perfect babies. Hannah had screwed all of that up. But Kyle was still here, practicing, hell-bent on making everyone better and dying a very old, happy man in his beloved hometown.

"I mean, she's not warm and fuzzy about it maybe," Derek went on. "But if you mess with someone she loves, you're going to have to deal with her."

Derek, on the other hand, didn't really have any plans beyond the next few hours. He was a whatever-feels-good-at-the-moment guy. He did a bunch of odd jobs around town—bartender, groundskeeper for the city, volunteer firefighter, EMT, and whatever else the town needed. His love for Sapphire Falls was as deep as Kyle's, and he too would die a happy old man right here, but he found that happiness differently. And there were no great loves in his past. Derek had plenty of love, just not the forever—or even more than a couple of weekends—kind.

Scott scratched his neck, feeling a little befuddled. Not about what Derek was saying. He was right on about all of it. But Scott was surprised that *Derek* was saying it.

"And I know all about her messed-up home life," Derek said. "But seems to me that if she didn't worry about her parents, at least a little, and love this town and the people here, it sure would have been a lot easier to just get the hell out, you know? But she's stuck around in spite of it all."

Scott felt a tightness wrapping around his chest. Damn, Derek was good.

That was all true. Peyton was a tough girl on the outside, but when she loved, she loved big and hard and loud. And that was exactly what he wanted from her—all of her passion, her energy, her inability to hold back, directed at him. Not just him—he appreciated her love for her friends and the town. But definitely at him *too*.

"That's what I love," Scott said. Hell, if he couldn't say this to these guys, who could he say it to? "In spite of how rough things were growing up and how easy it would be to just say 'fuck it all' and be cynical and hard and bitchy, she's...so full of life. She loves to have fun, *makes* other people have fun. She just lives so big, you know? It's like her go-to way of dealing with the shit is to be happy."

Kyle and Derek looked at one another and then back at Scott. Okay, so maybe he just shouldn't say that stuff to anyone. He frowned at them both. "What?"

Kyle shrugged. "It's just that all of *that* is why you shouldn't be so worried about sleeping with her."

Scott felt his scowl deepen. "What does that mean? I'm not worried about it."

Derek laughed and Kyle shook his head.

"Yeah, you are," Kyle said. "She's got a messed-up home life and that makes you all protective and makes you think of her as vulnerable, and because of the shit you did in Omaha, that gets to you."

Kyle and Derek were the only people in Sapphire Falls who really knew all about Scott's time with the sex trafficking task force. He didn't really want people to know. He'd prefer to keep everyone he knew in the dark about...the darkness. The disturbing, horrible stuff that went on in other places. At the same time, he needed to talk about it sometimes. Especially after he'd been out on an assignment. He was grateful to have friends who would listen and supported the work. In fact, there were times when Scott had been sure that Kyle and Derek would have absolutely joined him on the job if they could have.

In fact, they'd been on his ass about getting back to it. He'd taken a much-needed break. But it had been nearly eight months now since he'd helped with an operation and both Kyle and Derek thought he needed to get back to that work. They understood why he needed Sapphire Falls too, but they knew that he needed to fight a bigger fight once in a while, to celebrate what he had here by trying to make the rest of the world a little better.

"But you gotta remember," Derek continued, "Peyton isn't one of those girls you've saved. Or," he said, his voice gentling slightly and his gaze becoming more direct, "the girls you *haven't* saved."

Scott felt his chest tighten again. Yeah, okay, these guys knew him well. He thought about the girls he'd helped save. But he had nightmares about the ones he hadn't.

"Peyton takes care of herself *and* other people," Derek said. "She'd tell you, in no uncertain terms, if you did something to piss her off or scare her, and she'd kick your ass if you didn't listen."

And with that, Scott was 100% positive that his friends had discussed this—without him and possibly at length—before.

But they were right. Very right. He'd seen a lot of very vulnerable girls who had been victimized and taken advantage of. They didn't all have bad home lives, of course, but that was not an uncommon denominator. And that didn't even matter. The girls had been used, plain and simple. No matter where they came from, they'd been hurt—physically, emotionally, and mentally—in ways that would stick with them for the rest of their lives. He'd helped get them out, doing things that turned his stomach in some cases to do it, but he couldn't totally help and heal them.

Which was definitely one of the reasons he was drawn to Peyton Wells. She'd been hurt emotionally, but she not only still found joy and fun in life, she spread it around like feel-good-party-girl confetti. And she knew herself. She knew what she wanted, what she needed, and she would ask for it. Physically, sexually, he didn't have to worry about crossing any lines or pushing her too far. She'd let him know if that happened, and she'd enjoy the hell out of everything up to that point. He needed to be with someone like that, someone who owned her sexuality, and had no trouble telling him exactly where he stood.

He just worried about her emotional state sometimes. That was a little more vulnerable than she liked to let on.

"You been paying a lot of attention to Peyton," Scott commented. He wasn't the jealous type—well, he didn't *like* being the jealous type. And he wasn't, really. But it bugged him a little that Derek and Kyle had noticed these things about Peyton. Of course, one was a doctor. He was kind of trained to see people and notice subtle things. And the other was a bartender. Not trained, exactly, but certainly experienced in seeing people in various emotional states.

"Well, I see a lot of Peyton," Derek said with a laugh.

Everyone knew that the Come Again was one of Peyton's favorite places. She was a night owl, for one thing, and it was the only place in town open past six. She was also very social. And, being the only place open after six, the Come Again was where a lot of people ended up on any given night.

Or was it that she didn't like being alone? That seemed more accurate, for whatever reason.

"And I'm not all wrapped up in trying *not* to sleep with her for a bunch of deep, psychologically complicated reasons," Derek added, "so, I can see it all clearly."

"You are definitely not psychologically complicated," Kyle agreed.

"Not at all. Total straight-shooter. If that girl came at *me* in a naughty nurse's costume, no way I'd be worried about a thing except if I have enough condoms to last the night."

"Watch yourself, Wright," Scott cautioned with a scowl. "It's only my leg that's not one hundred percent." Not that he was concerned about Derek and Peyton.

Derek grinned. "You'd have to catch me first, old man."

Scott was only a year older than Derek, but the younger guy loved to point it out whenever he had the chance. "My Taser would absolutely catch you."

Derek pushed up out of the recliner and stretched. "Well, like I said, you've got the girl. I think you need to quit thinking so much and maybe just start *doing*."

"You out of here?" Kyle asked, as Derek picked up his beer can and plate and headed for the kitchen.

"Yeah, told Bryan I'd close up and then Mitch is stopping by."

"You guys really going to add on?" Scott asked. Derek had been playing with the idea of adding on to the Come Again. He had a grand scheme of adding a pizza kitchen and expanding the business. The Stop had pizza but it was...pizza. Nothing special. Derek seemed to think that Sapphire Falls was ready for something more.

Derek came back into the living room. "Yep, Bryan's on board. Said we can do a partnership where I manage the pizza business and keep whatever profits come in as long as I also pay all the bills for it. He keeps the bar business."

"And Mitch is going to do the work?" Kyle asked.

Derek nodded. "He said he and Andi will do it after hours and it won't disrupt business."

Mitch Dugan and Andrea Gallo were two of the best contractors and builders in the area. Both from Sapphire Falls, and best friends, they'd started their business about two years ago. They were getting busier, and doing something like the addition to the Come Again would get a lot of attention.

"Sounds great," Kyle said. "And like I told you, if you need an investor, just let me know."

Derek clapped his friend on the shoulder as he went by. "You're a good guy, no matter what they say," he told him. "And you," he said to Scott. "Quit torturing Peyton."

Scott laughed at that. *He* was torturing Peyton? Yeah.

He and Kyle both focused back on the baseball game on TV, but Scott couldn't stop thinking about Peyton actually caring about him. Of course she did. He knew that.

His phone pinged with a text message. He looked down. And smiled. Peyton.

Did you take your pill?

She was checking up on him.

Before he could answer, Kyle's phone pinged. He looked down where he had it resting on the arm of his chair. Being the only physician in Sapphire Falls, he was pretty much on call twenty-four-seven. He frowned and opened the message. Then he looked up at Scott with brows raised.

"Peyton wants to know if you've been drinking because you shouldn't do that while taking pain pills."

Scott snorted. "Good thing you've got her to remind you of that, Doc," he said.

Kyle just rolled his eyes. "Seriously, man, just sleep with her."

"You think I should?" Scott asked. Derek was one thing. He didn't harbor any hopes for a deeper relationship. Scott had thought Kyle understood his side though.

"She's *texting* me about your pain pills," Kyle said, typing something into his phone. "I've got real stuff to worry about."

"I can't control her and who she texts."

"But if you were home with her right now, letting her take care of you, she wouldn't be texting me." He set his phone back down and focused on the TV.

"Peyton's not really the staying-home type," Scott said.

"Maybe she just doesn't have anything to stay home *for*," Kyle said, eyes still on the TV.

Which was good, because then he couldn't see Scott's reaction to that. *Maybe she just doesn't have anything to stay home for*. Bingo. With her family life, no doubt she'd been coming up with ways and reasons to be out of the house from a very young age. Maybe it was a habit to not be home.

"I want her to be happy," he said.

Kyle glanced over. "I know, man."

"So maybe I need to do things her way."

Kyle cocked a brow. "Convenient that her way involves a lot of naked time."

Yeah, well, perks. "I just realized that *no one* does things with Peyton's happiness in mind. Everyone has another priority."

"Hope's there for her," Kyle said. "And Heather and Tess and Lucy and Brooke."

Scott nodded to all of that. "But Peyton isn't their main priority. They all have their lives, work, other relationships. When they're with her, she has a good time, of course. They all do. But she's the one making the good time happen. Has anyone ever just showed up at her house with a pizza? Or called up and said, 'I want to take you out for a drink because you're always there for me'? Or planned a surprise party for her?"

The realizations were coming to him as he talked. And the answer to all of that was no. He knew that Peyton would show up on a friend's doorstep with a bottle of tequila if the friend had had a crappy week at work. He knew she'd show up with ice cream if the friend had been dumped. She'd get people together at the river to celebrate someone's birthday. She was always the first on the dance floor or up on the stage for karaoke at the Come Again. Peyton made the good times happen. People went along with it all, of course. They all loved being around her. But no one ever made a point of making a good time happen for her.

"Peyton is always the one planning things, calling people up, getting people together. She's the party girl, right? So everyone expects her to initiate things. But wouldn't it be nice for someone to show that they wanted to be with her enough to make the plans?"

"So Peyton is *your* main priority?" Kyle asked.

"Yep." She was. From here on out. He was done resisting her and the urges to be with her all the time and to show her just exactly how much he wanted her.

"And that means you should sleep with her?"

"It means that I fully intend to show her that she is very wanted. I want her to be happy."

Kyle chuckled. "Yep, very convenient that she's happiest naked with you."

Scott just grinned. Peyton Wells was going to be in his bed that night, and he couldn't wait to tell her that he was lifting the pajamas-on-at-all-times rule.

———

I t sucked that Heather was still in Baltimore. Peyton would prefer tequila right now.

Instead, she was stuck with sugar, flour, and eggs.

She sighed. Yeah, tequila would be better. She should not do this. This was ridiculous.

Still, she had the definite urge to bake something.

She'd already tossed the meatloaf she'd put together for dinner after finding out Scott was going to Kyle's. She'd rushed into the kitchen to get rid of the evidence that she'd planned to cook for him. Thankfully she hadn't put it in the oven yet or he would have smelled it.

But now she was contemplating making him cookies. With frosting Band-Aids and crutches and pill bottles filled with little red hots for the pills in them.

Baking was what she did when she didn't know what else to do. She wasn't so great at words or other displays of concern or affection. She didn't say things like "I'm so happy you're okay" or "I'm glad you were born" or "I wish there was something I could do" to people, so instead, she baked.

It was silly. She knew that. But making cookies and cakes and cupcakes and pies and bread made her feel good. There was something therapeutic about creating something that was, literally, sweet and colorful, and knowing that it would make someone smile no matter what they were going through. And fortunately, because everyone loved carbs, she didn't have to feel self-conscious about it. People were too caught up in *oh this is so cute!* and *oh my God this is so good!* to think too much about the person behind it.

Hell, for all she knew, most of the people in Sapphire Falls thought Adrianne did all of the baking that made them all happy and feel good. Peyton didn't care. She liked that she had a simple, straightforward way of putting some good out into the world that didn't get any more complicated than getting just the right shade of icing for the occasion. And heck, even then, if it wasn't right, she could scrape it off and start over.

That was really the beauty of baking. As long as you had

enough ingredients, eventually you could get anything to turn out right. She wished more things in life were like that, frankly.

But she should not make Scott cookies. Because one, he'd definitely know they were from her, and two, she had the sneaking suspicion that he *would* think about what was behind them. They wouldn't be a simple sugar rush for him. No, he'd have to make them *mean* something.

Peyton chewed on her lip. She knew Heather would be at the wedding reception in Baltimore by now. Heather and Seth had been having an amazing time—even outside of the expensive silk sheets inside the fancy hotel suite. Heather had texted her a photo of the dress she'd chosen—or rather, that Seth had chosen for her—and her friend's smile had been huge.

But Heather would pick up if Peyton called, she was sure. She wouldn't keep her long.

"Help me," she said, when Heather answered.

Peyton could hear music and laughter in the background.

"What's wrong? Are you okay? Is Scott okay?" Heather asked.

Peyton rubbed her forehead. "Yes, yes, sorry. Everything is fine. I'm sorry to call."

"Don't be silly. I just slipped out to go to the bathroom. It's fine. What's up?"

"Are you having fun?" Peyton asked first.

"Yes, *so* much."

Peyton could hear the smile in her friend's voice.

"Seth is amazing. This night has been amazing. I can't wait to tell you all about it. But what do *you* need?"

Peyton's heart warmed. She might not do a lot of things right, but she picked awesome friends. "I'm thinking about making Scott cookies. But I shouldn't make him cookies if I don't want to keep him, right?"

"Um."

Peyton knew her friend didn't totally get her adamant refusal to get involved with Scott. Heather knew about Peyton's parents and everything, but she wasn't from Sapphire Falls, so she didn't *really* know the history like most of the town did.

Flat-out, Peyton hadn't really had parents. She'd had two people who had given birth to her and let her live in their house until she was old enough to leave. And a dad who had come to pick her up at the police station when they called. Of course, it would sometimes take him hours to get there. Peyton's crush on Scott had really started when she saw how angry that made him, and when he'd first pulled her dad aside and chewed his ass about it. She hadn't heard what Scott had said to Dan, but she'd read the body language. Scott had been defending her.

"I'm afraid he'll read too much into the cookies," she said.

Like she wanted to take care of him, and even making him a sandwich that he'd liked had made her happy, and watching him sleep had been a moment of realization for her. She'd liked *watching him sleep.* That was stupid. And maybe a little creepy. The fact that she'd felt happy and relaxed in his house, working while he slept, moving things around in his living room, familiarizing herself with his kitchen, making herself at home, had made her admit that there were things about Scott she was drawn to that went beyond the physical.

"Yeah, okay, if you're *sure* you don't want to keep him, definitely don't make the cookies," Heather said. "Do something else. Do laundry or something. Something that needs to be done, so it doesn't seem like anything too thoughtful or personal, but will still make you feel like you're helping."

"I don't need to feel like I'm helping him," Peyton said.

"Yes, you do. Him getting shot made you realize that you care about him more than you thought, and now you want to take care of him but you don't want him to realize it because, in your words, you're not sure you want to keep him."

"I *am* sure," Peyton protested. "I *don't* want to keep him." She was such a liar. She didn't think she *should* keep him. That was different.

And Heather was wrong. About one thing, at least. Peyton had realized she cared about him more than she thought before he'd gotten shot.

"But you're making him cookies."

"I'm *almost* making him cookies. I'm calling my best friend to talk me out of it."

"Well, I think you should make them," Heather said. "But I also think you should keep him, so there's that. Because if you give the guy a cookiegasm, you'll never be rid of him."

Peyton laughed in spite of herself. Heather always said she had cookiegasms after eating Peyton's. She really was good at cookies. "So I definitely need to kill time somewhere other than the bakery."

"Oh, you're at the bakery. Well, that's a little better than his house. If he walks into that smell, he'll never let you leave. Though sex in cookie dough could, and should, totally be a thing."

Peyton laughed again. "Stop. Thinking about cookies and sex together is *not* helping me."

Heather laughed too. "Why are you killing time? You couldn't just hang at Scott's and watch TV?"

"I didn't want him to think I was just sitting around, waiting for him to come home." She'd come to the bakery to work, and she had. Everything was prepped for tomorrow. And then some. But it still wasn't time to go back to Scott's. Peyton and time on her hands were almost always a recipe for trouble.

Heather sighed. "Scott would kind of love to know you were just sitting around."

"I know." Peyton chewed on her bottom lip.

"Peyton," Heather said gently, no longer laughing. "You can

give in to Scott. He'll take care of you. He'll be there no matter what. He's proven that over and over. You can trust him."

Peyton felt tears stinging her eyes and she blinked several times. "I know," she said. "That's the problem. He'll be just like my dad, and he'll never leave, no matter how bad it gets or how horrible I am or how miserable he is." Scott was completely the type to stick with something. Or someone.

"You're *not* going to make him miserable," Heather said firmly. "You're amazing. You have to quit thinking that there's some monster inside just waiting to bust out and terrorize everyone you know."

But there might be. Not like her mom. Peyton had worried—still did from time to time—that she'd inherited some of Jo's affliction, but so far she could only chalk up her emotional swings to being a little high-strung and having a short fuse. And sometimes Booze. But there was something about her mother with her dad that she absolutely saw in herself with Scott—she loved being the center of his attention.

Peyton pulled in a breath. "Leaning on Scott would be amazing," she finally said. "Him being there for me over and over again has always felt so good. For a while there, I got into trouble just so he would come and get me."

"I know," Heather said softly.

"But I'm past that. I need to take care of myself. And I realized that that feeds into *his* issues."

"Scott has issues?" Heather asked.

"He's this big save-the-world hero and gets off on helping people, and the thing is, if I turn into this needy woman who wants him around all the time and calls him for every little thing and doesn't want him to have his own life, then he'll get sucked in. Part of him will love it. My dad does. But he deserves better than that. He deserves to be with someone who doesn't just *need* him."

Heather was quiet for a moment. Then she asked, "You really think you would turn into that woman?"

"I already feel it," Peyton said, feeling her emotions welling up—panic, mostly, with a touch of self-loathing. "I've been staying with him for *one day* and I was already disappointed that he went to Kyle's tonight. I've already texted him *and* Kyle, checking up on him."

Heather laughed. "You texted his doctor to check up on him?"

"I did. I'm a mess."

"You're not a mess," Heather said loyally. "And Scott really cares about you."

Peyton knew that. It was part of the problem.

She heard the laughter on Heather's end of the phone and then a deep voice asking if everything was okay.

"You need to go," Peyton told her. "Call me when you get back to town."

"Okay. Everything will be okay. Just don't fall the rest of the way in love with him before I get back."

Peyton laughed. "You're coming home tomorrow."

"Exactly," Heather said. And she didn't sound like she was laughing.

Peyton sobered up and nodded, even though her friend couldn't see her. "Okay. Yeah."

"And...probably don't make the cookies."

"Yeah."

7

Peyton was still wound up after she made three batches of cookies.

She'd finally given in to the urge, telling herself that she didn't have to give them to Scott. She did want him to get over her. Probably. So she couldn't make him cookies. And not because of the possible cookiegasms, but because Scott would definitely realize that they were more than the best combination of flour and sugar he'd ever tasted.

So, instead she'd made cookies. Not cookies *for* Scott. Not cookies shaped or decorated like anything special. Just round cookies with colored frosting. And they now filled the trays in the front display case of the bakery. Cookiegasms for everyone *but* Scott.

But she was still wound up. It was late. He was home—Kyle had texted to tell her he'd dropped Scott off and done his dressing change. And yes, she totally heard the sarcasm in Kyle's text. But she wasn't quite ready to go and be all girlfriend-y. Worse, she wasn't ready to go there to try to seduce him.

Which was the weirdest thing of all. That was the deal, the

plan. He was going to push the relationship thing. She was going to push the sex thing. They both knew it. But she was hesitant, and she couldn't quite put her finger on why.

So she was driving very slowly toward his house and hoping to remember that she needed to do something else that would keep her out and busy for a while.

The lights were still on in the Come Again as she turned onto the highway, taking the very long and not-at-all-direct route to Scott's. It was after midnight, and while, in Nebraska, bars could stay open until two, the Come Again was almost always shut down by midnight. There was the occasional party or special event, and during the summer festival it stayed open later, but after midnight was only for the real diehards on regular weekends, and there weren't many real diehards in little Sapphire Falls.

But if the lights were on, that meant people. And Peyton could use some people right now. She'd been alone with her own thoughts far too long. That was, clearly, not a good thing.

She pulled in, parking next to Derek's truck. Well, he'd likely tell Scott she'd stopped down here, but she didn't care. As long as she could keep the bartender talking about anything *other* than his friend, she'd be good. And Derek was totally the type of guy she could threaten with "say the name Scott to me and I'll start buying my liquor in Kingston instead of here". Frankly, that would put a noticeable dent in Derek's budget.

Peyton grabbed her bag and started for the door, relieved to find it unlocked and all of the lights in the main room blazing. But no people.

She stepped into the room, letting the door shut behind her. Then she heard voices coming from the back room.

The Come Again was the kind of place where everyone felt at home. And considering she'd known the owner, Bryan Murray, another Sapphire Falls native, her entire life, Peyton was completely comfortable rounding the bar and poking her head through the swinging door that separated the bar area from the back, where the kitchen and storage were.

Derek was there with Mitch Dugan.

"Hey, guys."

They both swiveled. "Hey, Peyton," Derek greeted. "Thought you'd be rushing home to your patient."

She shrugged, trying to look completely nonchalant about how the words "rushing home" hit her. Home was the tiny house she rented from Mrs. Bernard. It was fine. All of her stuff fit. She had a bed and a shower and a kitchen. And a garage—that was big during the winter in Nebraska.

But it was just a house. A house where she had her stuff. Where she could do her online business and sleep safely and hang out doing home pedicures with her girlfriends with margaritas once in a while. But it was never a place she was excited to go.

She was excited to go to Scott's.

Which was why she was here instead.

"Kyle said he took care of the bandages and he took his medication, so he'll probably be out pretty fast," she said. All of which was true. And not why she was here instead of there.

"He looked a little worn out," Derek agreed. "Weird to see big old Scott get tired from sitting on the couch."

"Well, he was just *shot* yesterday," she said.

Derek held up a hand. "Don't come at me, wildcat. I know. I get it. You don't need to defend your boy to me."

She frowned. She hadn't been coming at him. She might have snapped a little more than necessary...

"You guys hanging out here for a while?" she asked.

Derek nodded. "Mitch and Andi are adding on for me."

"Adding on?" Peyton asked, moving farther into the room.

"We're putting in a brick oven for pizzas," Derek said with a wide grin. "And some other stuff. We need more space, so Mitch and Andi are doing an addition."

"Wow, that's cool," Peyton said. "It's kind of late for hammering and sawing, isn't it?"

"We're far enough away from any residential areas, we shouldn't make a lot of noise," Mitch said. "Working after closing means we don't have to disrupt business hours and we can still do other jobs during the day."

"You and Andi don't need to sleep?" Peyton asked. Andi and Mitch were older than her by a couple of years, but she knew them both pretty well. They showed up at river parties from time to time and were hilarious. Come to think of it, Peyton couldn't remember ever seeing either of them at a social event without the other.

"We'll sleep after the business is up and really running," Mitch said. "For now, we're taking on every project we can, and Derek's promised to keep the coffeepot on."

"Ooh, coffee," Peyton said. She turned to Derek. "As long as you guys are going to be here anyway, do you mind if I take one of your tables? I have some work to do and my house is too quiet."

"And Scott's house is too full of Scott?" Derek guessed.

"Something like that," Peyton agreed without elaborating.

Fortunately, Derek Wright wasn't really an elaborating kind of guy. "Sure, whatever you want. As long as Mitch's music doesn't bother you."

Mitch gave her a grin as he crossed to crank the volume on his beat-up radio that was covered with paint splatters, glue and what almost looked like tar. Classic AC/DC spilled out, and Peyton nodded.

"I can live with that."

It wasn't often that these four walls heard anything that wasn't country, which Peyton appreciated, but she could handle classic rock.

This music made her think of her dad, and the music he listened to while he messed with their car in the driveway or did yard or housework when she'd been growing up. Stupid, considering everything between her and her parents, but it made her a little nostalgic and tightened her chest. Probably because when Dan had been doing that kind of work, he was truly happy. He smiled and would sing along and would beckon Peyton off the top porch step and teach her about motors and weeding and gardening and fixing shutters and cleaning out gutters and all of the things he did to keep the house up. And to avoid being cooped up inside.

Winter had been the worst—fewer outdoor projects and weather that made it tough to be out anyway. He'd worked in his little shop in the basement, but he hadn't been able to crank up the music and sing along inside. Outside, he'd been in control—mowing the lawn in perfect lines, planting the tomatoes in perfect rows, keeping the house painted and fixed up and looking nice.

Because inside, things were...chaotic at worst, unpredictable at best. He could control things and keep them neat outside. Inside, he couldn't do any of that. Either Jo was depressed and in bed, sometimes for days, and they kept quiet and tried to keep things peaceful; or she was manic and excited—which could go from her suddenly wanting to paint the kitchen pink to her not sleeping for a couple of days at a time.

Peyton never had been convinced that she and her dad really handled Jo well in any of her swings, but they did what they could to try to help. Sometimes she let them. Sometimes she threw plates.

There was certainly never a dull day, which made Peyton wonder, not for the first time, if that was why she had a hell of a time sitting still, being quiet and just...being.

"Well, make yourself at home," Derek said, waving to the front. "Mi bar-o es su bar-o."

She laughed. "I don't think that's how you say that in Spanish."

He gave her a wink. "El café está en el frente."

She got that one. The coffee was in front. She poured a cup and took her favorite table. It was the perfect distance between the bar and the stage where people performed live once a month, and she always took the chair where she could see the door—and the people coming and going.

She opened her computer, took a deep breath, and opened the nursing school site.

She was going to do this. She was going to take the classes.

An hour later, Peyton yawned. She realized that she hadn't even finished her cup of coffee and it was after one a.m. She needed to get to Scott's. He was very likely deep asleep, but if he woke up and she wasn't there, he'd worry.

A warmth spiraled through her with that thought. It was nice to think that someone would worry when she wasn't home. Or even notice, for that matter. And maybe even more than that, he'd be disappointed she wasn't there. Peyton smiled as she packed up her stuff, dumped out the cold coffee, and said goodnight to Derek and Mitch.

She wasn't a big fan of going home, usually. Growing up, she'd purposefully spent extra time at school—not necessarily studying or participating in chess club, but there were always activities going on until well after dinnertime. And detention worked too. She'd become a cheerleader, not because she was full of pep and school spirit exactly, but cheerleading practice, games, and weekend clinics and competitions kept her away from home. She'd also spent a lot of time at friends' houses, and when girl-friends weren't around or available, boyfriends always were. Sure, she'd done more kissing with the boyfriends, but that was a small price to pay.

Now, as an adult, she didn't like going home any more than she had as a kid. Her house was dark and empty. So, the Come Again, the bakery, and again, friends' places and boyfriends' houses were her go-tos. She was even kind of looking forward to Hope having her baby so that Peyton could babysit. That would be a great excuse for hanging out at their place.

But going to Scott's was a whole new thing. Going to Scott's didn't feel just like a way of avoiding being home alone. She had a reason for being there. He needed her. And, yeah, it felt nice to think that he wanted her there. Her friends and boyfriends always liked to see her, of course. She was welcome in any of their houses anytime, really. But Scott wanted her in a way that no one else ever had. And while it worried her at times, and drove her a little crazy, it mostly made her feel special and cared for.

She could definitely feel how risky this was. Already. The more time she spent with him and the more she liked it, the needier and more dependent she could get.

Peyton scowled as she pulled into Scott's driveway. She did not want to be someone Scott took care of because she couldn't handle being alone or function without someone looking out for her. And he would do that. Just as she'd told Heather on the phone. Scott took care of people. He especially felt compelled to take care of *her*.

They could both get sucked into this never-ending circle of neediness.

But, she could make sure that didn't happen. Probably. Maybe. One thing her mother had never done was take care of Dan. Their relationship was sadly one-sided.

Maybe if Peyton was taking care of Scott too, then all of that dependence and clinginess wouldn't happen. Or it would happen equally. But she needed to work on making her side equal. Then that would be okay, wouldn't it? He went to Kyle's tonight, she'd started her nursing classes, and now they were going to spoon all night in bed.

She could just ignore the part where she'd been disappointed that they weren't spending the evening together. She'd get over that. Next time, he'd hang with his friends and she'd spend time with hers, and it would be normal and not needy at all.

That last thought got her out of the car and into the house. But her heart was thumping hard as she brushed her teeth and put her pajamas on. She was about to go to bed with Scott Hansen. But real bed. Not sex bed.

She didn't do sleepovers. She didn't have guys spend the night and she rarely slept over at their houses. If she did, she did *not* cuddle. She liked her space. She didn't like to share blankets.

But when she slipped into Scott's room and took in the sight of him fast asleep, blanket kicked to one side, wearing only a pair of boxers, his hair tousled, the scruff on his face, his muscled arms and legs sprawled out across the bed, all she felt was her heart turn over in her chest and the anticipation of being up against that big, hot body. She wanted him, but she also wanted the way he made her feel safe and desired. And not even desired in a physical sense, but in a sense that made it seem he just wanted her with him, all the time, for...whatever.

When she did slide into the small space that was left in the bed, he rolled to his side toward her and settled one big hand on her stomach. It wasn't cuddling exactly, but it felt possessive, like he'd naturally reached out for her even in his sleep. And then he mumbled, "cookies," and she grinned.

And yeah, she felt the definite scary-but-I-don't-think-I-ever-want-to-shake-this feeling that she was finally *home*.

S cott woke slowly. He rolled to his back, squinting in the sunlight from the window. He flexed his hand. But it, and his bed, was empty beside him. So why did he feel as if he'd been holding on to something?

Then he smelled it. The distinct, oh-baby scent of pancakes.

Peyton was here.

Had she slept in here with him as promised? What time had she come in? Had she worn pajamas? All of those questions tripped through his head and the next thing he knew, he'd rolled and put his face into the pillow next to him.

Sure enough, it smelled like her. Cinnamon and sugar. His favorite.

He smiled. Then he frowned. Peyton Wells had been in his bed, and he hadn't even awakened for it?

Great.

He started to sit up, but his leg instantly reminded him of why Peyton was here in the first place and why he'd clearly slept later than he ever did. The sun was high and bright through the window. The pain pills had done their job, if part of the goal was him sleeping like the dead.

He was surprised he'd fallen asleep at all. He'd wanted to wait until Peyton had come in. He'd been half worried that she wouldn't come back at all. But the last thing he remembered was his head hitting the pillow.

Slowly, feeling like he was eighty, he got out of bed and pulled on a pair of sports shorts.

He grabbed his crutch, stopped in the bathroom, and then headed for the kitchen.

And came up short in the doorway. Peyton was still in her pajamas—such that they were. They consisted of a baby-blue spaghetti-strapped tank and a pair of shorts that hung loosely on her hips and barely covered the curve of her ass. They were also light blue and had puffy white sheep all over them. As she reached and bent and stirred and flipped the pancakes, eggs and bacon that she had all going at once, the top pulled up, exposing smooth, firm skin on her back and stomach. The shorts rode high one moment, then low the next, making Scott wonder if they'd slip right off with a twist in just the wrong—or right—direction.

And then, of course, there were the pancakes, bacon and eggs. He had never considered himself a guy whose heart was connected to his stomach. He'd been cooking for himself—and at times, others—for years now. He did not believe a woman's place was in the kitchen and he was not a caveman. But the sight of Peyton Wells cooking him breakfast after sleeping in his bed, even after *not* having sex in that bed—hell, maybe *because* they hadn't had sex in that bed—was the most gorgeous sight he'd ever seen. The woman could have *anything* from his at this moment. And if that made him a caveman, well...he'd just have to never admit it to anyone.

Especially the girl flipping pancakes at the moment. He knew for a fact she knew self-defense moves that could put him flat on his back. He'd taught her. And she knew how to shoot a gun, swing a baseball bat, and use a can of mace. None of which he'd taught her.

And she had a temper. And a what-the-hell streak a mile and a half wide. And didn't put up with a lot of shit from anyone.

He could imagine how much he'd hurt if he said something like "damn, baby, you can fry my bacon anytime."

She might actually fry his bacon.

But that was one of the things he loved about her. There was no guessing.

"'Mornin', Trouble," he said, moving farther into the kitchen.

She swung around, spatula in hand, dab of batter on her cheek, and gave him a huge smile. And Scott had to grab for the nearest chair before he fell over. Because he hadn't even realized that he had a Betty Crocker fantasy, but sure as hell, he was hard as steel at the sight of that spatula.

But then her smile died, and she looked as if she'd just forgotten how to breathe.

Her cheeks flushed, her eyes widened and her mouth opened. Her eyes roamed over him, and Scott felt as if she was actually touching his shoulders, chest, abs and lower.

He opened his mouth to say something—though *what*, he had no idea—but just then his eyes made it past her face and the spatula to take in the sight of her from the front.

And holy hell.

Her nipples poked against the soft, thin cotton of her shirt, a strip of bare belly showed below the top, and the waistband of her shorts clung to her curves of her hips, ready to slip down at any moment.

She was the personification of sex and breakfast. Two of Scott's favorite things.

"Um, you're not dressed," she finally said.

"You either."

She looked down. "I'm...dressed." She looked back up at him, then down at his lap. "Oh." Then she set the spatula down and headed for the bedroom. "Be right back."

He thought about grabbing her as she went past, but she was too quick and, interestingly, made a point of taking a wide path around him.

Okay, so something was up. He eased himself into the nearest chair, stretching his leg out under the table.

She was back in two minutes and went directly to the food and flipped things and scooped things and plated things, not missing a beat. But now she wore another pair of leggings, blue ones with what looked like cupcakes on them, and a zippered hoodie.

He frowned. She still looked hot—and smelled like pancakes

—but now she was more covered up. He wasn't sure what to do with that. Mostly because Peyton typically was trying to *uncover* when they were together.

"Here you go," she said, avoiding eye contact as she set a huge plate of food down in front of him.

"Thanks." Again, he thought about grabbing her, but she was already back across the kitchen, pouring him milk and coffee.

He was ready for her, though, when she set those down. He hooked an arm around her waist as she started to turn away and pulled her up against his side.

She let out a shaky breath.

"What are you doing?" he asked. She wouldn't look at him. She didn't try to push away from him either, but she was holding herself stiffly. He settled his palm on the curve of her hip.

"I'm just making breakfast."

"Breakfast could be cold cereal and toast."

"You don't like pancakes?"

"Don't be ridiculous," he said with a laugh. "I love pancakes. And bacon. And scrambled eggs."

"Well, then..." She shrugged. "Breakfast."

"But this is breakfast that takes a lot more time and effort," he pressed. "If your job is just to keep me alive until I heal, the cereal would have worked." Why did he so want to hear her admit that she'd gone above and beyond here? He wasn't sure exactly, but something was definitely compelling him to push.

"I just...thought I'd do something nice," she said.

She wasn't looking at him, but Scott noticed the most astonishing thing when he looked up into her face. She seemed embarrassed. Or unsure. That was more accurate. She seemed almost—dare he even think it?—*shy* about making him a big breakfast.

And if hard nipples and spatulas got him going in the morning, then Peyton Wells acting shy about something made him want to spread her out on the table, cover her with pancake syrup and devour her from head to toe.

He squeezed her hip and tried to get himself under control. Ravishing a woman for being shy around him was probably not totally cool. "That's really sweet," he said.

"You're welcome."

"Sweet isn't really a word that applies to you often, Trouble," he said huskily. He still wanted her to admit that she'd done something special here. For him. And he knew she would take the comment as he'd meant it—affectionately. She tried *not* to be sweet, tried not to be too *nice*. Or predictable. Or any number of other words. But there were glimmers of the sweetness at times. A part of Scott could see it even when she was swinging a bat at a guy's headlights, because she was standing up for someone she loved.

Derek had been right last night. She did take care of her people. And she was taking care of Scott right now. Not just by helping him out with the basics because of his injury, but beyond that. He was one of her people. He really fucking liked that. But he also really wanted to hear her admit it.

"Well, I decided to show you that I can do more than cause you trouble," she said. Her voice was soft.

He swallowed and worked on not running his hand up under her hoodie. She probably still had that pajama top on. She hadn't been gone long enough to do more than pull these clothes on over the tiny top and shorts.

Instead, he turned his head and put his face against her stomach, breathing deep. She smelled like Peyton—the combo of her body wash and detergent that he was so used to—but she also smelled like pancakes and bacon and sugar and cinnamon and all kinds of delicious things. She was holding her breath as he rubbed his face back and forth, dragging the material of her hoodie across her skin.

"I want to eat you up," he said gruffly.

He heard her little gasp.

"And not just because I want you with every fiber of my body, and not just because you smell like everything I love, but because you *are* sweet to me, Peyton, even when you're not trying. And you being here in the morning when I wake up makes me happier than I can even believe."

He just rested his forehead on her stomach, breathing in and out, letting her absorb all of that.

Then, finally, he felt her hand slide up into his hair and rest on his head. Again, definitely not pushing him away. Maybe even holding him closer.

"What are you doing?" she asked.

Her voice was husky and soft as she spoke, and Scott felt his cock stir even from that.

"Just soaking you in," he said. He lifted his head and looked up at her. Watching her face, he slid his hands from her hips to her waist, then higher, inching up her hoodie and, sure enough, the pajama top underneath. He put his mouth against the smooth skin he bared just above her belly button and felt her fingers curl into his scalp.

"Scott."

"Peyton."

"Not Trouble?" she asked.

He looked up. "The best possible kind."

He kissed her, then licked, then kissed again. She tasted as good as she smelled. He didn't need pancake syrup. She was all he needed. He scooted his chair back with his good leg, then shifted her so she was directly in front of him, the table against her butt.

"Scott, I'm—"

He slid his hands higher, cupping her breasts. Those sweet little nipples pressed into his palms and he groaned. So did she.

But then her hands covered his. "Why?"

He grinned. "You did something normal by making me break-fast. So you get something sexy." That was kind of the deal. She was supposed to be the one pushing the sexy stuff, but honestly, he couldn't tell the difference between normal and sexy in the midst of spatulas and skimpy PJs. Making breakfast in her pajamas should have been one of the most normal things he'd ever seen Peyton do. But it was also easily the hottest. It was all mixing up into one gigantic ball of...want. And he was going to go with it.

"Pancakes make you horny?" There was a little more sass in her tone now.

"*You* make me horny, Peyton." He said it with sincerity.

"You're thinking about the syrup comment yesterday, right?" she asked.

Heat slammed into him, remembering her saying that she wouldn't have pancakes in bed with him without pouring syrup on his cock and licking it off. "Well, I—"

Suddenly she pushed away from the table and stepped out from between his legs.

He frowned. "What's going on?"

Peyton cleared her throat as she turned to face him again, her arms crossed now, the very picture of I'm-trying-to-be-tough-about-this. "So, the thing is, I might...like to see if we could maybe try...not sleeping together."

Scott felt his eyebrows rise. He tightened his fingers that were itching to touch her. She'd stumbled over all of that. Almost acting shy again. And then there was what she'd actually said. "Try *not* sleeping together," he repeated.

She nodded. "You know, do things...your way. The other not-sex stuff."

She sounded like she was talking about trying skydiving and

was really not sure it was a good idea at all, but she was trying to gather her courage.

Scott wasn't sure what to say to all of this. No, that wasn't true. He wasn't sure where to *start* saying things. "I thought you told me yesterday that any relationship with you would absolutely include sex. Like wake-the-neighbors sex," he said, proud that his voice sounded totally calm and composed. And not like he wanted to say "no fucking way are we not sleeping together". He'd just gotten to the point where *he* was ready to do things *her* way. And now she was changing her mind?

"Well, I did," she admitted. "But I say a lot of things before I think them through."

Okay, he couldn't argue with that.

"And I was thinking last night that..." She trailed off, wetting her lips, clearly hesitant.

"You were thinking what last night?"

He liked that she'd been thinking about him. About them. She hadn't just left his house and gone to work and done her thing. He'd been on her mind. And it had been about more than his pain pills.

She nodded. "That after all you've done for me, all the times you've been there when I needed you, that it maybe wouldn't be so bad for me to do things the way *you* need to do them. Or at least try to."

Scott cleared his throat. He appreciated the sentiment. Except that it meant not sleeping together, of course. "I don't know that that's necessary."

"It is," she insisted.

"Why?"

"Because that's *easy*. Because I've wanted to do that since I first saw you."

"You wanted to pour syrup on my cock since you first saw me? That's a very specific urge."

She shifted her weight and Scott let himself believe it was because hearing the word "cock" turned her on.

"I've wanted to do fun, crazy, sexy, *sticky* things with you since I first saw you," she said. "That's easy. And easy is my go-to. Instead of dealing with feelings and doing things the hard way— like getting to know you and opening up and risking that this whole thing could blow up and end terribly—I went easy, trying to get you into bed, mouthing off, getting into trouble so you would show up."

Scott got to his feet. He'd known that some of her trouble was to see if he'd show up again and again. She'd been testing him, because her dad hadn't shown up every time, her friends didn't show up every time. No one did. But he'd been determined to be different.

"Pey—"

"And now, I want to do it the hard way. I want to do this for you, the way you've wanted to from the beginning."

"For the record," he said, his voice low. "I've wanted to do fun, crazy, sexy, *sticky* things with you since I first saw you too."

She took a deep breath. "But you didn't. You wanted more. And that was hard—difficult, right?"

He nodded. "It was. Both."

She apparently decided not to comment on the hard thing. "So, I want to do that for you now." Her voice went soft. "Because I know how that made me feel."

"How did it make you feel?"

She held up a hand, holding him off. "Special. Like I was worth that effort. And I want you to feel that way."

Scott's heart slammed against his chest. God, this woman slayed him. She had no idea.

"Well, let me tell you something, Trouble," he said, low and firm. "You wanting me made me feel pretty fucking amazing too. I don't want you to think that resisting you all of these months wasn't the hardest fucking thing I've ever done. I want you to know that I want you more than I want my next breath. That the *idea* of touching you, kissing you, wrapping myself around you, makes me hard as a rock and ready to do *anything* to make it happen. That your mouth on mine is my idea of heaven. Yes, I want to eat dinner and breakfast with you, I want to text you when I'm out with my friends, I want to nap on the couch while you work on your computer, I want you to slide into bed next to me even if we go to bed at different times. But I also want to know every inch of your body, every sound you make, every place to touch you to make you completely *mine*. You can walk around this house in hoodies all you want, but nothing will make me *not* want you. You got that?"

She was breathing fast, her fingers digging into her arms where she had them crossed. She lifted her chin, but he could see the emotions swirling in her big blue eyes. Those eyes. He wanted to see it all in those blue depths—happiness, desire, contentment, love.

He wanted to give all of that to her.

"Well, you're going to have to hold all those thoughts," she finally said. "Because I have to do this. I need to do this the hard way, to prove that I can. That it's worth it."

"You don't have to prove anything to me," Scott said.

"I have to prove it to me," she said quietly. "I have to know that I have control over my emotions. I've never resisted something that I wanted and that felt good before. And I've never *invested* work and time and energy in a guy before."

Scott almost snorted at that. He was sure that was an understatement. Peyton was gorgeous and adventurous and fun and oozed a what-the-hell attitude that was addictive. Even to a guy like Scott, who valued rules and laws. To a bad boy, Peyton would be like crack.

"So you're going to do the relationship thing and *I'm* going to do the seduction thing?" he asked.

She raised an eyebrow. "You're not going to honor my wishes and lay off the sexy stuff?"

He raised a brow right back at her. "You mean the way you've always honored *my* wishes in that department?"

Did he love that she wanted to give this effort and try this relationship thing and that she wanted to show him that he was important to her? Of course. But he realized that he already knew all of that. Their relationship wasn't typical in any way, but it fit. There was no one else like Peyton, and being with her shouldn't be like it was with any other woman.

"Well, I guess we really are going to see who's the more stubborn of the two of us," she said.

"Guess so." He stretched, making sure to flex all of his muscles. She watched every bit of it. "So, you going to help me with my shower now?"

He predicted that it would take about five minutes to get Peyton's clothes off in the bathroom.

"You going to put swimming trunks on?" she asked.

"Uh. No."

"Then I guess we need to call Kyle or Derek."

"You can call, but I guarantee that Kyle and Derek are *not* going to help me with my shower," Scott said firmly.

"I can call your mom," she offered.

"She's not coming, she knows you're here. This is *your* job, Trouble."

"Well, I'm not going in that bathroom with you unless you have trunks on."

Scott ran a hand through his hair. Damn this woman and her crazy ideas. "I really do need a shower. I guess I'll just have to do it myself." He turned and started across the kitchen.

Three. Two. One.

"You're not doing it by yourself."

He grinned, then hid it as he turned back. "You're not giving me a lot of choices here."

"What if you fall over?"

"I might get hurt."

"And if you get your wound wet?"

"I could end up with a serious infection."

She narrowed her eyes. "I'm getting one of the plastic patio chairs for you to sit on."

"Sounds like a good idea."

"And I'll have to disinfect it before you sit on it."

"Okay."

"And then you think you're just going to sit in there in all your bare-assed glory?"

He shrugged. "I'll keep a towel on if you need me to."

"Need you to?"

"If you can't control yourself. I know that you've wanted this for a long time."

She gritted her teeth, then turned for the back patio and stomped outside. Scott headed for the bathroom. He dropped his shorts and wrapped a towel around his waist just as she returned, carrying one of his plastic patio chairs. She brushed past him as he balanced on his crutch, carrying the chair down the hall. A minute later, he heard the shower turn on and the sound of her opening and closing cupboard doors. She came back to the kitchen, bent to look under the sink, grabbed a bottle of cleaner, and went back into the bathroom.

Scott just stood there grinning.

When the chair was finally clean enough, she yelled, "Okay, let's get this over with."

He started down the hall, but she brushed past him on her way to the kitchen again. "I'm on my own after all?" he asked.

"Just getting the plastic wrap."

"The what?" he asked, turning back.

"We have to wrap your dressings so they don't get wet." She bent and retrieved the roll from his bottom drawer.

He took in the sight of her perfect ass in those fitted leggings and again cursed this idea that she wanted to make him feel special. He had some very specific, very special suggestions for her.

But when she straightened and gave him a soft smile and said, "I do really like being here to help you," his heart warmed and he felt some of his own stubbornness fade. This was a side of Peyton he knew was there—the soft, caring, sweet side—and that he really did want to see more of.

But he knew her. And he knew that about half of this sweet, big-eyed, I'm-all-about-you stuff was bullshit. But only half of it. And the half that was real, made him very, very happy.

"I'll meet you in there?" he asked.

"Right behind you."

In the bathroom, he found the chair in the tub and the showerhead was hanging from a long tube. "What's this?"

"It's a detachable showerhead," she said, giving him a look.

"Well, yeah, but I don't have a detachable showerhead."

She rolled her eyes. "You do now."

"You got me a new showerhead?"

"Well you can't get fully under the spray." She gave him a nudge. "Sit down."

"Did you install it?" he asked, sliding onto the chair.

"I did."

"You know how to do that?"

"Well, fortunately, they had pictures on the box," she said dryly.

So, she'd thought of, bought and installed the showerhead. Scott wasn't sure why he felt so stunned by that.

Maybe because he'd installed a new showerhead for her about a year ago.

"Prop your leg on the toilet."

He did, and she quickly wrapped plastic around his dressings, seemingly completely ignoring the fact that his cock was *right there*. And pretty happy to see her.

Then she picked up the showerhead and pointed it at his other leg. The towel got wet quickly, molding to everything underneath, but again Peyton seemed oblivious. She soaped his leg, then rinsed it, soaped an arm, then the other, then his back.

He groaned as her hands slid over his shoulders and neck. In part because he was trying to drive her nuts, part because it really did feel amazing.

"Stop it."

"Can't." He let his head fall forward.

Her hands rubbed up and down his neck again, kneading and eliciting another moan. She shampooed his hair, rinsed and then handed him the soap.

"What's this?"

"You do the rest."

"Why?"

She lifted her brows. "Because you can reach it all and don't need me to do it."

"Maybe I want you to do it."

She reached over and turned the temp of the water down, and pointed the nozzle at his foot.

"Hey!"

"Soap up, Officer Hansen. If I do it, it will be with cold water."

"Torturing your patients?" he asked, taking the soap. "I might write a letter to your nursing instructor."

"Yeah, you do that." She lifted the water stream to his calf, causing him to gasp.

He reached for the water control and turned the water up to a comfortable temp. "Okay, okay."

He ran the soap over his chest and abs. Peyton was studying the ceiling tiles. He grinned. And opened his towel.

Ceiling tiles or not, her peripheral vision was intact.

"Scott!"

"What?"

"Cover up."

"I gotta wash this stuff too. Unless you want to."

She didn't say anything to that.

He rubbed soap on his hands and continued to wash. But, of course, he was naked and Peyton was standing right there, and his body didn't really care that it was his hand and not hers on the important parts. In fact, his important parts were familiar with his hand and thoughts of Peyton going together. His cock was hard as he washed, the soap and his hand and Peyton all making a combination that was not a bad consolation if she was going to be stubborn.

"Oh my God," she groaned, almost to herself.

Scott met her eyes. And continued to stroke. Her lips parted and her tongue flicked out to wet them.

"That is really unfair," she told him. "I never did that in front of you when you were trying to not sleep with *me*."

"You never needed help in the shower."

"I should have thought of getting shot."

She was kidding, of course, but for just a second Scott's chest seized. Jesus, he would die if something like that ever happened to her.

He shook that off. They were messing around. He squeezed his cock and watched her eyes pull away...slowly.

"Get in here, Trouble." He would have also been a dead man if she'd ever done anything like this in front of him.

"I need to get to work."

She dropped the showerhead, water spraying everywhere, and stomped out of the room.

"You don't need to shower?" he called.

"I'll shower at my place," she yelled back.

"What if I slip getting out of here and get hurt?"

There was no response for a moment. Then he heard what sounded like her kicking the wall right outside of the bathroom. "Dammit, Scott!"

He grinned. "I'll just...finish up in here and let you know when I'm done."

"If you jack off in there while I'm standing right outside, I'm going to go home and use my vibrator in my shower. Think about that."

"That's gonna help me finish a little quicker in here, thanks."

She might have kicked the wall again, but Scott wasn't kidding. He was totally thinking about her and her vibrator in her shower and, thankfully, his much-needed release after sharing a house with Peyton for not quite twenty-four hours came quickly.

"Okay, ready to dry off," he called out a few minutes later.

She stomped back in, dried him off way harder than was necessary, helped him into the bedroom, and then left him to go home and shower before heading to the bakery.

But she did call out, "I'll be back to get you lunch!" before she slammed the door behind her.

8

Peyton was nearly to the bakery when her phone dinged with a text message. She swiped her thumb over the screen. It was a photo of Scott's abs. The first even semi-dirty text Scott had ever sent her. She smiled in spite of the fact that Scott was now trying to seduce her, and she was never going to survive.

This normal-relationship-versus-seduction thing was confusing. The normal stuff seemed sexy, the sexy stuff seemed normal —or at least really natural—and she wasn't sure which side she was on. Or he was on.

She was a little early to be getting to work, thanks to rushing out of his house after "helping" him shower, so she headed in the direction of the gazebo at the center of the town square. She took a few shots of the notes and drawings from the kids in Sapphire Falls that decorated the white wooden structure that many called the heart of the town. They were all get-well wishes for Scott. She sent them to him with a simple "aww, how sweet".

There. Little kid artwork. That had to be the opposite of sexy.

Peyton started for the bakery again, still smiling in spite of herself. She took a deep, contented breath at the sound of the little bell tinkling overhead as she pulled the door to Scott's Sweets open and stepped inside. Her eyes immediately went to the bakery case full of new, brightly frosted sugar cookies.

The plate of six she'd taken to Scott but hadn't really taken to Scott was still on the seat of her truck. Because the question remained—did she want to keep him? Or more accurately, *should* she keep him?

She'd decided somewhere between brushing her teeth last night and mixing pancake batter that morning, that she was going to at least meet him partway while they were playing house. He wanted more than sex. She could give him more. Or try.

She just did not want to be her mother. Scott was already Dan, more or less, so Peyton had to put some effort into being better, being a more equal partner than Jo had ever been, even if it was for only two weeks and was more of a flirtatious game between her and Scott than an honest-to-goodness commitment. She might not want to turn into her mother, but she still got itchy at the "C" word. Still, she could do better than naughty nurse costumes and going sans underwear around the house.

Like pancakes. And nice texts. And not getting him off in the shower...

"Morning!"

Peyton jerked her thoughts away from Scott's bathroom and back to the bakery. Where she was just standing and staring at the cookies she'd made last night. She looked up at Adrianne and pasted on a smile. "Hi."

"I see you were busy last night," Adrianne said, gesturing toward the bakery case.

"Yeah, I came in to get prepped for today and then had some time on my hands," Peyton said, moving around the front counter toward the back room.

"Well, they look amazing and the place smells divine," Adrianne said. "Thank you."

Peyton's smile was completely genuine as she took in the details of her boss's appearance. Adrianne's long blonde hair was pulled up into a ponytail, and tendrils were already escaping the elastic band. She had on light blue capris and a white T-shirt, but the shirt had a purple smudge on the hem that looked like a fingerprint made of grape jelly. The brown streak across the top of her right sandal was definitely dirt and she was wearing only one earring.

"You okay?" Peyton asked.

Adrianne nodded. "Sure."

"You, um, lost an earring."

Adrianne's hand flew up to her ear, then she laughed. "No. I just didn't put it in. I was in the middle of getting ready when Carver and Jefferson suddenly shouted "Eureka!"

Peyton grimaced then grinned. Carver and Jefferson, Adrianne and Mason's sons, had inherited their father's penchant for science and nearly uncontainable curiosity for how things worked and for actions and reactions. They were constantly mixing things together, taking things apart, putting things in the microwave, and throwing things out of windows to see what would happen. Even at their young ages. And, of course, there were the many living things they brought into the house. Peyton figured Adrianne had a lot of years of yelling things like "no, your brother can't fly!" and "whose three-headed-grasshopper is this?" and keeping a fire extinguisher very close by.

"Eureka is code for 'something bad just happened'?" Peyton asked.

Adrianne laughed, but her love for her boys was clear in her smile. "Or something bad is about to happen."

"Mason is out of town?"

"D.C. until Thursday," Adrianne confirmed. "The boys are

over at Phoebe's now. They're playing with Kaelyn and Joe this morning," Adrianne said of her best friend's daughter and husband.

"You know those boys are going to turn sweet little Kaelyn into a hellion," Peyton teased.

Adrianne snorted at that. "Sure. She'll be the one getting funding for them for all their crazy inventions."

Peyton loved that. It was true that Kaelyn was already showing all the signs of being the social, know-everyone-and-charm-them-into-doing-anything-you-want-them-to-do girl that her mother was.

Peyton's phone dinged with another text just then, and she smiled even before seeing that it was from Scott.

My house smells like you. Cinnamon and sugar. I'll never be able to eat another Snickerdoodle without getting hard.

She laughed lightly. That was sexy, but also funny and sweet. Dang, the guy was good. She walked to the bakery case and snapped a photo of one of the cinnamon rolls on the top rack. She sent it back to him with *imagine the fun we could have with some cream cheese frosting.*

She sent it and then froze. She swore under her breath. Crap, that was sexy and flirtatious. That wasn't normal and sweet.

She was going to have to focus.

"Everything okay?"

Peyton lifted her eyes to Adrianne again. And she'd forgotten her boss was standing right there. She could have sworn she felt her cheeks heating, even though she never blushed. Or almost never, anyway. "Yeah, everything is great," she said with a smile. And it was. It was confusing and she wasn't very good at *not* seducing Scott, evidently, but things were good anyway. "Sorry, Scott's just...hungry." Okay, her cheeks definitely heated at that.

Adrianne nodded. "That's right. I heard you were helping him out. How's he feeling?"

Sexy. Charming. Full of it.

Which were some of her favorite things.

"Good," she finally said. "Better overall. But still hurting some." She frowned as she thought about that. He had been *shot* only two days ago. He should be focusing on getting better, not getting her into bed.

"Well, take him anything he wants from here," Adrianne said.

"Thanks, I appreciate that."

"Of course. I'm going to get started on the truffles."

"Sounds good. I'll head to the back," Peyton told her.

Adrianne grabbed an apron from the hooks by the swinging door to the back room. She would work at the table behind the front counter and wait on customers for the morning. Peyton would be in back, mixing dough, baking and decorating until lunchtime.

Peyton grabbed an apron too, and was just tying it behind her back when her phone dinged again. She smiled automatically, anticipating Scott's reply to her frosting comment.

But the message wasn't from Scott. It was from Dan.

Your mom is going into rehab. I'm dropping her off on a Wednesday. Thought maybe we could have dinner Thursday night.

Peyton felt all of her euphoria dissolve instantly.

Jo was going to rehab. Again.

Peyton scrubbed a hand over her forehead. She did not want to have dinner with her father. That probably made her a bad person, but dammit. The only reason he wanted to see her was because he couldn't be alone. She never got dinner invitations when Jo was home.

She typed in a quick response—*can't do dinner, but maybe lunch.*

She couldn't just leave Scott on his own and have dinner with her dad. She had promised to be there to help Scott while he was healing. Yeah. That was why she couldn't have dinner with Dan.

Definitely. So what if Scott was getting around fine on his own and had a ton of friends and a mother who could help him out with meals if needed? Peyton had *promised* to be there and she would be, dammit.

And so what if it was a great excuse to avoid eating with Dan?

An hour later, she was still wound up about it. A mixture of guilt and frustration twisted through her. In spite of the brightly colored cookies she was decorating. And that pissed her off too. Decorating always calmed her down and made her happy.

Of course, maybe if she wasn't decorating, she'd be throwing things or swearing instead of just thumping mixing bowls and measuring cups down on the counter harder than necessary. Thankfully she was using the plastic ones.

"Everything okay?"

She looked up and felt herself blush as she found Adrianne standing in the doorway that led into the kitchen from the front of the bakery.

"Sorry. Just...grumpy."

Adrianne joined Peyton at the prep table and looked over the flower- and butterfly-shaped cookies that were cooling on the racks, waiting for frosting. "These are for Emma's garden club?" she asked.

Peyton nodded. "I have honeybees and ladybugs too," she said. "She wanted simple sugar cookies to go with the tea and coffee, but I showed her the decorated ladybugs and she loved them. I also talked her into doing dirt cups—chocolate pudding with crushed chocolate cookies on top and gummy worms."

Adrianne grinned. "That's awesome. What can I do to help?"

Peyton laughed and felt some of her frustration melt away. "You're the boss. You do whatever you want."

Adrianne shook her head. "This is your party. Just tell me what you need."

It was her party? Not really. It was Emma's. But the ideas to make it special and something Emma would love had been Peyton's. She had to admit that made her feel good. "Well, how about frosting butterflies? We need lots of yellow. It's Emma's favorite color."

Adrianne gave her a smile. "Wonderful."

They worked for almost five minutes without talking, applying different colored frostings and designs to the butterflies. But eventually Adrianne asked, "What happened?"

Peyton sighed. "To make me grumpy?" she asked.

"No offense," Adrianne said. "But I know you're staying with Scott. Sometimes suddenly being with someone almost twenty-four-seven is tough. And it's my experience that men who are not feeling well, or who are being told not to do things they want to do, can be especially difficult."

Peyton laughed at that, feeling something warm unfurl in her chest. Adrianne was talking to her woman to woman about men trouble. She almost wished Scott *was* her problem, so she could commiserate. Obviously, she was around Adrianne a lot and she was fascinated by Adrianne's relationship with her husband, Mason. Mason was a genius. Literally. Which made him different from the other guys in Sapphire Falls. In a really great way. But no, Peyton's issues were with another man entirely.

"It's my dad," she confessed. "Or my mom, actually."

Adrianne gave her a sheepish smile. "Sorry to assume it was Scott."

Peyton waved that off. "He hasn't been exactly *easy*, but..." She trailed off as she thought about Scott and how it had been to be essentially living with him. "Actually, he's been very...great," she finally said. It was hard to come up with the right word. It hadn't been easy, but it hadn't been a hardship either. It had been tempting. That part had been hard. But that part had also been fun. And frustrating. And yeah, actually, kind of great.

"So what's up with your dad?"

Peyton had never shied away from talking about her parents. Everyone knew everything anyway. Dan and Jo's relationship, Jo's illness, how Peyton figured in—or didn't—had been well-known facts in Sapphire Falls long before Peyton was old enough to tell, or keep, secrets. That was, strangely, something she'd always been kind of grateful for. She wasn't the type to hide her feelings. When Peyton was happy, people knew it. When she was pissed off, they knew it. She was terrible at poker.

"He just texted to say that Mom is going to rehab. Again. And he wants to have dinner while she's gone."

"That's great, right?" Adrianne asked.

Peyton wished it was great. She wished she could summon even a fraction of the hope and happiness she'd felt the first time Jo had decided to go to rehab.

But this was the fourth time. And all together, her stays equaled about fourteen days.

"Well, he only wants to see me because he doesn't have anything else to do while she's gone," Peyton said.

"How long is rehab?"

"It's supposed to be thirty days."

Adrianne didn't say anything, but she gave Peyton a questioning look.

"Jo's never stayed thirty days," Peyton said. "She's never even stayed seven in a row." Which was, of course, why it had never worked. Then again, it could have been the fact that Jo didn't really want it to work. After all, if she was stable and sane, Dan wouldn't have to be at her beck and call. "She always calls after a few days, tells him she's miserable, and he goes to get her," Peyton said. "He can't handle having her gone, so he never pushes her to stay. Usually she agrees to go after her doctor or therapist really insists, but that motivation only lasts so long. So, anyway, Dan will only invite me for dinner for the first couple of days. Because he knows she won't be there much longer than that."

Adrianne just nodded. Everyone knew how this went. Peyton was plan B. Maybe even C. And Dan almost never got beyond plan A. Jo. All the time. He went to work—though he took calls from her at least twice a shift, and he'd had issues with bosses because of it. But otherwise, he only did things that involved his wife.

"But you'll go," Adrianne said.

Peyton shrugged. "For lunch. But yeah."

"I think it's nice," Adrianne commented casually as she picked up a spoon and added some blue food coloring to the blue icing she was using, darkening the color.

"What?"

"That you'll have lunch with him. Even though it's crap that you only get time with him when your mom's gone and that it hurts your feelings a little. You'll still go because you know he needs someone to have lunch with."

Peyton sighed. "It's pathetic. But yeah, that's our routine."

"It's not pathetic, Peyton."

"To let someone treat you like that? To be there even when they don't really appreciate it and they're just using you?" she asked, willing herself not to cry as the words made all of the emotions well up suddenly. God, this sounded *way* too much like her and Scott, and it made her stomach knot. "For him to not realize that he's doing to *me* what Jo has always done to *him*?" she added, her voice quieter.

"What has she done?" Adrianne asked.

"Expected him to be there no matter how she's treated him, without thinking about how he never says no, without ever once saying 'I appreciate you'." She looked up at Adrianne, appalled that she was spilling all of this. But Adrianne Riley was a sweet, accepting, loving woman who saw people. She really *saw* people. It was what made her perfect for her quirky, genius husband, who had a hard time relating to people sometimes. Or a lot of the time. "That's the thing," Peyton said. "Jo says 'I need you' or 'I miss you' or 'help me', but she never says that she *appreciates* him or loves him. And there's a difference I think. Between needing someone and loving someone."

Adrianne seemed to think about that and then she nodded. "I think you're right."

"And part of the difference," Peyton went on, "is that if you *love* someone, you want to do things for them too."

Adrianne nodded. "Agreed."

"And Dan doesn't appreciate me or love me. He doesn't recip-rocate, not really," she said, feeling tired suddenly. "But I still show up."

They were quiet for a few minutes, silently frosting and deco-rating. Until finally, Adrianne said, "Loving someone when they don't deserve it, or even want it, is the hardest and best thing there is."

Peyton looked up. But strangely, it wasn't Dan and Jo she thought of with Adrianne's words. It was Scott.

He cared about her. She knew that, deep in her gut, and she hadn't really deserved it. Or wanted it.

And yet, it was one of the best things in her life.

God, she really was like her mom—she'd been going along just expecting Scott to be there, and she'd never said thank you. Or acknowledged that it meant so much to her.

Well, she was getting better about that. She was learning. Unlike her mom and rehab, *Peyton* could be made aware of some-thing and actually make a change. She was definitely taking him cookies tonight. No qualms or hesitation.

"Thank you," she finally said to her boss. "And just so you know—I appreciate *you*. I love this job."

Adrianne smiled at her. "I don't know what I'd do without you. The candy is my thing. You're the cake and cookie girl."

Peyton felt warmth swirl through her. She knew, of course,

that Adrianne preferred making the truffles and fudge and caramels, but she was glad that Adrianne liked Peyton's work. Adrianne had always been great about letting Peyton try new recipes and had encouraged her learning and practicing new things with cake decorating. "Actually, I wanted to show you my idea for Hope's shower cake," Peyton said.

The whole theme for Hope's baby shower had come to her one day while she'd been doing a chocolate and banana cupcake.

Five minutes later, Adrianne laughed and shook her head. "Wow. This is amazing. If you want to take on the whole shower, I know Delaney would be all for it."

It was true that Delaney Bennett, one of Hope's sisters-in-law, wasn't the party-planning, foodie type. Delaney built custom cupboards and cabinets. With her own two hands. She wore tool belts, she had calluses, and she made no excuses for barely knowing how to use the measuring cups in her kitchen. She didn't care.

"Well," Peyton said, feeling a touch shy. "I don't want to horn in."

"Honey, Hope is your sister. If you want to plan her shower, do it. Just let us all know what we owe you and what you need."

Hope's friends—Delaney, Adrianne, Phoebe Spencer—and her other sisters-in-law, Lauren and Hailey, were planning the shower. But when Adrianne had asked Peyton to do the cake, she'd been thrilled.

"I'd love to do it," she finally said.

"Awesome." Adrianne gave her a quick hug. "I'll tell the girls."

Peyton felt herself grinning as she returned to her cookies. In spite of Dan's text.

She might not own her own business, or get voted favorite teacher every year by her students, or fly to Washington, D.C., to lobby Congress like the other women in Sapphire Falls, but if there was a party going on within twenty miles, she was the go-to girl. And, even if she knew nothing else for certain, she did know that her parties always kicked ass.

S cott heard Peyton's truck pull into the driveway and he felt his body tighten.

Just from the sound of her truck.

Damn, he had it bad.

He forced himself to continue stirring the sauce, as if nothing out of the ordinary was happening. But as Peyton banged into the kitchen, making even coming through a door loud and attention-worthy, he admitted that this was *extraordinary*. Peyton Wells was coming home. To him.

Okay, maybe it was because she kind of had to. Maybe it was temporary—for now. But it was still something worth noting and appreciating.

He glanced over, playing it cool, to find her standing in the middle of his kitchen staring at him.

"Hey," he greeted her.

"You're making spaghetti?"

The scent of garlic and oregano filled the air, and the pan of garlic bread was cooling on the counter next to the stove, where a pot of noodles boiled. It seemed self-explanatory, but Scott nodded. "Yeah. Do you like spaghetti?"

He was stunned to see her eyes fill with tears. She dropped her purse on the floor next to her and crossed the room in three strides. She wrapped her arms around his waist and pressed her cheek into his chest.

Scott hesitated for only a second before folding his arms over her and hugging her close. He just held her for a few seconds, waiting to hear what was going on.

Finally, she pulled back and looked up at him. "You're fully clothed."

He was wearing sweatpants and a T-shirt, but his feet were bare. "Pretty much," he agreed.

"And you're cooking."

"Um, yeah."

"And you're not even trying to be sexy, are you?" she asked.

"Well...some things are really hard to help," he told her with a little grin. "But no, I guess not."

"And I still want to take all of my clothes off and beg you to do dirty things to me."

His body hardened almost instantly and he had to clear his throat. "Damn, girl."

She hugged him again, and then stepped back. "Do you know how long it's been since I walked in the door after work to dinner already being made? Not to mention a big hot guy doing it?"

His heart softened even as everything south of there stayed hard and on alert. "I'll do it every night."

She shook her head. "I'm so confused."

"About what?"

"I thought when you said you were going to be seducing me, it would include a lot of nakedness and dirty talk. I was prepared for that. But making me spaghetti...I mean, should the smell of oregano make me wet?"

Good God. And the thing was, she wasn't trying to be sexy right now either. This was Peyton, having a conversation with him and just saying what was on her mind. Without realizing that saying she was wet was making his tongue tingle for a taste that was definitely not oregano.

"I can honestly tell you that if the smell of oregano makes you wet," he said, noting his voice was definitely huskier now, "then you can expect to come home to a lot of pasta dishes in the future."

She gave him a smile that made his heart turn over in his chest. "Yeah, I'm definitely confused about the sexy thing and the relationship thing. One minute you're going for normal and I'm not wearing panties. The next minute, I'm flipping pancakes and you're jacking off in the shower. And now this. I'm turned on by something totally normal that you weren't even trying to make sexy. What side are you on, Hansen?"

He knew exactly what she meant. Her texting him the photo of the gazebo that morning had made him want her as much as having her hands on him in the shower had. He gave her a slow grin. "All sides. Every side."

"I'm in trouble," she said with a sigh.

He hoped so.

They ate at the table and talked. Peyton told him about Dan's text and Jo's planned trip to rehab. Scott told her that he really didn't want her to have lunch with Dan.

She frowned. "Why not?"

"Because he makes you feel bad," Scott said, trying not to grit his teeth. He'd had words with Dan in the past, but he'd gladly go over there and tell the man to back off. Of course, Peyton was his daughter and was a grown woman who could make her own decisions. Which was the only thing keeping him from driving to Dan's right now.

"I feel sorry for him," she said. "But it's also all his own fault. So I'm just torn."

After they were done eating, Peyton joined him at the sink and they rinsed and loaded the dishwasher together. Scott didn't say anything about it. For one, it was a strange thing to love and to be turned on by. For another, it just didn't require any talking. She put the last plate in the rack and closed the dishwasher, then turned to him with a sigh. "Well, I guess now you have to watch *Grey's Anatomy* with me."

Scott dried his hands on the dishtowel by the sink and then handed it to her to do the same. "*Grey's Anatomy*, huh?"

"Well, you were all sexy with the spaghetti and everything. Now we do something normal."

"And you watch *Grey's Anatomy*?"

"Religiously."

"Okay," he agreed, making it sound as if he was very put upon. "But you have to sit with me on the couch."

"Okay," she said, "but you have to keep your hands to yourself."

He grinned. "No can do."

She sighed, as if *she* were very put upon. "Fine. But every time you touch me, I'm going to tell you a fact about the show that you don't care about."

"Deal." He didn't know much about *Grey's*, but he did know it had been on for a long time. That meant lots of facts. And that meant he could do a lot of touching.

But two hours later, he was hooked.

On sitting with Peyton, watching TV. On rubbing her feet— and the little sounds she made when he did it. And on freaking *Grey's Anatomy*.

After finding out he'd never seen a single episode, she'd insisted they start at episode one, season one. She'd run to her house quickly to get the set of DVDs she owned and they'd settled in. Scott had been all about her purple toenail polish— even after she'd put socks on when he'd commented about how much the polish turned him on—and rubbing her feet, and just feeling her up against him. She sat close, with her legs stretched over his lap, even while maintaining she was on the couch with him only because he insisted. She ran her fingers through the back of his hair almost absentmindedly while she watched TV. And she simply smiled and gave a soft sigh whenever he turned his head and kissed the inside of her elbow, or her neck, or her cheek during commercial breaks.

But he hadn't pushed for more nakedness or said anything particularly sexy or even touched her anywhere else. For two reasons. One, she seemed completely content and happy, and damned if he was going to do anything to change that. Sex would be good—or fucking amazing—too, but he loved this peaceful-ness, and once he'd found out that Heather and Tess were the only people who had seen these DVDs with Peyton, he'd decided he was just fine like this, thank you.

Oh, and because he got into the show.

It would never be better than sex with Peyton, but it only took three episodes for him to be fully invested in Meredith and McDreamy and Izzie and everyone else.

But finally, he yawned and had to admit he was fading. It was the fucking pain pills, but he still needed them and he knew his body was still healing.

"Bedtime," Peyton said, pointing the remote at the TV and stopping the show.

"But—"

"You can watch more tomorrow while I'm at work," she told him.

Well, he probably wouldn't do that. He wasn't *that* into it. But he really did want to find out what George was thinking. Okay, so maybe he'd watch one episode. Two at the most.

"Fine."

"Let me help you up."

"You're coming to bed too, right?" he asked. She hesitated and he reached for her hand. "Spoon me, Trouble. That's all I ask."

She huffed out a laugh. "Well, okay, as long as there's no forking."

And even that made him hard. And soft. At the same time. In very different parts of his body.

S he was officially pathetic.

Watching the guy sleep had been a little creepy, but lying awake to listen to him *breathe*? God, help her.

She should get up. She should go to the Come Again and study.

But she didn't want to. She wanted to lie here, with Scott's hand on her boob, and listen to him breathe.

And not doing something she should, so that she could keep doing something easy that just felt good, was exactly what Jo would do. Which was the thought that pushed Peyton up to sitting and then out of the bed entirely.

She'd been listening to him breathe.

Fuck.

She quickly pulled on leggings and a hoodie, slipped on her tennis shoes, and grabbed her computer.

The Come Again. Coffee. People who weren't Scott. That was what she needed.

And that was what she got until about two a.m., when she slipped back into Scott's bed.

And listened to him breathe until two-thirty.

9

Scott got from the bedroom to the bathroom before realizing he'd done it without a crutch. He picked his leg up and set it back down. There was a little twinge there, but nothing bad. He wasn't sure he'd go much farther without the crutch, but this was good.

He ignored his bottle of pain pills and opened the cabinet to grab the ibuprofen instead. And there, on his bottle of mouthwash, was a note that said, *It's a fresh new day!*

Scott stared at it for almost a full minute. Peyton had left him a note. A perky, peppy, not-really-like-Peyton-at-all note. On his mouthwash. He wasn't sure what to make of that.

He grabbed his crutch from the bedroom before heading to the kitchen.

Which was empty. Then he looked at the clock. It was after nine. He'd slept like the dead. Again.

Dammit, one of these nights he was going to not sleep through having Peyton in his bed. That was a hell of a thing—he finally had the girl sleeping with him and they were only sleeping.

But he couldn't help but smile at the pan of muffins she'd left. She hadn't just hustled out of the house without a thought. She was still taking care of him. And then he saw the canister of creamer. And the note.

I know you like French vanilla, but try this...it's my favorite. I mean, caramel.

It was vanilla-caramel creamer. It was half-empty, which meant this container was from her house. She'd brought her favorite creamer over and was sharing it with him. And leaving him notes.

Really, really stupid to be turned on by that. But he was.

He pulled out his phone to text her, but his gaze landed on another scrap of paper on top of the coiled piece of elastic tubing on the table he was supposed to be using to exercise his leg. That note said, *Girls dig scars...but not flabby muscles. Do your exercises!*

Scott felt his grin stretch his mouth. That was more like Peyton. The mouthwash note had seemed forced. Like she wanted to leave him a note but wasn't sure what to say. Like she'd never left silly, sweet notes for someone before. He really fucking liked that. But the note on the creamer was a little more casual. And now this one. Yeah, that was more Peyton. Maybe she'd gotten into the note-writing thing with a little practice.

And then he went searching. Something told him there were more notes for him. He was maybe supposed to find them throughout the day as he was in and out of the different rooms of the house, but he wanted to see them all now.

Sure enough, on the remote in the living room there was a note that said, *There's a Die Hard marathon on channel 134 today...if you get tired of Grey's. Hot cop saving the day seems like your thing.*

There was also one on the window of his kitchen door. It read, *Turn around, go back to the couch and sit down. You need to heal.*

The final note was on the dresser mirror in the bedroom—*I ordered you a T-shirt. You're welcome.* With it, she'd hung a photo of the T-shirt. It said, "The last thing I want to do is hurt you...but it's still on the list."

He grinned. And was really glad his friends weren't around to see how much he fucking loved this. That note was all Peyton. Even if she hadn't actually ordered the T-shirt.

And this note had a smiley face. Peyton Wells had drawn him a smiley face.

Her notes were sweet, funny, and she was taking care of him. And drawing him smiley faces. Scott was ninety-nine percent sure she'd never left a note with a smiley face on it for any of the other guys she'd dated. That just wasn't really her style. Except that it was, deep down. Where she cared about *him*.

Grinning like an idiot, Scott took four muffins and a cup of coffee with vanilla-caramel creamer into the living room and flipped on the TV. Then he pulled out his phone and texted her.

Hot cop saving the day seems like YOUR thing.

Then he started on the next episode of *Grey's Anatomy*.

Her return text came a minute later. *You're right. I do have a thing for cops.*

He smiled and felt warmth spread through him. This was working. She was writing notes even though it was totally out of her comfort zone. The notes didn't have to be good. Just the fact she was writing them at all was amazing.

But they *were* good.

Then he bit into one of the muffins.

They were cinnamon. And beyond good. He moaned and grabbed his phone.

This is the sexiest muffin I've ever eaten. At least to date. And yes, I mean that in every dirty way possible.

She didn't respond right away, so he hit play on the DVD player. He didn't mind if she just thought about that for a little bit.

Ten minutes later her reply was *WHAT?! A muffin isn't sexy!*

He grinned. She hadn't been trying to be sexy but it seemed that she couldn't help it. At least not with him.

I even find your toothbrush beside my sink sexy, Trouble. There's nothing you can do that's NOT sexy. And you know what cinnamon does to me. Don't tell me you didn't make cinnamon muffins on purpose.

I didn't! I swear! I just...crap.

He laughed out loud. *Can you come home for lunch?*

No!

God, he liked her. *Then I guess I'll have to take care of myself. Again.*

Scott!!!!

Laughing even harder now, he replied, *What?* And added an angel emoticon. He didn't use emoticons. And definitely not angels.

The next text from her was a photo of the town square with Frank, Albert, Conrad and Larry, four of the older men in town who were some of the biggest gossips and funniest citizens, playing horseshoes. It looked like a Norman Rockwell painting. Her message said *Beautiful day out. You should go sit on the porch and read a book, or meditate, or call your mother.*

He laughed. And didn't reply.

Two minutes later, she texted again. *Maybe your MOM could come over for lunch.*

He grinned. His mom was a teacher. She couldn't come over for lunch with him. But Peyton knew that and was simply trying to put images of his mother in his head.

Another two minutes later, she sent, *Or your GRAND-MOTHER. You should have lunch with her.*

Yeah, well, he could do that, except that his grandmother was working too. She worked part-time at the flower shop. Also, he had a note on his back door telling him not to leave. But he wasn't responding just yet.

Finally, she sent, *You better not be jerking off while sniffing ground cinnamon or something!*

He laughed. She wasn't comfortable leaving sweet notes? Well, he wasn't all that great with sexy texting. He hadn't done it before. So, he'd been pondering what things to send her. Now he didn't have to. Their conversation was naturally sweet and sexy at the same time.

Couldn't find the cinnamon. Tried ginger. NOT the same reaction.

Her response was almost immediate and was simply six laughing face emoticons.

Scott settled back into the couch cushions and again started *Grey's* with a very similar look on his face.

Two hours later, he got a photo from Peyton of a vase of flowers. *Emma sent me these to say thanks for the cookies and ideas for her garden party this morning.*

The second text came immediately after that—*you better not find a way of making this dirty.*

He hesitated. He loved that Emma had sent Peyton flowers and, more, that she'd appreciated Peyton and was publicly showing it. But he also couldn't resist sending *Really? A garden party? How can that NOT be dirty?* He grinned as he hit send.

A moment later, he got another laughing emoticon.

It was crazy how much he loved the idea that he was making her laugh.

An hour later, she texted, *How are you feeling?*

You're thinking of me constantly. That's sexy too, he replied.

It is not! It's sweet. I'm concerned.

You being sweet to me is sexy. Sorry.

She sent a frowning emoticon that time. But Scott wasn't worried.

A minute later, she sent, *I'm making strawberry cupcakes today. Thought these were your favorites but I didn't know about the cinnamon thing.*

He replied honestly. *I didn't know about the cinnamon thing either. That's all because of you. My pillow smells like cinnamon since you've been staying here.*

And he wanted it to smell like cinnamon every day for the rest of his life. He didn't add that.

Ten minutes later, he still didn't have a reply back to that though.

You there? he asked.

Yeah.

You okay?

That was just...really sexy. And I can't think of something appropriate to say back.

He smiled at that. *Can you think of something inappropriate to say?*

Definitely.

Let's hear it.

No way. I'm trying to be sweet.

I know...that's really sexy.

ARGH!!

Scott finished season one of *Grey's Anatomy* with a huge, stupid smile on his face.

A little after two in the afternoon, Scott heard a knock at his front door.

He got up from the couch smoothly, pleased that there was only the slightest twinge in his leg. He limped slightly on his way across the room, but made it without his crutch and without it taking an inordinate amount of time. All in all, something to be proud of.

He pulled the door open. And straightened.

Chase Walker, the kid who had shot him, stood on the other

side. Holding a plate of brownies. And looking like he wanted to throw up.

"Hey, Chase," Scott said easily. He pushed the screen door open. "What's up?"

It was clear that the kid was not comfortable, but he held up the plate. "Peyton asked me to bring these over to you. Said you needed them today."

So, Peyton had sent the kid over.

"She did, huh?" He took the plate.

Chase nodded. "Said it was easier for someone to bring them over than for you to get out and go to the bakery yourself."

"Yeah. That's true for the time being."

Chase's eyes drifted to Scott's leg. The bandages were visible under the edge of Scott's shorts. He watched the kid swallow hard.

He wasn't sure if Peyton had sent Chase to make him face the consequence of his actions in person or to make the kid feel better that Scott was still alive and getting better, but it seemed like both things were happening.

"You know, I've been feeling pretty good the last couple of days," Scott said. "But I was wondering, since you're here, could you give me a hand with something?"

Chase looked up at him. "You really want my help?"

"Sure. If you're up for it."

"Yeah, definitely." Chase almost looked relieved. "I'll do anything you want me to."

Scott could tell the kid he was fine, that Scott had forgiven him, that he knew Chase had learned his lesson. But he knew that actually *doing* something for Scott would go a long way toward making the boy feel better.

Now he just needed to come up with something for the kid to do.

"Well, it's kind of a big job," Scott said, thinking fast.

"That's okay, I don't care. I'll do whatever," Chase said quickly.

"You ever wash a truck before?" Scott asked. He mostly drove his squad car, so rarely had little use for his F-150. But he was a Sapphire Falls boy, so he still had to own one.

"I've helped my dad," Chase said.

"Great. My truck could use a wash. The hose is on the back of the house, buckets in the shed. I'll grab the soap and rags and meet you in the drive, okay?"

"Okay!" Chase turned to descend the steps, but looked back. "Thanks."

Scott gave him a smile. "And after you're done, I'll show you the bullet hole. It's pretty cool. And gross."

Chase's eyes flickered to Scott's leg again, but a small smile tugged at his mouth. "Yeah?"

"Yeah." Scott figured seeing the damage a bullet could cause would be something that would stick with Chase, but seeing it would also prove to the kid Scott was healing.

"Okay. Cool." Chase headed around the corner of the house at a run.

Scott shook his head. It was good that Chase was here. That was a pretty amazing thing Peyton had done. Damn, he'd been crazy about her for so long it was hard to remember a time he hadn't been, but it seemed every day she gave him another reason to want her. For good.

He made his way to the kitchen and gathered the rest of the supplies Chase would need. His phone rang just as he was carrying them outside. Setting everything on the pavement by the bucket Chase was filling with water, Scott glanced at the phone screen.

He'd hoped it was Peyton, but it was an Omaha number. "Hansen," he answered.

"Scott. It's Lance Shepard."

"Hey, Lance."

Lance was an FBI agent who had worked with Scott and the task force a number of times.

"Heard you got yourself shot," Lance said, a touch of humor in his tone.

Scott laughed. "Yeah, taking a bit of a vacation." It didn't surprise him that the news had reached Shepard. The world of law enforcement was a small one, a tight brotherhood, and it really would have only taken Ed mentioning it to one other officer for it to spread, even as far as Omaha.

"How soon are you going to be back at it?" Lance asked.

"Not sure. Few more weeks probably," Scott answered. "Why?" Lance wasn't a guy to beat around the bush. He was not just calling to check in on a past task force member.

"We have a situation. North Dakota. I'd love for you to be a part of the team."

Scott felt his heart thump. As it always did when he was called for a special operation. "North Dakota? That's not really our area."

"They want our team," Lance said simply. "Told them I'd be in contact with everyone. We're meeting in two weeks. I'd like for you to be there. In fact, I'd like you to go in with me and do the initial stay."

"In North Dakota?" Scott asked.

"Yep."

"Don't know if I'll be up to it in two weeks," Scott said, his mind spinning.

He wanted to go. That was the clearest thought. He always wanted to go when they called him. And nine out of ten times he did go. But they were usually more local ops, and the last couple had been short and sweet. They'd gone off of solid intel and been able to bust in and make the arrests. This time Lance wanted Scott to be one of the guys gathering that intel. That was a lot longer process. It could take weeks. It would involve being away from Sapphire Falls, his work...Peyton.

Sapphire Falls was very supportive. Ed, TJ, Hailey, everyone involved in figuring things out when he was gone with the task force, were great about making sure he could do that work occasionally. But it had always been just a few days at a time before.

"You don't have to be up to much. At least at first," Lance said. "We're going to go into a little town called Cedar Downs. It's almost to the Canadian border. They'll think we're coming in to check things out for a possible takeover of the local lumber mill. That will give us a chance to hang out in town and talk to a lot of locals."

"What's going on?" Scott asked.

"Two girls have disappeared from there in the past month," Lance said. "Three other unsolved disappearances in the past year in a hundred-mile radius. Two supposed runaways, but apparently local law enforcement is suspicious."

"Why there?" Scott asked.

"That's what we need to go find out."

Scott watched Chase hosing down his truck, but his mind was only minimally on the boy. North Dakota? For an indefinite amount of time?

"You're one of the best ones for the job," Lance said. "You know how small towns work. You know what to look for. And you're too shot up to be chasing all those bad guys through the streets of Sapphire Falls anyway. Come hang out with me in a pub in North Dakota so we can bust some bad guys."

Scott scrubbed a hand over his face. "Let me think on it."

"We meet in two weeks."

"Got it."

They disconnected and Scott tried to focus on Chase. But the kid was doing a great job. And Scott's mind wouldn't stop. He hadn't done any task force work for a while. And while he'd never had much of an urge to go to North Dakota before, now he couldn't stop thinking about who in that little town he'd want to talk to, what he'd want to look at, and how damned much he wanted to clean up whatever was going on there. Cedar Downs might not be Sapphire Falls— the town he'd sworn to himself he'd protect no matter what— but he'd bet all of the cookies at Scott's Sweets that people in Cedar Downs showed up for the high school football games whether their kid was playing or not, and that they had some big Christmas tradition in town, and that parents loved the fact that their kids could ride their bikes up and down the neighborhood sidewalks without fear.

Fuck. Every town should be like that. And the people who went in and ruined that sense of peace and safety and happiness should be brought down.

Peyton walked in the door just after five. And just like that, Scott felt the churning in his gut stop. He'd been wound up ever since Lance's call, but Peyton coming in through his back door like she owned the place, made it all better.

Scott turned from taking the homemade pizza out of the oven.

She took a deep breath of the oregano scented air and groaned. "Really?"

He nodded. "Really. How are your panties?"

She sighed. "So this is how it's going to be."

"Absolutely." Yeah, he needed this. He needed her. To make him forget about the bad stuff out in the world for a while.

"Okay, then," she said.

She came toward him and Scott tensed. Not in a bad, way but in a very good, instantly hard-as-a-rock, I'm-so-ready-for-this way.

But instead of wrapping herself around him, Peyton bent to grab another pizza pan from the cupboard. She transferred the pizza from the hot pan to the cold one, picked it up and started for the door.

"You're kidnapping my pizza?" he asked.

"Nope. You sexied the kitchen up with oregano and pizza. So, I'm going to *sweeten* this up by making it a picnic while we watch the sunset."

He couldn't have been more surprised if she'd said she wanted to give the pizza to the squirrels in his backyard. "A picnic?"

"Come on, tough guy, you've been on a picnic before, right?" she asked with a mischievous smile.

Oh, yeah, he was all over this. "Actually, not since I was a kid," he said, moving toward the cupboards where he stored his liquor. They might be going for a romantic drive to watch the sunset, but after the sun went down, the stars came up, and he had some ideas. "Have you been on a lot of picnics?"

He glanced at her when she didn't respond right away. She was frowning.

"Now that you mention it, no," she said. "Huh."

He grinned. "You didn't realize that you haven't been on a lot of picnics?"

She shrugged. "The idea just came to me automatically. That's kind of weird."

It wasn't one bit weird, but he wasn't going to get into that. Peyton was still a little squeamish about things like being head over heels for him.

"I guess I'm better at the sweet stuff in person," she said.

"What's that mean?" he asked, moving to stand in front of her, a bottle of blue curacao in one hand and a bottle of peach schnapps in the other.

She lifted her shoulder again. "I kind of blew it with the sweet texts, but I think I can counter your sexiness in person."

She'd done a hell of a job with the texting, but again, he wasn't sure she was ready to hear all about how head over heels *he* was either.

"You're better at dirty texting?" he asked. He didn't really want her to answer that. He didn't want to know about her texting with other guys, dirty or otherwise.

But she shook her head. "I've never really done dirty texting."

"Really?"

"I text things like 'meet you at seven'. Maybe a sexy selfie after a couple of shots but not really...words." She frowned as if this was all a very thought-provoking realization for her too.

That made him smile. All of it made him smile. That she'd never dirty texted with anyone else. That she was surprised by that. He really wanted to just get her naked. Right now. Right here.

But he needed to give her a chance to pull this off. Hell, they were both out of their comfort zones here. He was only succeeding at sexy consistently because she found oregano a turn-on. And had a few erogenous zones on her feet. And liked his abs. It wasn't as if he was really an expert at dirty texting either.

"Okay, let's go, then," she said.

"Right behind you."

"Where's your crutch?"

It was propped up next to the stove several steps away, actually. "I keep forgetting it as I get around," he admitted.

She frowned. "Is that okay?"

"Yeah, they said to do what I felt like I could do."

She chewed her bottom lip. "Maybe I'll just text Kyle quick."

"No. Do not text Kyle." Lord, he was already getting enough shit from his friends about protective Peyton.

"Just to check," she said.

"No." He frowned down at her. "We're going for a *drive*. And then we'll be parking. I don't intend to do a lot of standing or walking around, okay?"

She didn't look happy, but she finally nodded and turned toward the door. He followed her out to her truck, grabbing a cap off the hook by the door. She set the pizza on the floor behind her seat and watched like a hawk as he climbed up into the passenger seat. He worked on not grimacing. It wasn't difficult. It didn't hurt that much, but he was stiff. He set the bottles on the seat between them and pulled his cap on. When he was finally settled on the seat, she climbed up behind the wheel.

They drove for nearly ten minutes without talking. Scott didn't know where exactly she was taking him, but it wasn't the most common make-out spot, Klein's Hill, nor was it the park, or the river.

She turned off the highway onto a gravel road, then off the gravel onto a narrow dirt path leading through a field. They bumped along until they came to the top of a hill that looked down not onto the river, as most of the party spots did, but onto the town of Sapphire Falls.

The town was nestled in among the rolling rises and dips of the prairie. It was surrounded on all sides with fields and farms. Trees, fences, dirt roads, the highway, the river to the north, all added to the landscape. The deep greens and browns of the land and crops, the spots of color of houses and buildings, and the sky —the blue deepening as the sun sank, the western horizon streaked with pinks and oranges—looked like a painting. This was called the heartland for a reason. And Scott felt his chest tighten.

"Wow," he said simply.

Peyton didn't say anything. He glanced over. Her eyes were

fixed out the windshield, and she had her bottom lip pulled between her teeth.

"This is gorgeous," he told her.

She nodded. "It's my favorite place."

This was her favorite place. Not the Come Again, not the river, not her house. This hill that looked down over her hometown.

He had not been expecting that.

Scott flashed back to when Derek had said that it seemed that leaving would have been easier on Peyton but that there must have been something keeping her here.

"You come here a lot?"

She sighed. "Used to." She looked over. "I come here alone. Usually."

Scott wasn't sure why she felt compelled to tell him that. But he was glad she had. He also wasn't sure why she'd chosen to bring him here, rather than keeping it to herself. But he was glad she had.

He reached for the pizza. He was going to make this as casual and easy as he could. It was either eat pizza and look at the view, or grab her and make love to her right here on the front seat of her truck. He was pretty sure she'd go for the sex. In fact, he was positive she would. That would make it easy for her to pretend that she'd brought him here to make out. But she could have taken him a million other places for that. And he wasn't sure she'd realized that yet. Or if she had, he didn't want her thinking about it too hard. But he didn't want her to turn this place into a make-out spot just to cover up that she was feeling more than that.

He handed her a piece and took one for himself. For a second, it seemed as if she wasn't sure what to do with it. But finally she bit into it, sighed, and chewed.

They both got through half a piece before she spoke again.

"I would come out here when things got particularly crazy or confusing at home," she said. "This view reminded me that there were bigger things than what was going on in my house."

Scott swallowed. "That doesn't mean that what was going on wasn't important."

She nodded. "Yeah. I know. I mean, it was. But I needed there to be more. Something bigger. I couldn't let that...bubble...turn into everything I thought about. I needed to remember that the sun would rise and set the next day, that somewhere in that same town people were laughing, and kissing, and being thankful, and saying I love you. And in that same town, other people were arguing or were getting bad news or were making mistakes. It was just so good to look out there and think that I wasn't..."

"Alone," he said into the gigantic pause.

She looked over. "Yeah. It's easy to think that what's happening to you is the worst thing to ever happen, or to think that you got the short end of the stick, or to think that it will never get better."

"And looking out over Sapphire Falls made you realize that everyone has shit going on in their lives."

She shrugged. "Yeah. And..."

"And what?" he said, trying to make it sound encouraging and not the *tell me now, I have to know* that he felt swirling through his chest.

"The first time I came up here was during the festival," she said. "And I was looking down on the town with all the lights and all the people and all the...happiness. I just was thinking that yeah, everyone has shit in their lives. People have arguments and people get sick and people hurt each other's feelings and pets die and...a million bad things. But they still celebrate." She looked over at him again. "You know what I mean? People still have birthday parties and weddings and summer camping trips and book clubs and soup and pie suppers and Christmas pageants and *festivals*. I mean, our ability to keep celebrating is amazing. We crave it. When you have a bad day, you want to hang with your friends and have a beer. When someone dies, we all hang around afterward and talk and tell stories and spend time with other people. You could get fired the day before Christmas, but if you go to the town square and get a peppermint hot chocolate and listen to the little kids sing carols in the gazebo, you can't *not* smile. I just... People always celebrate. We don't all just hole up in our houses and wallow in our sadness and forget about the Fourth of July and Halloween and," her mouth curled up at the corners, "St. Patrick's Day."

St. Patty's Day. His new favorite holiday ever.

Scott was watching her with such a combination of emotions pounding through his brain and body that he didn't know where to start.

"We invented all of these holidays and turned them into the crazy parties that they are now. Halloween was some religious holiday, but we added candy and costumes and decorations and turned it into this big *thing*. And then you come to Sapphire Falls and it's even crazier." Her lips stretched into a full-blown smile. "I mean, we can't just trick-or-treat here. We have to have zombie paintball tournaments."

They sure did. Sapphire Falls did have a tendency to take every holiday and blow it up into something huge and fun.

And suddenly, Scott got it. Sapphire Falls was the Peyton Wells of small towns.

He grinned at her and she blinked. "What?"

"No wonder you stick around here. This is your place, Trouble."

She smiled but her eyebrows still pulled together as if she was confused. "You think so?"

"You appreciate celebrating life. Nobody does that better than Sapphire Falls."

She sat looking at him for a long moment. Then she crawled out from behind the wheel. The glass bottles between them clinked together when the seat dipped as she climbed over them and into his lap.

She straddled his thighs, and his hands settled on her hips naturally. She pushed his hat back, cupped his face between her hands, and kissed him. Just like that.

Her mouth was soft on his for nearly a minute. Then she slicked her tongue along his lower lip, and Scott's fingers curled into her hips. She gave a little moan and wiggle, and he couldn't help but press her more firmly against his fly. Her moan was louder that time and when her lips parted, he took advantage, sweeping his tongue into her mouth. He splayed one hand in the middle of her back, bringing her closer and tangling his other hand in her hair, holding her head still so he could slowly, firmly, fully stroke her tongue. The way he wanted to stroke the rest of her.

After nearly five minutes of just deep, hot kissing, she pulled back. Her breaths came fast, and she was looking at him as if her mind was spinning with ideas.

"Where is your favorite place in Sapphire Falls?" she asked.

It took him a second to process that she wasn't saying "take your pants off."

"Uh..."

"I told you this was my favorite place," she said. "Where's yours?"

"Probably—"

"And do *not* say 'wherever you are' or something," she said.

He laughed. "Okay. Probably the square." He lifted a shoulder. "I know a lot of people would say that and maybe it seems cliché, but the square is at the heart of it all."

She nodded. "I love the square too." They sat for a second. Then she added, "Now you kiss me again."

He lifted a brow. "Oh, sorry. I didn't know the rules here."

"I do or say something sweet—like asking you about good memories here in Sapphire Falls—and then you do something that makes me want to take my clothes off."

"Got it." He brought her in for a kiss, but just before their lips met, he said, "I know just the thing."

She blinked, clearly surprised to have *not* gotten her kiss. But Scott reached for the two bottles of liquor he'd brought along.

"What's this?" she asked, as he unscrewed the lid on the schnapps.

"Derek and I invented a shot."

"Really?"

"The Sapphire Shooter. It's got more than this in it, but blue curacao and peach schnapps are the main things." He tipped the schnapps back, taking a mouthful. Then he did the same with the curacao, mixing the two in his mouth. Then he brought Peyton forward, putting his lips to hers. He kissed her and then opened his mouth and gave her the shot of liquor.

She was clearly surprised, but she swallowed, then pulled back. "That's how you do a Sapphire Shooter, huh?"

"It's one way," he said. "You can be boring and use a glass, I guess."

She laughed. "It's good."

"I know."

"But you shouldn't have any. You're taking pain pills."

He shook his head. "Last ones were last night. Haven't even had ibruprofen today."

She tipped her head. "Honest?"

"Promise."

Finally, she nodded. "Okay."

"Want another?" He lifted the bottle.

"Yeah. But first you have to tell me something else."

"Like what?"

She thought about it for a second. "If you weren't a cop, what would you want to be?"

"Easy. Teacher and coach," he said.

"Really?"

He nodded. "Definitely. Perfect way to interact with everyone, be a positive influence on the kids, be a part of the community."

"That's a really big deal to you, isn't it? Positively influencing the town."

"Of course." All towns. The whole fucking world, if he could. But Sapphire Falls for sure.

"You didn't come right back to Sapphire Falls though," she said. "You were in Omaha for a while, right?"

He lifted the bottles. He could use a shot or two if they were going to talk about Omaha. "Come on now, that's more than one question."

"We're doing a shot per question?" she asked. "We're going to be wasted."

"You really feeling talkative tonight?"

That made her pause. Her eyes got a little wide and then she nodded. "Guess so. I want to *talk* to you, Hansen. What's that about?"

He pinched her butt and handed her the schnapps. "I'm more than a pretty face and a rock-hard body."

She tipped both bottles back, then leaned in and kissed him. The sweet liquor from her mouth warmed more than the path down his throat. Especially when she stroked her tongue along his, giving him a good, deep taste.

She sat back. "Yeah, you are," she said belatedly.

He palmed her butt cheek. "But I'm a rock-hard body too."

She wiggled on his lap. "Yeah, you are."

Scott ran a hand up and down her back, then slipped under the hem of her shirt and repeated the motion with his hand on her bare skin. She shivered at his touch.

"You gotta talk if you're going to touch," she told him.

"What do you want to know? Because I'm definitely touching."

"How long were you in Omaha?"

"Four years." He ran his fingers under the back strap of her bra, then back and forth along the elastic band. "After the academy." He flicked the tiny hooks open and her bra loosened.

"Wow, that was smooth."

He grinned. "Stick around."

She wiggled again. "I'm not going anywhere."

He ran his hand around to the front, cupping her breast and rubbing his thumb over the nipple.

She pulled in a quick breath and arched slightly, but said, "I would think Omaha was pretty different from Sapphire Falls."

He plucked at the hardened tip, watching her eyes flutter shut. "Very different."

"Why'd you come home?" Her voice was breathless now.

"I always intended to come home."

"Why didn't you come home right away then?"

"I was recruited to a task force that I really believed in."

Her head tipped back and she pressed closer to his hand as he tugged on her nipple. "Why..." She cleared her throat. "Um... what task force?"

Scott wondered if she was having a hard time concentrating on the conversation. "Sex trafficking."

There was a beat, and then her head snapped up and her gaze pinned his. "What?"

Well, that had been fun. Scott pulled his hand from under her shirt. "Sex trafficking," he repeated. "I worked with a task force along I-80, through Illinois, Iowa, Nebraska and Colorado."

"But..." She frowned. "Sex trafficking? Really?"

He nodded. "There's a lot of it. All along that corridor."

"And you worked on stopping it?"

"Yep."

"And...did you?"

He sighed. "Some of it. But it's not something we ever felt like we really got in front of."

"But..." She put her hands on his shoulders and looked into his eyes. "This is happening here?"

"It happens everywhere. But not Sapphire Falls," he said firmly. "Never here. I'll make sure."

"But nearby."

"Too nearby."

"And why did you leave it?"

"Burnout," he said with a deep breath in and out. "The cruelty, the devastation, the trauma...it was a lot to deal with. I still jump in on special ops." His chest tightened thinking about the invitation from Lance. He wasn't sure he could say no. But he wasn't sure he could say yes either. "But I'm not doing it full time," he went on. "And I haven't done any undercover work in a long time."

She looked at him for several beats. Then she leaned in and wrapped her arms around his neck and put her face against his shoulder. And she just hugged him.

Scott slowly felt the tension ebbing out of his neck and shoulders. He moved his hands to her back again, pressing her closer. He took a big breath in, the scent of cinnamon lifting from her hair and enveloping him. And he closed his eyes and just held her.

Peyton ran her hands up into his hair, then back down, stroking his neck. Her breath warmed his skin through his shirt, and he slowly became aware of everywhere they were touching, from her butt on his lap, to her breasts against his chest, to her hair against his cheek.

She fit against him perfectly.

"Most of the time, I love the things about Sapphire Falls that you were talking about before," he said, almost before he realized he was going to speak. He sounded like he was pushing his voice past sandpaper. "I love the festival and the holidays and the celebrations. I came back here because of things like that—the happiness and joy."

"But?" she asked softly.

"Sometimes it doesn't feel right," he admitted. "There's so much darkness. So many horrible things going on. It feels like partying, when there are people...*kids*...being kept as slaves. I mean, bound to these people emotionally and financially in a way that takes away any hope for anything else." He pulled in a breath. "And people hurting each other and killing each other. Sometimes it just feels like the parties are sacrilegious or something. Or we're naïve here, thinking that *this* is real life. Like we're not taking things seriously enough. Like we should be putting that time and money and effort toward something else. Something more important."

Peyton didn't say anything at first, and Scott just worked on moving air in and out of his lungs. That was enough for right now. He couldn't charge out there and save the entire world tonight. Or any night. He could only do his part in his corner of the world. And pray that others were doing their parts in the other corners. He knew that. The therapist he'd seen just before moving back to Sapphire Falls had talked to him about that at length.

Was North Dakota in his corner? And even if it wasn't, was there someone in that corner to do it? And if not, then he should do it. Right?

He couldn't stop the thought swirling in his head and cursed Lance for calling and stirring up his conscience.

Finally, Peyton lifted her head and looked at him. "I don't think it's sacrilegious," she said. "And I don't think we're naïve. We're not having celebrations and having fun and making the holidays a huge deal because we think the whole world is this bright, wonderful place with unicorns running around pooping rainbows."

Scott gave her a half smile.

"We do it because we know the world is *not* that. We do it because the world can be a horrible, hard, hurtful place," she said. "We do it because if there are no parties, no balloons, no peppermint hot chocolate, no zombie paintball wars, then what the hell is the point?"

He felt her fingers digging into his shoulders and realized she was feeling the wave of emotions he was. God...if he hadn't loved her before, he did now. She made him believe all of that. Hell, she almost made him believe in rainbow-pooping unicorns.

"We're fighting the hate and the cruelty and the pain by proving that people can still care about each other, people can still put aside their differences and their worries to have a Leprechaun Launch on St. Patrick's Day or drink a love potion on Valentine's Day or get together to stitch an American flag big enough to cover the gazebo like a tent on Memorial Day, just because it feels good. We watch old movies on the side of city hall every Saturday in the summer, and we bring in a Ferris wheel once a year, and we have hayrack rides in the fall because that's how it *should* be, and by God, we're not going to let the bad guys take that away or make us forget."

Scott stared at her, a million thoughts going through his mind. But first and foremost was the realization that she was absolutely right, and he loved that she knew all of that even better than he did. And that he needed to go to North Dakota.

"And that's why I stayed here," she said, her voice quieter. "Because yes, this is my place. This is the place that is good, and happy, and right, in spite of it all. This is the place that was outside my front door every time I left the house. Walking out my front door wasn't just an escape. Here, it made me a part of something bigger and better."

Scott swallowed hard. Then he wrapped his arms around her, brought her in, and kissed her.

But this time there was no liquor, no tongues, and he slipped his hands under her shirt and re-hooked her bra.

Then Peyton drove them home. And for the first time, Scott was fully conscious when she slipped into bed next to him, and he pulled her up against his side.

"I want inside this house to be as good as outside," he said, gruffly against her hair.

And he felt her kiss his shoulder in response and he knew in his soul that it would be. As long as they were in it together.

10

She spelled *anniversary* wrong. Twice.

Peyton blew her hair out of her eyes and shook her head. Damn. She'd never been this distracted at work before. She'd been hungover. She'd come in after an hour of sleep. She'd worked with a migraine before. And she'd never had this much trouble getting her stuff done.

She swiped the *Annniversary* off of the cake and redid it for the third time, finally getting it right.

Then she wrote *Kathy and Scott.* Instead of *Kathy and Steve.*

She growled softly, fixed the error, and decided it was time for lunch. Even if it was only ten forty-five.

"Is it okay if I head out early for lunch?" she asked Adrianne, as she stepped into the front of the bakery. "I have an errand to run today."

"Of course," Adrianne said, looking up from the caramels she was dipping in chocolate.

"I'll be back in an hour." The second her shoes hit the pavement outside of the bakery, Peyton turned for the Come Again. She hoped that the bar wouldn't be too busy at this time of day.

They did burgers and basic sandwiches, but most people headed to Dottie's for lunch, saving the Come Again for the late-night munchies.

Her phone dinged in her pocket as she crossed the square. She silenced it, assuming it was another sexy text from Scott. She'd already gotten three, referencing things he'd like to do with strawberry yogurt, dill pickles and peanut butter. Not necessarily all at once. And she should have been expecting them.

She'd left notes around the house again today. Like a note on the jar of pickles in the fridge that said, *there's never a dill day with you,* and one on a container of strawberry yogurt that said, *yogurt a great butt.* She'd also stuck one on the jar of peanut butter that read, *I'm nuts about you,* even though that was really close to sharing feelings she wasn't quite sure she was ready to share. She'd almost gone back inside to throw it away, but she'd been afraid of waking him.

She just wasn't quite ready to see him today. Her thoughts were still spinning from last night—from the things she'd shared with him and the things he'd told her. And she needed more information. Because frankly, she was ready to jump him and do all kinds of dirty things to him and just deal with the relationship debris that would occur in the wake later.

Scott had worked to stop sex trafficking and save victims? He'd gone undercover? He'd pulled young girls out of horrible situations and kicked major bad-guy butt? Oh, yeah, she could totally see that. But how had she not known about it?

But she had a pretty good idea why. She'd never paid *that* much attention to him.

She'd assumed that she knew the important things, and she'd been focused on making it all about the physical between them. She'd definitely taken inventory of his great ass and his wide shoulders and his big hands and his general gruff, protective, bossy attitude that did delicious things to her hormones. But she hadn't really paid attention to *him*. The things he cared about—other than *her*. The things he spent time on—other than *her*. The things he talked about—other than *her*.

Ugh. It all made her stomach roil. As long as his attention had been on her, she hadn't cared what else *he'd* cared about or thought about or did.

She was more and more like her mother every day.

Peyton hit the door to the Come Again with enough force to send it bouncing against the wall inside.

"I add holes in the drywall to bar tabs," Derek said from behind the bar where he was drying glasses. "Just so you know."

"We need to talk," Peyton told him as she slid up onto a stool.

"Is this iced tea talking, beer talking, or tequila talking?" Derek asked, seeming unfazed by her slamming his door open or stomping inside. At least before noon. She'd done some slamming and stomping around in here before. But it was almost always after ten p.m.

"Iced tea," she said. "But only because I have to go back to work."

He pulled the pitcher of tea from the fridge behind the bar and poured her a glass. "So it should be a tequila talk?"

"Definitely."

"Then I'm guessing this has to do with Scott somehow." Derek gave her a grin and propped a hip against the bar. "What did he do?"

"Told me about the sex trafficking work he did," she said. "Told me he worked undercover to bust up sex trafficking along I-80 and save all those kids. Told me he came back here because he got burnt out. Told me that he would never let anything bad like that happen here."

Derek straightened away from the bar, his half grin melting away. "Oh."

Peyton nodded. "So that's all true."

Derek shrugged. "Well, yeah. I mean, he did that task force work for a few years, but when he had a chance to come back here to work, and only help out with the special ops once in a while, he took it."

Peyton ran her thumb through the condensation on the side of her glass. Then she lifted her gaze and looked at one of Scott's best friends in the world. Derek was a laid-back, get-by-on-his-charm-and-good-looks kind of guy. But there were a few things he took very seriously—the Come Again, Sapphire Falls, and his friends and family.

"Do you think Sapphire Falls is enough for him?" Peyton asked.

Derek's eyes flickered with surprise for a moment, but then he gave her a slow nod. "In some ways."

"But not in every way," she said. She blew out a breath. "I mean, of course it's not. Scott is...too big for Sapphire Falls, don't you think?"

"What do you mean by too big?"

"I mean, I get that he loves it here and that this is the perfect place to come after seeing all of the horrible shit he's seen. But, is he really going to be happy just breaking up beer parties and making sure people don't speed down Main and doing crowd control during the festivals?"

Derek frowned. "I think he is very happy doing those things." He took a breath. "I think that there's nothing more important to Scott than keeping this town and the people here as far away from the bad shit he's seen as possible. I think his goal is to maintain Sapphire Falls as the...haven that it is."

Peyton thought about that. Yeah, that made sense. And damn, if she didn't love Scott even more for keeping this town the way it was, the way *she* needed it to be.

"And you think that he can be fulfilled by that for good?" she asked.

Derek seemed to be debating about what he was going to say next. "Okay, honestly?" he asked. "I've wondered the same things you have. I think that the work he did was really important to him, and it fed a need in him to save people and right the wrongs and make the world better. But, I also think that when he saw how close some of the shit was—the sex trafficking, the drugs that go with it, the guns, the...everything—when he saw that up and down that interstate so close to home, I think that made him all the more determined to come back and become our own personal sentinel. Nothing's getting in here as long as we have Scott."

Derek's words hit her directly in the chest. He was absolutely right on with all of it.

She wet her lips, wondering if she should ask the question that was on the tip of her tongue. But finally, she couldn't help it. For all his laid-back, good-time ways, Derek Wright was someone she could trust. He probably kept more secrets than anyone in this town.

"And do you think that a lot of Scott's attraction to *me* is that I'm the girl in town most in need of saving?"

She really wanted to be more than that to Scott, but since he claimed to be interested in more than her boobs and healthy sexual appetite, she couldn't help but wonder what he really saw in her.

The most obvious answer seemed to be that he saw her as someone who needed a protector and a warrior.

She risked looking up at Derek, afraid to see agreement, and maybe pity, in his eyes. But he was smiling at her.

"You really don't know why he likes you?" Derek asked.

"Well, I look really great in tight jeans and short skirts," she quipped. Then regretted it. She wanted an honest answer here.

Derek laughed. "That you do," he agreed. "And yeah, okay, he likes being your hero too. But there's more to it."

Peyton felt her heart trip in her chest. She *really* wanted there to be more to it. "Yeah?"

"Yeah. You and this town are the epitome of everything he's fighting for and wants to save."

Peyton felt her eyes widen. "What do you mean?"

"I mean, you make him happy, Peyton."

"I do?"

"You laugh and you live big and you love hard and you have fun. You're secure enough in yourself and in this town to say what you think and do what you want, and you aren't afraid. That's what he wants...hell, for *everyone* in the entire world, I swear. He wants people to be happy and safe and unafraid."

Peyton felt her chest tightening. "You don't think he sees me as sad and pathetic and as a damsel in distress?"

Derek snorted at that. "*Nobody* sees you as a damsel in distress, Peyton. And no, sad and pathetic are definitely not words Scott, or anyone else, uses."

She wasn't sure what to say to that. She was so freaking *relieved*.

"But," Derek added, and Peyton felt her brows raise. "I do think you have a point."

"I do?" she asked. "About what?"

"Scott. I do think that he should be doing more with the task force and special operations. I get that it's hard, but damn. That kind of stuff is his shit."

Peyton agreed. "And he's got us. He's got Sapphire Falls to come home to. I think that would make a difference this time if he went out and did more of that work."

Derek gave her a smile that was unlike the smiles she'd seen from him in the past. Usually he looked entertained by her. He even got flirtatious with her from time to time, though mostly because he simply couldn't help it when there was a female within ten yards. But this smile seemed completely affectionate.

"I think you're right," Derek said. "He's got us now."

Damn right he did.

The rest of her day went well. She spelled everything right, she sent Scott a couple of witty texts—rather than saying *I'm totally falling in love with you and freaking out a little bit about it* as she was tempted to—and she agreed on a day and time to have lunch with her dad. Overall, she felt accomplished and like she had her crap together.

And then she walked into the house to find Scott working out.

He was dressed in only gym shorts and was lifting weights in his dining room. He was standing, legs braced, crutch nearby but not under his arm.

She did not have her crap as together as she had hoped.

She was wound up and completely turned on by...just *him*. In the past, she'd been attracted and turned on. But that had been before she really knew him. Not that she'd realized it. But now, after not even a week of living with him, she'd seen a sweet, sexy, funny side of him she hadn't known before. And now she knew about his task force work and that he was an even bigger hero than she'd thought and...she just *wanted* him. So much more than she even had before. This was scary stuff.

His back was to her, and she just stared for several long, delicious moments as he curled the huge dumbbell, arms, shoulders and back muscles bunching and lengthening, his skin glistening slightly with sweat, as Miranda Lambert belted from the stereo system in the living room. Miranda. Peyton's favorite bad-girl diva.

Peyton swiped a hand over her chin, making sure she wasn't drooling. She could just sit and watch this for a few minutes. Or an hour. Or two.

Lord, there was a lot of skin and muscle going on there.

She took a deep breath, turned around, and left the house.

She was going to give in. She was going to take her clothes off and beg Scott to do wonderfully dirty things to her. But now it was going to be a really big deal. Or rather now, she *realized* that it was going to be a really big deal.

So, Peyton was up on a ladder cleaning the gutters when Scott came around the corner of the house an hour later.

"What the hell are you doing?"

She frowned down at him. He had his crutch with him, but she could tell he was more or less just carrying it rather than using it. He also had a shirt on now and his hair was wet.

"Wait, did you shower?"

He ran a hand through his hair and looked sheepish for a very brief moment. "What are you doing up on that ladder?"

"You *showered*?" she demanded. "By yourself? You didn't even know I was here!"

"Maybe I was hoping you'd *get* here and walk in on me."

She propped a hand on one hip while holding the gutter with the other. "You did not. And if you're trying to get away with something, you should start sooner or buy a blow dryer so I don't see the wet hair."

He sighed.

"I don't like that. What else have you been doing that you shouldn't be?" she asked.

"Nothing."

"Scott," she said warningly. "I've been sneaking around and getting away with stuff for way longer than you have and you're not very good at it. Don't lie to me."

"I went for a drive yesterday."

"Scott!"

"I'm going crazy!" he exclaimed. "Sitting around here all day, doing nothing?"

"You have to be careful! You have to *heal*. I know it's hard, but you can't push this. You could hurt yourself."

"I'm fine."

"You shouldn't be driving on those meds."

"I'm not taking the meds during the day."

"You could get sleepy or—" She stopped. "You're not? At all?" She knew that he hadn't taken much yesterday, but she didn't realize that had become a regular thing.

He shook his head. "I take them at night because my leg gets really achy by morning, but during the day I'm doing okay. And I didn't take them last night at all. In fact, I talked to Ed, and I'm going to go in and do some desk work starting next week."

"Did you ask Kyle?"

Scott sighed. "Not yet."

"You need to ask him first. And I'll tell Ed that he can't—"

"Leave Ed alone," Scott said.

"But he needs—"

"Peyton," Scott said, low and firm. "Leave Ed alone. And don't go talking to Dottie about delivering lunch to me while I'm at the office. And don't go talking to TJ about how we need to have a backup plan for Ed and me. And don't ask Kyle or Derek or Hope or anyone else to check in on me at the office."

She scowled. "You make it sound like I want to *take care of you* or something."

He moved to the base of the ladder and gripped one of the rungs. "Tell you what—you want to be sure I eat lunch and that I'm taking it easy? *You* come to the office to check on me."

She blinked down at him. "Yeah?"

"Yeah. And if you bring me ham and cheese that you made yourself, I'll even set you up on my desk and kiss you."

She felt a little shiver go through her. She had a thing about him and his official police business stuff—his car, his uniform, his desk. His handcuffs. "Promise?"

"Definitely." His voice had gotten husky.

"Well, in that case, can you go back to work tomorrow?"

He grinned, but his eyes scanned up and down the ladder. "Trouble, what are you doing on my ladder?"

"Cleaning out your gutters."

He lifted that one brow in that sexy way that said he was pretty sure she was full of shit but he liked her anyway. She loved that look.

"You're cleaning out my gutters?"

"They're not actually too bad," she said. It was April so there weren't a lot of leaves to worry about, and it was clear that he had kept the gutters cleaned himself. Which made sense because...

"I clean *your* gutters."

Yeah, he did. "I know."

"But you thought you needed to clean mine?"

She shrugged. "I needed something to do, and I checked everything else out and there wasn't really anything to fix or clean so, I climbed up here."

"What else would you have fixed or cleaned?" he asked.

"Shutters, shingles, shed, lawn mower," she said, naming off the things she'd checked out in her desperate attempt to stay out of the house.

Sure, her *reason* for getting out of the house was very different than her father's had been, but she'd learned from the best about how to putter around and find out-of-the-house projects to work on. She'd been debating the wisdom of taking Scott's lawn mower apart so she could put it back together. She was pretty sure she'd be able to get it back together correctly. Mostly.

"You would have cleaned my shed?" Scott was looking at her like he wasn't sure who she was.

"I wouldn't have *loved* it," she told him dryly. "But yeah, I know how to use a broom."

"And why would you have done this?"

"To uh...help you out."

"I can give you a very short list of ways you can help me out, Trouble. And not one of them includes a broom."

God, that low, sexy tone did it to her every time. She swallowed hard as heat swirled through her. *Girlfriend stuff. Relationship stuff. You're getting the hang of it. Kind of. Maybe. Don't blow it now by saying something crazy dirty.* But *if you pulled my shorts down and put your mouth between my legs right here on this ladder, you'd be my favorite person ever* was right on the tip of her tongue.

And speaking of tongues... She shook her head and took a breath. "I like doing this stuff too."

"Oh really?"

"Yeah." Well, she didn't *mind* doing this stuff. Not as much as she'd like doing the mouth-between-her-legs stuff or the stuff Scott had in mind. But that was the point, right? To show him she was about more than that?

"Peyton?"

"Yeah?"

"Come here."

Oh, boy. He was going to kiss her. She could *feel* it. His voice, his eyes... "I don't think I should."

"You most definitely should."

She *really* wanted him to kiss her. She was weak and needy and at the moment, she didn't care a bit. She scooted down until she was at eye level with him.

He braced a hand on either side of the ladder, caging her in. "If you know how to do all of those things you mentioned," he said, "how come I've been cleaning your gutters out for two years?"

Oh, that's what he was thinking about. She made herself grin and said, "I like having a man slave."

He shook his head slowly, eyes locked on hers. "Why really?"

She felt her smile die. How did this guy know her so well? She wet her lips and said honestly, "Because *you* needed to do those things."

He didn't deny it. He didn't frown. He didn't smile. He didn't move. But he did ask, "How do you know that?"

"Because you take care of people. That's your thing. And you like that I'm needy and dependent on you."

And that right there was the issue. He did like that. And she kind of liked being that way. Except that this past week, she'd really liked being the one taking care of him and getting to know him and learning more about him.

Maybe he was going to have to get used to a little of that.

"I do like taking care of people," he finally said. "But I did those things for you because I thought you needed them and I didn't want you to have to depend on your dad."

Peyton felt like he'd just sucked all of the air from her lungs. She stared at him. He'd been trying to keep her from needing her dad? "Why?" she asked softly.

"Because I saw too many times when you needed, or wanted, him to be there and he didn't show."

Yeah, he *had* seen that. There had been a few times when she'd gotten into trouble, had to call her dad, and then sat around waiting for him. She'd ended up sleeping in the cell at the jail one night. Scott had opened the door. He'd brought her food. He'd told her she could go. But where was she going to go? She'd still been living at home at that point. And yeah, she could have walked home from the jail, but there had been something that made her feel like she'd rather be in *jail*, at least kind of in jail, with Scott, than at home with her parents. So she'd curled up on the bed in the cell and gone to sleep. The next morning, when Dan had finally strolled in, she honestly thought Scott was going to take his head off.

"Is that why you gave me your number to call whenever I

needed anything?" she asked. "Because you didn't think my dad was dependable?"

"I wanted that to be the reason. I wanted to see you as this poor little thing that didn't have anyone else."

She looked at his chin instead of into his eyes. Pity. That was one thing she definitely didn't want from Scott Hansen. "Well, I appreciated it."

"But," he said, putting a finger under her chin and tipping her head up to look at him again. "I felt that for about three minutes."

She shouldn't ask. She should keep her mouth shut. Or kiss him. Use the sex thing as a distraction. *That* she was really good at. But she heard her voice say, "So what did you feel?"

"Fascinated. Drawn in. Impressed." He paused, then said gruffly, "Addicted."

Peyton felt her heart warm and swell in her chest, and she fought not to let that all show on her face. "A cop who has a thing for bad girls. A little cliché, Officer."

"You think that's what it is?"

"Maybe."

"I don't think so. I've known bad girls before. And good girls. And I've never wanted anyone the way I want you, Peyton."

She didn't know what to say to that. This was so much more than chemistry or even them being friends who wanted to sleep together or sort-of friends who liked to fight and wanted to sleep together.

"And you let me take care of you because you knew *I* needed that," he said, almost to himself. He moved his hand to drag his thumb across her lower lip.

She wanted to suck it into her mouth so bad. But she made herself sit perfectly still.

"I did need that," he said, a moment later, his eyes still on hers. "I needed to do something for you that you couldn't do for yourself. But I'm starting to think there isn't anything like that."

For some reason, Peyton felt tears stinging at the back of her eyes. Yes, she was self-sufficient. But she couldn't deny feeling like she *needed* Scott.

"Just because I can clean gutters out, doesn't mean I don't need anything from you." She was going down. She was losing the game of chicken. And it was going to be glorious.

He gave a single nod. "And just because my gutters are already clean doesn't mean I don't need anything from *you*."

"What do you need from me?" she asked.

"For you to let me handcuff you to my headboard."

Want shot through her so fast and hot that Peyton actually felt a little dizzy. "You want to handcuff me to your headboard?"

He shook his head. "It was *want to* a week ago. Now it's *need to*."

"I've been sweet," she said softly.

"Yep. I'm pretty sure it was the sticky notes that totally did me in."

She'd felt silly about those more than anything. "Yeah?"

"I was in trouble when you made me breakfast even that first time. Then it got worse when you started texting me. But then you left me sticky notes and I was done for."

Peyton grinned, pleasure spinning through her. This was a new kind of pleasure though. She wasn't sure she'd ever felt anything like it. "Those were okay?"

"Those were very okay," he said gruffly.

She wrapped her arms around his neck, feeling almost giddy. "Well, then, Officer Hansen, I really think I need to be hand-cuffed. For being *good*."

He gave her a naughty, very bad-boy grin. "Imagine that."

Then he kissed her. And Peyton actually felt her toes curl. She didn't know that that could really happen, but right there in her tennis shoes, Scott Hansen curled her toes.

His mouth was hungry on hers, his tongue hot and possessive, as were the big hands that scooped under her butt and pulled her off the ladder. He set her on the ground and then cupped her head, holding her still while he kissed her as if he'd never get enough.

Peyton found herself gripping his biceps and going up on tiptoe to get closer. This was why she wore heels. She was too damned short for this.

He pulled back as she made a sort-of-turned-on, sort-of-frustrated groaning noise.

"I wish like hell I could pick you up and carry you into my bedroom."

Yeah, she wished like hell he could do that too. "Well, the good stuff happens *after* we get to the bedroom," she told him. "I assume you can handle everything once we're there?"

His eyes darkened and he leaned in, his mouth nearly on hers. "I promise you, if I tell you to get on and ride me, you won't know if it's because my leg is hurting or because I just really want to see you on top, playing with your nipples and making yourself come on my cock."

Peyton felt her panties begin to melt. But she concentrated on what he'd said—before the nipples and cock stuff. "Is your leg hurting?"

"I'm barely aware I have a leg."

"Do you think this will hurt it?"

"I think that I don't care and I promise that you won't either."

She blew out a short breath. "Scott—"

"Peyton, I fucking love that you're all into taking care of me," he said, shutting her up. "But here is how you can take care of me right now—take off your clothes, get on my bed, put your arms over your head, and don't hold back one moan, request, demand or 'oh my God, Scott, you're the best I've ever had'. Got it?"

She swallowed hard. "Leg? What leg?"

"That's my girl."

Peyton felt her heart squeeze at that and gave him one last hard kiss. "Let's do this thing." Then she leaned back and pulled her shirt off over her head.

He gave a pained half laugh, half groan. "In the house, Trouble. Strip down *in the house*."

She grinned. "Right. Okay."

He stepped back and she slipped around him, heading for the door. She looked back when she didn't feel or hear him right behind her. He was on his way across the lawn to his car.

"Come on, Big Shot." She reached behind and unclasped her bra as she climbed the front steps of his porch.

"Gotta grab my cuffs."

Peyton felt her body go soft. Handcuffed to his bed. Yes, please. And she wasn't really the type to let someone take over like that. But Scott? Oh, yeah, no question. He'd used them on her on St. Patrick's Day too, and that had been the hottest experience of her life. Now on his bed? With him able to do so much more than he could on the hood of his car in the dark? Peyton practically ran to the bedroom, praying that his leg wouldn't keep him from some of the things she really hoped he'd do.

11

————

S cott paused at his car, braced a hand on the hood and took a deep breath. Peyton was going to kill him. The moment he got her completely naked, in his bed, handcuffed to his headboard, it was very likely that his head—or his heart—was going to explode. So he needed a second.

He'd never felt lust like this before, but he knew why. Because it wasn't just lust. He was falling for her. *Had* fallen for her. Hard and deep.

And yeah, it was the freaking sticky notes that had sealed the deal. He'd liked her for a long time, he'd wanted her for what seemed like forever, he knew things about her that he suspected she didn't even know about herself. But he hadn't admitted that he was in love with her.

Until he saw the sticky note that said *never a dill moment with you* on the jar of dill pickles in his fridge. How was he supposed to *not* love a girl who would leave him a very bad pickle pun?

And then she was cleaning out his gutters? After letting him do the same at her house for years? Because she knew that he needed to *do* things for her. She'd been taking care of him, by letting him take care of her.

Scott scrubbed a hand over his face. And she was now going to let him handcuff her to his bed. Because yeah, he fucking *needed* that. He needed her completely into this, making this choice, trusting him, and knowing that he would take care of her.

Yeah, *something* was going to explode.

He grabbed his cuffs out of his car, gripping them tightly as he started up the walk to the porch. He was feeling a hell of a lot better, stronger, had less pain, and was getting antsy to get out of his house. But getting out or going to work were not the first things he intended to do with his renewed strength.

His heart was pounding as he approached his bedroom door. He'd never been this jacked up for sex. The buildup here had been long and intense, but he didn't remember being this *ready* for someone.

Then he stepped through his bedroom door. And it was completely perfect.

Peyton was lying in the middle of his bed, bare naked, her hands already clutching the wooden slats above the pillows. Her clothes were strewn over the floor. She hadn't even pulled the comforter down. And her going all in, all at once, was so typical that he felt his heart expand, almost painfully, and his grin stretch his mouth, even as his cock pulsed and ached.

"Maybe I don't need these," he said, tossing the cuffs onto the bed next to her hip. He stripped his shirt off, tossing it on top of her clothes, the action strangely intimate.

"Oh, you do," she said emphatically. "Because you get much closer and there's no way my hands are staying up here if I have anything to say about it."

He pushed his shorts and underwear to the floor and kicked them away. "Oh yeah?"

"Come here and I'll show you."

He put a knee on the mattress and climbed up next to her. He was already hard and aching, and he thought about just rolling on a condom and going for it. The foreplay had been going on for days. Years, really.

But then she squirmed, her legs parting, her back arching, her breasts rising, and Scott knew he couldn't jump ahead. Didn't want to. He'd been inside of her sweet body. And that had been heaven. No question. But he hadn't been able to worship her body, make her crazy, make her *his*.

He reached for the handcuffs as she reached for him. She ran her hand down his chest, her fingers trailing over his pecs, nipples, and abs. Scott held his breath as her hand drifted lower and then clasped his cock.

He groaned as she sighed, squeezing him gently, then stroking tip to base. Then she shifted, curling quickly so she could replace her hand with her mouth.

"Holy... *Peyton*." His hand went to her head, tangling in her hair to stop her from sucking him deeper into the hot, wet paradise of her mouth. But he hesitated. He could let her go for a minute. Or two.

She licked and swirled and sucked, and Scott felt his fingers tightening in her hair, as the pleasure built and threatened to pull him under.

"Peyton..."

She shifted back and looked up at him. "I have wanted to do this for so long,"

And just like that he was on the edge of coming.

He tugged on her hair. "Can't do it. Hands up."

She gave him a look. "You know I've been thinking about this since the other day during your shower."

"Yeah, me too," he told her. "And a few other things. So put your hands up."

She grinned and shifted to lie back on the bed. "That's funny from a cop, you know."

He gave a little growl and grabbed her wrists, pulling them over her head. He wrapped the cuffs around one slat in the headboard, then around her wrists and clicked them into place.

She wiggled and he looked down to find her already breathing harder. She liked this. A lot.

"God, you're a dream come true," he told her, running one hand over her hair, down her shoulder and then farther, over her breast, stomach, brushing over her mound, then down her thigh.

She sighed, as if his touch was actually comforting her, and shifted her legs apart. "Please do every dirty thing that you've been bottling up for the past two years. *Please*."

He chuckled. Of course she might be handcuffed to his bed, but she would still use everything else she had to make him crazy. Like her mouth.

He kissed her, holding her chin and ravaging her mouth, his tongue stroking deep, tasting her, giving her a hint about what his tongue would be doing very, very soon on another part of her body. He'd had her, but he hadn't *really* had her. Hadn't put his mouth on every inch, hadn't erased every thought of any other man, hadn't made her mindless with pleasure.

And that all ended now.

He cupped one breast, thumbing over her nipple until the point was stiff, then lowered his mouth, licking and sucking. She encouraged him with soft moans and yeses and more wiggling. Her hips didn't stop. Like she was looking for something, needed something. He put a hand between her legs, just cupping her as he sucked and gently bit one nipple.

Her breath hissed out and he felt her lifting into his hand.

The way she moved her hips was already making him crazy.

"Scott, seriously, please," she begged.

Already. Peyton didn't seem the type to beg. But if she lost her mind a little bit with him? Yeah, he was good with that. He circled the pad of his finger over her clit. "What do you want, Trouble? A little more of this?"

Her neck arched as she pressed her head back into the pillow. "Yes, oh yes, please."

He grinned. He'd barely gotten started. "You're wound tight," he told her, circling again and pressing gently.

"I am," she agreed. "For you. Because of you. I've been staring at your naked chest, I'm thinking about you while I'm at work. Every time I'm in the shower. Whenever I've got my vibrator. But it doesn't go deep enough. It doesn't fill me up like you can."

Fire licked along his limbs even as he realized what she was doing. He raised his head from her breast and stopped his finger from moving.

She froze and looked at him.

"Yeah, I'm onto you," he told her.

"What do you mean?"

"You're trying to rush me along."

"I don't know what you're talking about."

"You know damned well that the image of you getting yourself off in the shower while thinking about me makes me want to put your knees up by your ears and fuck you until the only word you know or care about is *Scott*."

Her breathing hitched and her eyes got wide. "Yes, do that."

"But," he said, "I don't want to do that. Yet."

"Why not? I'm *very* flexible."

Jesus, she was going to kill him. He shook his head. "Because I need you to come on my finger, and then on my tongue, and *then* beg me to fuck you with my cock. Got it? In that order. And I mean real begging. Not this stuff where you know exactly what to say to get me to do what you want, but real begging where I'm the only thing on your mind and if you *don't* come, you'll die."

Her mouth fell open and she stared at him for nearly a full

thirty seconds, but then she narrowed her eyes. "I've already come on your finger. Can we skip that part?"

He chuckled, but the sound was less humorous and maybe a touch ominous. "Maybe we could have skipped that part if you'd put American cheese on my ham sandwich instead of Swiss." He swirled his finger over her clit. "But you didn't. You used Swiss. My favorite."

"You always get Swiss on your burgers," she said, her voice hitching. "I just assumed that's what you liked."

"And that," he said, leaning over to kiss her, and then trailing his scruffy jaw down her throat, over her chest, and across one breast to suck on her nipple again. "Is why I have to make you come on my finger first."

"Because I was *nice* and paid attention?"

He nodded. "It's only fair. Because..." He gave her clit a little more friction, then dipped one finger just inside of her silky heat. "I know that you love when I finger you. It's kind of your Swiss cheese."

"No," she said, though her voice was breathless as he slid his finger deeper. "My Swiss cheese is your cock, for sure."

He laughed. "Who do you think you're talking to here?" he asked, sliding deep again and then dragging his finger out along the sensitive sweet spot that made her moan. "My fingers, deep inside of you, thrusting while I play with your clit? That is definitely your Swiss cheese, Trouble. My *mouth*, on the other hand, is going to be your strawberry cupcake."

She arched up, closer to his hand, even as she asked, "What are you talking about?"

"I love Swiss cheese," he said. "It's my favorite cheese. But I love the strawberry cupcakes you make at the bakery even more."

"So your *cock*," she said, "is *my* strawberry cupcake."

He shook his head, adding a finger and relishing her moan as he thrust deep, nice and slow and steady. "No, I love the strawberry cupcakes, but my *favorite* food of all, the thing I want more than all the others, even as much as I love those? Fried chicken."

Peyton laughed at that. All of a sudden, surprising them both, she laughed. "Oh my God, we're talking about fried chicken in bed?"

He grinned. "My cock is going to be to you what fried chicken is to me," he said. "The thing that you *want*, the thing you *crave*, the thing you can't get enough of."

She shook her head. "You're crazy, you know that?"

"Maybe," he agreed, lowering his head to her nipple again and taking a hard suck. "Because I think I'm about to find something I crave even more than fried chicken. And I'm going to want to have it every day."

She laughed again lightly. "I'm not sure I'm going to be able to ever see fried chicken again and not think of you—and this."

He picked up the speed between her legs. "You make me fried chicken and you can probably have anything you want from me."

"What if I throw in strawberry cupcakes for dessert?" she asked, starting to pant slightly.

"Then I'm yours forever."

Of course, he already was.

He circled her clit and moved his fingers, making her gasp and moan. Then he put his mouth against her ear and said, "Come for me, Trouble."

She turned her head, captured his lips with hers. And then her body clamped onto his fingers and she let the orgasm happen, her cry muffled against his mouth.

Scott kissed her back, pouring not just his overwhelming desire for her into the kiss, but the sheer awe of having her here, in his bed, at his mercy. But then he had to go on. He had to taste her, he had to make her come apart again. He kissed his way down her body, lingering over her nipples again, before licking over her stomach, and then cupping her butt in his hands and bringing her to his mouth, as he sprawled on his stomach between her knees.

"Your leg—" She started.

But he looked up and said, "That doesn't sound anything like 'Scott, you're amazing' or 'Oh my God, I'm coming again.'" And he set to work licking and sucking, sliding, thrusting, nibbling and then starting all over again, until she was wiggling in his hands and repeating the first three words over and over. And only the first two repetitions sounded sarcastic. Then finally, she said those magical six words and she came apart on his tongue.

He rose up on his knees—and yeah, his leg protested slightly, but *nothing* was going to stop this—and rolled on the condom he'd tossed onto the mattress.

She watched him, her breathing ragged, her cheeks pink, her hair tousled.

"I have never seen anything more gorgeous," he told her. "You are absolutely everything I've ever wanted and more."

She gave him a smile that was new. He couldn't quite put his finger on what was different about it, but it was sexy and soft and almost...affectionate. Or something.

"It's easy to say you're amazing when you have your mouth between my legs," she said with that smile. "But seriously, you really are. I don't know why you want to be with me so badly, but I'm really, really glad that you do."

And Scott felt something happen that had, maybe sadly, never happened during sex before. His heart opened up and got totally involved.

He stretched up and undid the handcuffs, pulling her arms down, massaging them, and making sure all the blood was flowing again. Then he pulled her up into sitting, wrapped her arms around his neck, and hugged her.

With a condom on, with a raging erection, with the taste of her still on his tongue, he just held her. And she held him back.

And when she finally wiggled and he grasped her hips and lifted her onto him and they both groaned as he filled her, and when she moved herself on him slowly and languorously, and when he gripped her hips and thrust deep and hard and his eyes were nearly crossing with the pleasure, and when they both came hard, each other's names on their lips, and when they fell onto the pillows and drifted to sleep, wrapped up in one another, it still kind of felt like they were hugging.

F ive nights later, Peyton bent over on the edge of the bed to pull her shoe on.

A big arm wrapped around her waist and hauled her back to the middle of the mattress and up against Scott's hot body.

"Where you think you're going, Trouble?" he mumbled sleepily.

She sighed and felt herself melting into him. Never having been much of a cuddler, she was shocked by how much she loved having his heavy arm across her in the night. In fact, his favorite position seemed to be with his hand under her shirt and resting on one breast. But it wasn't sexual. He was dead asleep and seemed to just find that position subconsciously. She had never slept better in her life than she did in Scott's bed with him next to her with his hands on her.

"Just going to do some studying," she told him. She'd been going to bed with him every night, but after he slipped off to sleep, she got up and headed to the Come Again to get a couple of hours of studying in. Something about being there with the music in the back room and the coffee percolating and other people being up and around and working, helped her focus. It wasn't that she *couldn't* read her lessons and take notes at Scott's, but when she was here, she liked...being with Scott.

They watched TV, and ate popcorn, and teased, and talked and...yeah, had lots of mind-blowing, amazingly good sex. Sometimes slow on the couch, sometimes fast on the kitchen table, sometimes a little bit of both in the shower.

So she preferred all of that, then slipping out to the Come Again to hit her virtual books, and Scott slept through her leaving and coming back again.

Usually.

"You're studying? Now?" he asked, peering at the clock on the table beside the bed. It was just after midnight.

"Yeah. I have a test I have to do and turn in online before six a.m."

He ran his hand back and forth over her belly and Peyton felt her body heating. "Can you take the test in, say, an hour?"

She laughed. Heather was meeting her at the bar, actually. She hadn't been sleeping well since her new boyfriend, Seth, the cop from Baltimore, had left. He'd come after her when she'd returned to Sapphire Falls, professing his love and staying for a few days so that he could meet her friends and see the town. But he was back in Baltimore now, and Heather didn't move back there until after school was out. Peyton was going to miss her terribly, and so the idea for Heather to catch up on grading papers while Peyton did her online class stuff at the Come Again seemed perfect.

The Come Again was a much mellower place after hours. There was no blaring jukebox or live band. Just the muted sound of classic rock from the back room where Mitch and Andi worked. Along with the sound of a saw and hammers and drills.

Otherwise, it was quiet. Almost library-like. And Peyton was no longer the only person seeking a place that was open after midnight. Each night, someone new had wandered in. Now there were three other tables occupied regularly. One by Riley Ames, Kyle's little sister, who was back in town after spending the last few years out in California; one by Hannah McIntire, another Sapphire Falls native who was now home, but only for a visit to help her grandmother after her hip surgery. And some guy that Hannah had brought with her. He sat at a corner table and tapped on his laptop almost nonstop.

Riley and Hannah were a little older than Peyton but she'd always liked them. And she felt a little sorry for Kyle right now with his little sister—who could be a bit of a handful—his ex and some guy his ex had brought with her, all here in Sapphire Falls and spending a lot of time in one of Kyle's favorite places.

"You need your sleep," Peyton told Scott, rolling to her side to face him.

"I need *you*."

She felt a warm shiver go through her. She was never going to get enough of him saying stuff like that in that tone of voice. "Well...I can give you twenty minutes."

He rolled her underneath him before she even got all the words out. Bracing himself on his elbows on either side of her head, he pressed his already-thick erection against the seam of her leggings. "Forty-five."

"Thirt—"

But then he kissed her and started touching her and started saying all of the things that turned her bones to liquid.

And sixty-five minutes later, she walked into the Come Again.

"Where have you—" Heather got a good look at her. "Oh."

Peyton grinned and pulled a chair out at the table where Heather already had her papers all spread out. "He woke up this time."

Heather sighed. "I'm so jealous of you right now."

Peyton laughed. "You've got Seth."

"Seth is in Baltimore," Heather said. "And I've found out I don't really like sexting."

Peyton shook her head. "Then you're doing it wrong."

"Hey, I loved my vibrator. Before I met Seth. Now it's just not the same."

Peyton loved that she had a friend who would say something like that to her. "You should try phone sex—like hearing his actual voice—instead of texting," she said. "That might be better."

Heather shrugged. "Probably. And maybe video chatting."

"There you go," Peyton said. "Way to be a problem solver."

Heather giggled. "I'm pretty thrilled that my biggest problem right now is that my boyfriend gives better orgasms than my Rabbit."

Peyton took in Heather's bright smile and the general glow—sure enough, it was real—about her. "I'm really happy for you."

It was funny because Seth was supposed to have been Peyton's date to that wedding in Baltimore. Now he was madly in love with Heather, and Peyton had finally admitted that she was crazy about Scott.

Heather's smile softened. "Ditto, babe. You so deserve to be happy. And you picked a great guy to do it with. Scott is the best."

He really was.

Peyton felt a vaguely familiar emotion ripple through her. It was the same feeling she got when she stepped back from a decorating job to see that it had turned out exactly the way she'd pictured it. Or when the customer came to pick up a cake they'd ordered and lit up when they first saw it. It was like pride and happiness all rolled together. But pride didn't quite fit for her and Scott. It was a gut-deep sense of *yeah, this is exactly right*.

"Wow, that was a very contented sigh," Heather commented.

Peyton hadn't even realized she'd sighed. But yes, *contented*, that was the perfect word for how she felt.

She smiled at Heather. "I'm content. Completely. And that's weird."

"Weird?" Heather asked.

"I'm never content. I'm always looking for something to do, people to be with, a party to start. Content isn't a normal word for me."

Heather nodded. "I guess that's true."

"But I never had all the things I have with Scott," Peyton said. "I've never wanted to go home, and stay home, before."

Heather squeezed her hand. "That's awesome, Peyton."

"It is." She swallowed hard. "I mean, we don't even really *do* anything. We watch TV and talk and cook and do laundry. I've been going to bed around eleven every night. I've eaten more meals at a kitchen table in the past few days than I have in the last few *years* combined. It's all just really normal, boring stuff. And it's so...nice."

"You seem stunned by that."

"I am," Peyton agreed. "Who would have believed that *I* would be so happy being normal?"

Heather didn't laugh. She sat back in her chair and looked at Peyton thoughtfully. "I completely believe it."

"It doesn't seem strange?"

"Not at all. It's what you've always wanted," she said. "A normal home and family life. Some people don't get to go out much, so having a night on the town is a treat. Some people never get to travel, so they dream of seeing the world. Your dream is the normal, contented life that you didn't have growing up and staying home doing nothing is your treat."

Peyton nodded. Heather was exactly right. "I'll tell you, not doing the whole hair and makeup thing every night *is* a treat. And my feet feel great since I haven't had heels on in over a week."

Heather laughed. "I really am happy for you."

Peyton grinned and glanced down at her computer. The test she needed to take was up on the screen. She looked over at the coffee cup that sat to the right of the keyboard, then up at her friend.

"Do you know how many shots we've done at this table?" she asked Heather.

"I'm not sure I can count that high."

Peyton chuckled. "And now here we are, drinking coffee, working, talking about our relationships, and how nice it is to stay in. What happened to us?"

Heather sat forward, also looking very content. "We fell in love."

Peyton felt her eyes widen. In love? She knew Heather was in love with Seth, but her and Scott? She knew she was crazy about him. She knew that she was maybe *falling* in love with him. But was she already there?

"You do know that you're in love with Scott, right?" Heather asked, clearly reading Peyton's expression.

Peyton felt her head nodding slowly. "Yeah. Okay."

Heather snorted. "You're not actually surprised by that, are you? I think you've been in love with him for a really long time."

Peyton thought about that. Heather might have a point. It would explain a lot. Like how bossy she let him get. And how her heart rate kicked up every time she saw him. And how she could still feel the icy coldness coursing through her when she'd heard "Scott's been shot".

"Wow," she finally said.

"Wow?" Heather repeated. "That's it?"

Scott had been so in her face about taking care of her and wanting more from her that it was a little surprising to find out that he'd actually snuck up on her. "I guess I would have expected to *realize* I was already in love."

Heather gave her an affectionate smile. "Scott made it easy and comfortable. Just like he does everything for you."

And Peyton felt her heart expand. That was so true. "Heather?"

"Yeah?"

"I think that maybe this—" Peyton swept her hand over the table, indicating everything from her coffee-cup-instead-of-a-shot-glass to her computer to their conversation. "—might be what being grown-up and mature is like."

Heather laughed. "Well, I'll be damned."

12

_____

S cott approached the door to the Come Again with trepidation. He didn't know what the hell was going on in there, but Peyton's truck was parked out front, so he was going in.

He stepped into the bar, expecting to see the usual crowd of people and hear the usual loud country music, laughter and conversation.

But the place was mostly empty and quiet. Well, except for the guy behind the bar, the guy sitting at the bar, and the four occupied tables. And what sounded like a muted electric drill.

And the place smelled like coffee.

What. The. Hell.

His eyes immediately found Peyton. She was already on her feet and coming toward him. Scott completely ignored Kyle and Derek—the guy behind the bar and the guy sitting at the bar—as he met her halfway across the Come Again.

Of course, they were mostly just looking at him with knowing grins, so ignoring them was pretty easy.

"What are you doing here?" she asked as she came to stand in front of him, head tipped back to meet his eyes. She was wearing slip-on tennis shoes rather than the heels or boots she typically wore here, and she only came up to his chest without that extra lift. "You should be in bed."

God, he just wanted to wrap her up in his arms. He didn't need to even kiss her. He just wanted to touch her. He'd not touched her for so long that now the dam had broken, he couldn't stop the flood of *want*.

"I always check it out when you're not where I expect you to be, Trouble," he said, settling for tucking a strand of hair that had escaped her bun behind her ear. "Seems to save me headaches later."

She didn't smile but she didn't frown either. She was studying him as if searching for something. Or as if she'd just realized something. "I've been studying down here for a while."

"Yeah, guess I kind of thought when you said you were getting up to study that you meant at the kitchen table or something."

She looked around and a faint smile touched her lips. "The first couple of nights, it was just me—and Derek and Mitch and Andi—but more and more people keep showing up."

He followed her gaze, actually taking in the other people in the room for the first time. When he realized who was there, he swung his gaze to look back at Derek and Kyle. Kyle's sister and his ex were both back in town? Derek was grinning his usual shit-eating grin. Kyle looked, predictably, exasperated. Scott needed to get the story here.

"So you're taking your test?" he asked, focusing on her again.

"Yeah, just, um...getting ready to."

He looked over to where Heather sat. She gave him a little wave and he lifted a hand, then grinned down at Peyton. "Were you talking about me, Trouble?" he asked.

She crossed her arms. "Yeah, but nothing good."

He moved in closer and put his finger under her chin. "I don't believe you."

She lifted a brow. "It's true."

"Then you didn't tell her about the maple syrup, and that you didn't even make it out of the pantry with it." He was gratified to see her suck in a little breath. He grinned and leaned in, kissing her softly and taking a slow swipe over her lower lip with his tongue. He lifted his head and gave her a wink. "Go kick ass on your test."

He watched her hesitate, wondering over that brief pause where it felt like she was going to say something—or do something. But she finally turned on her heel and headed back to her table.

As she settled in front of her computer, her eyes came up to his again. Satisfaction coursed through him. He'd drifted back to sleep after she'd left his bed, but not for long. He'd found himself reaching for her and then going to find her in the kitchen—appropriate, he'd thought, considering he was still hungry for her. But she'd been nowhere. He'd dressed and headed for her house, thinking she must have gone home to study. But passing the Come Again, he'd seen her truck and he'd of course had to pull in.

He took a seat at the bar across from Derek and next to Kyle. Derek, that stupid grin still on his face, pushed a cup toward Scott.

There was a light foam on the top and a sprinkle of...

"Is that cinnamon?" Scott asked, looking up at his friend.

"Nutmeg, actually," Derek said, "though I'm not sure you, or I, could really tell the difference."

He wasn't so sure about that. He had a big thing for cinnamon. "So this would be a..." Scott trailed off, intending Derek to fill in the blank.

"You don't know what cappuccino is?" Kyle asked. "Really?"

Kyle was definitely grumpy, and Scott had a pretty good idea why. And he sympathized. Kyle's little sister, Riley, was home, and then there was Hannah—the one that got away. Yeah, Scott would be grumpy too. But the thing was...he was in love. And he didn't care if it was a little insensitive to be incredibly happy in the face of his friend's stress.

"I just wanted to be sure that my friend who is a *bartender* is actually making cappuccinos and then sprinkling shit on top," Scott said, picking the cup up and taking a sip. "Not bad."

"Spoken by the guy who uses flavored creamer," Kyle muttered, picking up his cup of black coffee.

Scott laughed. "Maybe Doc here needs something stronger than coffee," he said to Derek.

"Bar's closed," Derek said, shaking his head. "Coffee, tea, cappuccino, soda, water."

"Yeah, what exactly is going on here?" Scott asked, swiveling to take in the room again. He'd mostly been focused on Peyton, and had then noticed Heather, and then Riley and Hannah. But Conrad and Frank, two of the older guys in Sapphire Falls who were involved in *everything*, sat at the table talking with Hannah, and there was also a guy at the corner table Scott had never seen before.

"Frank and Conrad are out kind of late, aren't they?" Scott asked. Considering the guys were part of the group that met at the diner every morning for coffee at six a.m., he was shocked to see the guys out at one a.m.

"They're here getting advice from Hannah," Derek said, his mouth stretching into a huge grin as he looked at Kyle.

Scott looked at the good doctor as well, but Kyle was glaring at his coffee.

"What's up with that?" Scott asked Derek.

"They came in because they heard Hannah's been in here the past couple of nights. They wanted to ask her some questions but didn't want Dr. Ames to find out."

Scott looked at Kyle again. "And yet, Dr. Ames is right here."

"Yep," Derek said. "Here he is. Weird, when he has rounds at the hospital bright and early in," Derek glanced at the clock on the wall, "a little over six hours from now."

Scott turned toward Kyle and rested his elbow on the bar. "Yeah, that *is* weird."

"But I guess if someone's in town trying to take some of your business away, you'd probably want to keep tabs," Derek said.

"Hannah's trying to take some of Kyle's business?" Scott asked.

"Well, it didn't really start out that way," Derek said, leaning on the bar with both forearms. "It's actually kind of a funny story."

"It's really not that funny," Kyle said.

"Well, it's probably in how the story is told," Derek said.

"He has a point," Scott said, totally rolling along with this. It was pretty fucking fun to make Kyle uncomfortable. Kyle was a perfectionist, and everything always worked out for him, and he rarely had so much as a wrinkle in his shirt. Even a hint that something might not be going exactly according to plan for him was enough for his friends to jump all over.

"Well, it was Kyle's idea that they talk to her," Derek said.

"Shut up, Derek."

But they both knew there was no way Derek was going to shut up. "Kyle wanted to show her that it's really nice to be involved in taking care of the people in your hometown. You know, kind of rub it in that she didn't come home to practice like she'd promised. But he wanted her to talk to them as a physical therapist."

"Because she *is* a physical therapist, right?" Scott asked.

"Yeah, but Hannah's not talking to them about physical therapy. She's telling them all about acupuncture and massage and immersion therapy and stuff," Derek said, shooting a look at Kyle as he said it.

"Immersion therapy?" Scott repeated.

"Oh, you'll have to have Hannah explain it. She gets *really* excited talking about it," Derek said with a smirk.

Kyle's eye roll was big enough to be seen across the room.

Derek went on, "She's very anti-pain medication and, well, pills in general it seems. So she's telling our old guys with arthritis and gout all about how to change their diets and to use meditation and massage and other stuff instead. Which, of course, kind of rubs our doc the wrong way. Pun totally intended."

Scott processed all of that. Including the pun. Which was actually pretty funny. "So," he said to Kyle. "She came to town, *you* sent people to talk to her to show her what she's been missing, and now she's telling them the opposite of what you've been telling them," Scott summarized. "And on top of that, they're sneaking around and meeting her after hours to avoid you."

Kyle just lifted his cup, but Derek said, "Pretty much."

Scott couldn't help it. He laughed. Everything always went Kyle's way—except Hannah.

"How long is she back?" Scott asked.

"Her grandma had her hip replaced, so she's here to help with her rehab. I guess she'll be here for, what, another six weeks or so, Doc?"

Kyle nodded. "Or so."

"And Riley's back too?" Scott asked. "When did that happen?"

Derek shot a look at the gorgeous redhead in the corner, tapping away on her computer. "A few days ago too. She's staying with her parents while she gets back on her feet."

"I heard all the charges were dropped," Scott said. Riley had been in jail. For computer hacking. Always smarter than a whip, Riley had gotten into computers early. She'd been chomping at the bit to get out of tiny Sapphire Falls and had headed straight to California out of high school. But she'd run into some trouble recently. She' been framed and eventually the cops had cleared her, but she'd been arrested and spent some time in jail before all of that could be proven.

"They were, but it's hard to get a job in the computer world after something like that," Derek said.

"But she didn't do anything wrong," Scott said.

"Well, she did—it just wasn't her fault," Derek said. "She was set up." He grinned. "But everyone now knows that she's *capable* of hacking the biggest, most secure companies. Her skills make potential employers nervous in spite of her intentions."

"Got it," Scott said. And he didn't say anything about how impressed Derek seemed or how his gaze had lingered on Riley. At least, not with Riley's protective older brother sitting right here. That didn't mean he wouldn't say something later.

"So she can't get a job," Kyle said flatly. "Which means she can't pay her rent or buy food or, you know, take care of herself, so she's back—living with my parents and doing web design until she can find something else."

"And she hates every minute of it," Derek added. "Well, except hanging out in here, because her family isn't here being judgmental and giving her unsolicited advice. Until now, of course." He gave Kyle a look. "But Dr. Ames just couldn't stay away. I just haven't figured out which girl he's here for."

"Both," Kyle muttered, pushing his cup toward Derek for a refill.

"You could leave," Derek suggested, pouring the coffee.

Kyle didn't reply.

Scott found Peyton again. She was now focused on her computer. She was biting her bottom lip and staring at the screen. She looked...adorable. That wasn't a typical word he assigned to Peyton but yeah, her hair up in that messy bun, her leggings, her one foot tucked up underneath her on the chair, no makeup, a gigantic cup of coffee by her elbow—she looked every bit the student. Young and optimistic and on the verge of something fresh and new. And he wanted to take her home, strip her down, and kiss every inch of her body until she was begging him to fuck her.

He cleared his throat and tuned back into his friends. To find that they were both watching him with eyebrows up.

"Shut up," he told them, lifting his cup.

Derek chuckled. "I don't know which of you is more entertaining. Calm, cool, to-do-list Kyle being all grumpy and wrinkled and annoyed, or by-the-book, all-his-shit-together Scott being all gaga over a girl."

Scott and Kyle looked at each other.

"We really do have our shit together," Scott said.

"Absolutely. You're as calm and cool as I am," Kyle said.

"So why are we friends with Derek again?"

They both looked at the bartender.

"Beats the shit out of me," Kyle said.

But Derek wasn't bothered. He straightened from the bar and gave them a smile. "Fine. Just remember that I also know how to make you *not* calm and cool," Derek said. "Scott, ask Kyle who the guy is at the computer over in that other corner."

"You bastard," Kyle said.

Scott glanced at the guy. "Why? Who is he?"

"He came to town with Hannah. They're even sharing a room over at Ty's," Derek said.

Ty Bennett had bought the house right next door to Hailey Conner when he'd moved back to town. He'd figured it was the easiest way to show her that he was all-in on the relationship that he wanted and she didn't. Now that they were married, they were living in Hailey's house and they used Ty's as a sort-of boarding house. As an Olympic medalist in the triathlon, Ty brought athletes to town to train and learn from him, and they stayed there. But there were six rooms in the house, and when they weren't full of triathletes, other people could rent them. There was a bed-and-breakfast in town, but Ty's was really for longer-term tenants than the ones who came to town for a weekend here and there and stayed at the Rise and Shine.

So Hannah was staying at Ty's while she was in town? And sharing her room with this guy? "Why isn't she staying at her mom and dad's?" Scott asked.

"Seems that when she didn't come home as planned, Kyle wasn't the only one she ticked off," Derek said.

Yeah, Kyle had been less ticked off and more...heartbroken.

"And she brought this guy with her?" Scott asked. Ouch. "Boyfriend?"

Derek shrugged. "We're assuming. Right, Kyle?"

"I don't fucking care."

Derek gave Scott a look that said "yeah, right". "But you know who that is, right?" Derek asked.

Scott looked at the guy again. "No, should I?"

"You ever heard of Michael Kade?" Derek asked.

Scott nodded. "Sure. The writer. He does thrillers and stuff, right?"

"Yep. And that's him."

Scott looked again. He wasn't sure he'd ever seen a photo of Michael Kade, or even read one of his books, but he was one of those guys who was big enough that you'd heard of him, even if you didn't really follow him. "No shit?"

"No shit. That is Michael Kade, the *New York Times* bestselling author, and he is here in Sapphire Falls with Hannah for as long as she's here. He calls her his muse."

Oh, boy, that was...interesting.

But Scott's brain completely shut down whatever the guys had been saying when he saw Peyton headed his way. She had a huge grin on her face, and he felt his heart rate accelerate in response. That happy, sassy look really did something to him.

Without even looking at Kyle, Peyton looped her bag over the back of Scott's bar stool, slipped between him and Kyle, and wedged herself next to Scott.

"Hey."

"Hey yourself." He swiveled, and she moved between his knees and up against him as if she had every right.

And she did. He was hers. He wasn't sure she completely realized that yet—or maybe it was that he wasn't sure she completely *believed* it yet—but he was all hers.

She rested her hands on his thighs and looked up at him, and his whole body tightened. "So I finished my test."

"Good. How'd it go?"

She shrugged. "Okay, I guess. But that's not what I'm thinking about right now."

"No?" He could give her a very short list of things he was thinking about right now. And every one of them involved her being naked.

"I've had a fantasy about you and this bar for a long time," she said.

"Yeah? I've had a fantasy about you and several things for a long time now."

She grinned. "I don't know how many times I've looked across this room at you and wished I could just walk up and kiss you."

He moved a hand to rest on the back of her neck. "What stopped you?"

She shook her head, more serious now. "I'm not really sure."

"How about now?"

And the smile was back. "Yeah, now seems really good."

She went up on tiptoe, gripping his shirt in her hands while he pulled her forward and bent his head. His hand felt huge on the back of her neck, and he was able to tip her head with his thumb on the edge of her jaw.

She seemed to melt into him, pressing close against his fly, where his cock was, as always, very happy to see—or feel —her again.

She opened her mouth before he even urged her to, her tongue stroking along his lower lip. She kissed him hungrily and Scott absorbed every bit of it. Having her in his arms was one thing; driving her crazy, touching and kissing and talking dirty to her was another. But the best thing of all? When she came into his arms and made *him* crazy.

Finally, she settled back on her heels, running her tongue over her own lip and smiling up at him.

"Good thing you got your test done," he said.

"Yeah?"

"Yeah. Because that was a take-me-home-right-now kiss."

13

D ottie's was busy two days later as Peyton made her way to the table where Dan was already seated.

"Hey," she greeted.

Her father gave her a sincere smile. "Hi."

She took a breath. She was glad she'd decided to meet him for lunch. She was. This would be great.

"Um, so, I can't stay," Dan said, as she started to slide into the booth.

Peyton froze halfway across the bench and stared at him. Okay, so it wouldn't be great. Because it wasn't going to happen. Then she shook her head and sighed, moving the rest of the way into the booth. "I'm shocked," she said dryly.

"Your mom needs me to come pick her up."

Peyton nodded. "It's been four days."

"Yeah."

"*Only* four days," she added. Then wondered why she bothered.

"She's unhappy," Dan said with a shrug.

"And you're lonely."

Dan was the one to sigh this time. "Yeah."

A prickle of guilt niggled at Peyton's mind. She could have seen him before this. She could have taken dinner over last night, or the night before. But she'd been spending time with Scott. And she hadn't really wanted to have lunch with her dad.

"Can we just...talk?" she asked Dan. "Just for a minute?"

She wasn't sure where that had come from. She and Dan hadn't sat and talked for a really long time. Or maybe ever. But she'd been doing a lot of talking lately and it wasn't so bad.

Dan nodded. "Yeah, okay."

Peyton knew that Dan wouldn't give her much more than the few minutes, so she leaned her forearms onto the tabletop and jumped right in. "Don't you think the rehab would be good for her?"

Dan didn't look surprised by the topic, but he didn't look thrilled with it either. "I don't know," he finally answered. "Seems like it should be."

Peyton nodded. "Yes. It really does."

"But I don't know how effective it can be if she's miserable and doesn't want to be there."

"It's not unusual for people to not like doing things that are good for them," Peyton pointed out. She really hated running. Her friend Tess had tried to get her into it, but Peyton hated it. Even though she knew it was good for her. Of course, she hadn't stuck with it. Or the gluten-free thing she'd tried. Or cutting back on her drinking. Or getting a degree before now. All of which also would have been good for her. But she hadn't liked any of it. Peyton shook all of those thoughts off. This was about Jo. And Dan.

Dan slumped slightly in his seat. "I know. But I can't handle it when she's unhappy."

Peyton frowned and leaned in. "What is that about?"

He frowned back. "She's my wife. I love her."

Peyton shook her head. "No, this is more than that. You know rehab would be *good* for her. That she could be even happier when it's over. But you don't encourage it. You don't push her. You show up the second she's not having a good time. Is it really because you miss her that much? You really can't be alone, even if it's for her own good?"

She had never gone into this with her father. Peyton hadn't been surprised even the first time Jo had quit rehab. Jo had gone on and off of her meds, started and stopped therapy, started and stopped support groups, all of Peyton's life. She'd tried everything from meditation to adopting pets to trying Hope's essential oils. She'd never stuck with anything. And Dan had never pushed. He'd never made her do anything that was difficult or that made her even a little unhappy.

Again, Peyton thought about all the things *she'd* started and quit in the past, and then shook it off. She could think about all of that later. Maybe.

Dan was tracing his finger up and down the butter knife by his hand. It almost killed her, but Peyton stayed quiet, hoping that he would answer her. And that when it came, the answer would make sense. Because her parents and their craziness—some of it literal—had been a cloud she couldn't shake. She would love some actual insight into the whole thing. She would also love to think that Dan *had* some actual insight.

Finally, he looked up. "That woman isn't easy," he said. "She's got a lot of problems. Some that she can't help, some she can. And I don't think very many people would have stuck around for her. But I make her happy. And I made her a promise, to always be there. In a world where everything seems to be working against happiness and people sticking around and keeping promises, that's something that's made me proud for a long time."

Peyton felt like she was holding her breath. That was kind of like what she and Scott had talked about the night on the hill—the fact that there was so much fighting *against* the happiness and that it was really important to do things to keep it going.

Without overthinking it, she reached over and covered her dad's hand. "You've given up so much, though. Are *you* happy?"

Dan was clearly surprised by Peyton's touch. He lifted his eyes to hers. "Yeah, I have given things up. That's why it's important that I'm here for her. She needs me."

Something in his voice made her pause. She looked closer. He looked...she wasn't sure. But not sad or upset. He looked determined.

"So you don't want it to be different? You don't want her to get help and get better?"

He took a deep breath. "Well, that's not going to happen. So that makes my decision to stay matter."

Peyton frowned, thinking about what he'd said. "Your decision to stay? You mean, instead of leaving Sapphire Falls with Melody?"

Melody was Hope's mother. She'd spent a summer in Sapphire Falls and had met and had a fling with Dan. When she was ready to leave at the end of the summer, he'd chosen to stay in Sapphire Falls. With Jo. He hadn't known he had a daughter with Melody until Melody passed away and Hope came looking for him.

Dan finally nodded. "Yeah."

"You loved her, didn't you?" Peyton asked.

"I did," he admitted. "But she didn't need me. Jo did. So I stayed."

"And if Jo stops needing you, then all of that sacrifice was for nothing," Peyton said, putting the pieces together as she spoke.

Dan didn't confirm that. But he didn't really have to.

"You don't want Jo to get better," Peyton said quietly, stunned. "You want her to need you."

He shrugged. "She can't get totally better, Peyton."

"And that's okay with you."

"We're making it work," Dan said.

Except that they really weren't. Jo was dependent, Dan was an enabler, and their daughter had been on her own almost from the beginning.

Peyton pulled her hand back. "I guess I never realized...that this really *is* what you want," she said.

"It's my life," Dan said. "I've done my best. That's really all anyone can ask, you know?"

Peyton swallowed hard. She was *not* going to point out all of the things he hadn't done well, all of the ways she could name that he'd failed, the mistakes. Because maybe, just maybe, he really had done his best.

She took a second to consider that. She supposed it was possible that Dan and Jo just weren't cut out to be parents, and that they'd done the best they could. And maybe it didn't matter anymore. They were happy. At least, by their own definition. Who was she to tell them that was wrong? *She* knew that there should be more, could be more, and maybe that was all that mattered.

"I need to go," he said.

She nodded. "I know."

Dan slid out of the booth and stood. Then he shocked her— and maybe himself a little as well—by leaning over and kissing the top of her head.

Before she'd really recovered, he was across the diner and out the door.

They'd made it past two weeks.

Scott looked at the date he'd just written on the check to the electric company, then up at the woman sitting next to him at the kitchen table working on her computer.

He was paying bills and she was studying. They'd finished dinner about an hour ago, done the dishes, and were now settled at the table. If tonight went according to the routine they'd already established, they would be here for a couple of hours, then head to the couch for some TV time, before going to bed, making love, and sleeping all night wrapped up together.

They had a routine. Full of some of the most normal, everyday stuff that two people could do together.

And he was suddenly filled with the urge to give a loud *hell yeah*.

Instead, he reached over and ran a hand over her hair.

She looked up and gave him a little smile that made his heart kick in his chest.

He wanted this for the rest of his life. He opened his mouth, wondering even as he did it, if it was the right time. It was fast. Kind of. He wasn't going to propose, exactly, but he was going to ask her to stay. Like this. Forever.

So, okay, that would be sort of like a proposal.

But he didn't want to spook her. He didn't want to do anything that would rock this boat. This perfectly normal, routine, could-be-boring-but-it-wasn't boat.

"Pey—"

Just then his phone rang. And he was split between frustration at being interrupted, and relief at being interrupted. He leaned in, kissed her quickly on the mouth, then pulled his phone out.

"Hansen."

"North Dakota. You and me. It's all set up."

It was Lance. Shit.

Scott glanced at Peyton. "Um, I haven't set things up here."

"Dammit, Hansen," Lance said. "Come on."

Scott sighed. "Thought we were having a meeting first."

"Yeah, tomorrow. And your ass better be there. We head out the next day."

"The next day?" Scott repeated.

"What? You need to get a mani-pedi before we go? We don't have time to waste here," Lance said.

"It's just...not a good time." Scott saw Peyton frown slightly.

"Yeah, well, it's not really a good time for those girls that are missing either."

Scott scowled at the tabletop. "That was low."

"I don't fucking care. I want you on this with me."

Scott blew out a breath. "I appreciate that. I just can't really... drop things right now."

"So don't drop them. Put them on hold. For fuck's sake, Hansen, I can't believe I'm even having to ask more than once."

Scott felt a squeeze on his hand and looked up into Peyton's eyes.

"You okay?" she asked quietly.

He wasn't.

He wanted to go to North Dakota. He needed to go. But things here were just getting solid. How could he pick up and leave Peyton when he was just now able to show her how good and steady this was? That was what Peyton had never had...a home that was good and steady. Where she could count on the people and the routine to be the same, no matter what else happened. She'd had to *leave* her childhood home to find the good things that made her feel better. He wanted those good things she needed to be inside these four walls.

He had to make a decision here though. "I'll call you right

back," he told Lance. Then he disconnected before the other man could give him any more grief.

"What's going on?" Peyton looked legitimately concerned.

"It's...the task force," Scott told her. Might as well be honest about it. Damn, why couldn't this be two or three months from now? Or six? Or twelve? He wanted things stable here before he left to make something—someone—else his priority. Even temporarily.

"They need you?" she asked.

He nodded.

"Why did you tell him this wasn't a good time?" she asked. "Is your leg bothering you too much?"

"My leg's not an issue," he said. There'd be no kicking down doors or running down back alleys. At least, not at first.

"So then you have to go."

"The op is in North Dakota," he said. "And I'll be gone two weeks, minimum. Maybe more. And totally cut off, at least for part of it. I don't know when I'll be able to call or even text."

"Oh." That seemed to make her think. She straightened after a moment. "Well, you still have to go. If that's where they need you, that's where you have to go."

"I told him I had to think about it."

"What's to think about?"

Okay, fine. Scott leaned in, pinning her with a direct gaze. "You and me. And all of this."

"All of this?"

"Us being together. We're just getting started," he told her.

She didn't laugh, but she did smile. Sweetly. And not even a little sarcastically. "We started a long time ago, Scott."

"And it took me a hell of a time to get you to this point," he said. "And I don't know if the time we've had is enough to keep things solid."

She leaned in too. "Well, where am I going to go? You've ruined me for all other men. You've got that new showerhead that I love. You make the best homemade pizza I've ever had. You go get the bad guys and save the day, then come home. I'll be here."

Her words rocked through him. Yeah, the ones about ruining her for other men were good. He liked those. A lot. But it was the *I'll be here* that made his heart feel like it might pound right out of his chest. He'd said that to her a hundred times. But she'd never said it to him.

She was here. With him. She was good. Happy. Content. And Sapphire Falls was good. It was the safe, happy, peaceful place he wanted, no *needed*, it to be.

That was all he'd ever really wanted. Home. And her.

Everything was different now than the last time he'd been on an extended op. He could go to North Dakota, do the work, make it really matter, and then, after all the dirt and darkness, he could come home. To Sapphire Falls and to Peyton.

He reached out and snagged her by the wrist, pulling her into his lap. "What if you need me?" he asked, putting his nose into her hair and breathing deep.

She wrapped an arm around his neck and snuggled close. "Well, I'm not going to lie and tell you my vibrator is going to stay in the drawer," she said.

"Not what I mean."

"Why would I ne—" She stopped and pulled back to look at him. "Wait a second, you mean, like a ride home from a party or bail money?"

He lifted a shoulder. "Anything."

"I did ninety percent of the shit I did so I could have your attention," she said with a small frown. "You know that."

Yeah, he did. It didn't matter. He wanted to be the one she could call no matter what. And that couldn't happen if he was in

North Dakota for God knew how long. "Not when you were in Vegas," he said.

"I'm not planning another trip to Vegas."

"You didn't plan *that* trip to Vegas." That had been a last minute, hey-I've-got-an-idea Peyton move.

She sighed. "Okay, I promise not to go to Vegas."

"That was hardly the first or last time you needed me, Trouble."

She suddenly pushed back off of his lap and frowned down at him. "Okay. But I don't understand what that has to do with North Dakota. I'm not going to be drinking and partying while you're gone. Is that what you want me to say?"

He sighed. "I just want to be around. In case."

Her eyes widened. "In case of emergency," she said, almost to herself. She frowned. "Like in my phone," she said, referring to putting his number in under ICE on her phone so he'd be the first call anyone made if she was in trouble.

"Yeah." He scrubbed a hand over his face.

"You really get off on that."

"On being someone you can count on? Yeah. You matter to me, Peyton."

"Well, thank you. And I know that," she said. "But you do realize that I'm not going to start questioning that just because you're not around to give me a ride home sometime."

Scott clenched his jaw, then forced himself to relax. He wanted her to be okay. Better than okay. He *needed* her to be good, safe, healthy and happy. And if he wanted something done right —like Peyton protected and cared for—then he had to do it himself. No one else had ever done it very fucking well. "It matters to me to be there for you."

"You can't come running every time I have a hangnail, Scott."

"I wish I could," he shot back. "That I could fix." Then he froze. Fuck, why had he said that?

She seemed stunned too. "My stuff does seem pretty easy to fix, doesn't it?" she said after a moment.

"That's not what—"

She held up a hand. "No, seriously." She seemed to be thinking as she spoke. "You worked on a task force where, no matter how many people you saved and how many bad guys you put away, there was always more. You never really felt like you completely fixed anything. And then you came to Sapphire Falls. Where you could fix the noise complaints and the speeding and the littering. And you found me—a girl you *could* save. Because what I needed was someone who would show up, over and over, no matter what I did wrong or how I screwed up."

"Peyton, that is *not*—"

"No, hang on," she said. "This is really it, Scott. I needed you. And I let you think I needed you even more than I did because I knew that's what *you* needed. You needed to clean out gutters and give rides home and give self-defense lessons to someone because you needed to feel like you were actually making things better for someone."

Jesus. His heart was aching as he watched her process everything going through her head. But he didn't try to stop her again. Because she was kind of right.

"Derek said that he didn't think you liked me just because I was the girl in town who was the most trouble," she said. "But that's part of it, isn't it?"

"You talked to Derek about this?"

She nodded. "I needed to know if I was the only one who saw that you needed more than Sapphire Falls."

"I don't," he said firmly. "Everything I need and want is right here."

"Am I the reason you haven't been doing as much work with the task force?" she asked. "Have you been sticking around

Sapphire Falls because of me and how much I get into trouble? And because I was giving you problems to fix?"

"I came back to Sapphire Falls because I was burned out," he said. "I told you that."

"Yes." She crossed her arms. "But you didn't tell me what's kept you here after you got over the burnout."

"Maybe I'm not over it."

"You are. You want to go to North Dakota. I know you do. I know the work is hard, but the other night when we were talking about it, I could see how much it means to you."

He didn't answer that.

"So if you're over the burnout, why aren't you going back?"

"I like it here. I want to take care of Sapphire Falls."

"Okay. But we don't need you twenty-four-seven three-sixty-five, Scott. This is *Sapphire Falls*. You can go and do the other stuff too."

"*You* need me twenty-four-seven three-sixty-five," he finally said. "You don't have anyone else like that in your life. That's me. That's my job."

She frowned harder.

"Hell, I fell in love with you, Peyton. I want to be here. With you. Is that really so bad?"

She just looked at him for a long moment. But finally she nodded. "Yeah, that is so bad."

"*What*?"

"Well, first of all, I don't love that this is the way you tell me you love me."

He grimaced. Yeah, okay.

"And second of all, and maybe more importantly, I don't love hearing that you loving me is keeping you from doing other things you're passionate about. Things that other people need you to do. You can't stay here in Sapphire Falls all the time because you're afraid to leave me. You can't do something that's only partially fulfilling because *I* don't have my shit together."

"That's not what I meant."

"But it's true," she said. "You've been staying here, not going on longer operations, because you're afraid that at some point I might need somebody and you're worried that no one else will be there for me."

He sighed. "Yeah. Kind of."

She didn't say anything for a long moment. Scott sat, watching her, trying to read her expression. Damn, this had gotten fucked-up fast. He knew it sounded pathetic that he'd wanted to stay close to take care of her. But he'd promised to be there for her. Any time. He couldn't fulfill that promise if he was hundreds of miles away undercover and not answering his phone.

"I can't be the reason that you're not doing everything you can and want to do," she finally told him. "I'll admit that I'm part of this problem. I watched my mom *need* my dad and my dad respond to that. It seemed to make him happy. So, I did the same things, trying to get his attention. It didn't really work with him. But it worked on *you*. And I loved having your attention so I didn't change it. But, I don't want to be like my mom and dad. My dad is there because she needs him. Not because he wants to be, but because he feels obligated. I don't want that from you. I want you with me because you choose to be. Not because you feel like you can't leave me and you feel responsible. I don't want to be nothing but troub—trouble, for you."

She stuttered over the word and Scott felt like his chest was cracking in two. "Peyton, I never meant that like that."

She pressed her lips together and nodded. Then she blinked hard and said, "I know."

"I *want* to be with you, Peyton. Jesus, I've never wanted anything more in my life." He could feel the need to *do* something coiling in his gut, but he had no fucking idea what to do. Besides lay his heart on the line.

"Then go to North Dakota."

He sucked in a breath. Why did he feel like if he left, he'd lose this? Her?

She wet her lips and then said, "And I'm going back to my house."

Scott felt his eyebrows slam together. "*No*."

"Yes." She lifted her chin. "You can be my ICE, but clogged gutters and hangnails are not emergencies."

"Fine," he blew out a breath. "But stay and...not need me *here*."

She shook her head. "I need to spend some time alone."

"No you don't. It's—"

"We've done the two weeks," she interrupted. "We said we'd do this thing where I try to seduce you and you show me what a real relationship is like for two weeks."

He gritted his teeth. They had said that. "You don't have to leave."

"I do. We made an agreement. Now we need to see where we want to go next."

"I know exactly where I want to go next," he practically growled. "I want you. Here. With me. For good."

Her expression softened for a moment, and he could see in her eyes that she wanted to give in. But she stiffened her spine and said, "We'll talk when you get back."

Fuck.

He would always do two things—whatever made Peyton happy and whatever he said he would do. They had said two weeks. That had been the testing period. So he had to let her go. At least temporarily.

That need to do something coiled tighter in his gut. He wanted to keep her here, to make her stay, to bind her to him somehow. What if she realized she really *didn't* need him? What if there were no more emergencies? What if there was nothing for him to save her from? Would *she* want *him* then?

"What if I don't go?" he asked stubbornly. "You move back to your place and we take some time to think about what we want. But I stay here while we do it?"

"Those girls need you, Scott. I know it kills you a little that you can't save them all in one fell swoop, but every single one you do save is worth it."

His heart squeezed. Dammit.

"And as a girl who you've fixed a lot of things for, let me tell you, seeing you come through the door, all big and bad and determined to right every wrong, is something those girls deserve to see."

Love and need and desire pulsed through him with her words. She believed in his work. She could help him see the good in the midst of the horrible crap. And she *had* to be here when he got home. She had to be. Coming home to her was what would hold him together for the next few weeks.

He reached out and circled her wrist with his fingers, pulling her close, just needing to *feel* her. She stepped between his knees and reached up and ran her hand over his hair, like he so often did to her.

It was that action that broke the final wall that was holding back the completely, almost irrationally, possessive part of him that needed to make her *his* before he left.

He came to his feet, grasped her hips and lifted her up onto the table in one fluid movement. He stripped her T-shirt over her head and lowered his mouth to take hers in a hot, deep kiss.

As his tongue stroked firmly, possessively along hers, he undid her bra, tossing it to the floor, and cupped her breasts, plucking and teasing the nipples until she was moaning into his mouth and wiggling on the tabletop.

He released her lips only so he could say firmly, "Take your pants off."

"What are you doing?" she asked, as he reached past her to set her computer on the chair and tossing his bills and paperwork to the floor. "I thought we were kind of breaking up."

The fuck if they were. "I'm ruining you for your vibrator too," he told her. He kissed her again, laying her back on the table. He hooked his thumbs in the waistband of her leggings, pulling them and her panties down her legs and dropping them on the floor.

With her totally naked and laid out on the table, he straightened and reached for the bottle of maple syrup they hadn't put away that morning.

Her eyes widened as he popped the lid. His gaze locked on hers, he tipped the bottle, drizzling the amber liquid over her stomach and then lower. She gasped as the syrup slid between her legs. Scott set the bottle to the side, parted her knees, and lowered his head, licking and sucking. She came before he'd even gotten it all lapped up, but he kept going, and after her second orgasm, finally pulled her ass to the edge of the table.

He dug a condom from his pocket and lowered his fly. He handed the foil packet to her. Without a word, she tore it open and reached for him. He gritted his teeth as she stroked him a few times before rolling the protection on.

"Even if this is all you ever need me for again," he said. "I *will* give you this. Whenever you want it. Over and over. As often as you'll let me."

"Scott." But that was all she said as he slid deep a moment later.

They both groaned. Nothing had ever been this good, or this right, and after they'd both come apart in each other's arms, he carried her, and the bottle of syrup, to the bedroom, and they did it all over again, getting his sheets as sticky as she'd promised on that very first day.

Several hours later, Scott was aware of the mattress dipping and the sheet shifting as Peyton got out of bed. But he kept his eyes shut. She was leaving. He'd known she would. He was heading to Omaha tomorrow and then to Cedar Downs. Having her in his bed, or his kitchen—and God help him if she had a spatula in hand—would have made it nearly impossible to leave.

But before she left, he felt her lips on his. And she kissed him like she wasn't going to see him for a long time. And like she was just maybe going to miss him terribly while he was gone.

14

There was really only one time and place where Peyton ever felt what it might be like to be quiet and shy.

And that was with Hope Bennett and her friends.

Adrianne, Hailey, Lauren, Phoebe, Kate, and Delaney, along with most of the female population of Sapphire Falls, had gathered at the community center for Hope's baby shower. It had been planned for after the baby was born, but so far, TJ Bennett's child was proving to be as stubborn as he was, and was taking his or her sweet time about showing up.

But they'd gone ahead with the party anyway. Lauren was due in D.C. next week, Delaney's boys had baseball tournaments all next weekend, and Hailey had to...do something amazing somewhere. So rescheduling wasn't an option.

Peyton stood off to one side near the food table, watching them all and trying not to be overcome by the general kick-assery in the room. People—women mostly—talked about the testosterone overload when these women's husbands got together, but the confidence and beauty and sheer OMG-I-want-to-be-her in the room was ridiculous when these women were in the same place at the same time.

"I kind of want to hate them all."

Peyton turned with a carrot stick between her teeth to see that Tessa had finally shown up. She bit the carrot off. "Thank God you're here."

"Sorry I'm late. Went for a run and didn't get back when I'd planned." Tess was a half-marathoner. She also helped Hailey Conner Bennett run the town. Tess fit right in here. She was beautiful, accomplished, independent, and madly in love with Bryan Murray, a Sapphire Falls boy who was equally beloved.

Still, Peyton always felt better when Tess showed up. She was a little younger than the other women, like Peyton, and was one of Peyton's closest friends.

Tess was still surveying the room.

"By the way," Peyton said. "I kind of want to hate them all too."

"But we can't," Tess said.

"Nope. Because they can't just be beautiful and successful, they all have to be super sweet too."

"Yeah."

They both sighed and again looked out over the room. Peyton crunched on her carrot and Tessa grabbed a chocolate-dipped banana.

Peyton was used to being in the middle of the party. Whatever the party. She was also used to having something to say. Always. So she was pretty out of her element here with the teachers and scientists and business owners who had wrangled some of the most eligible bachelors in the state and made beautiful babies with them. All while continuing to rule the world.

She and Tessa called it being "overwhelmed by the awesome" and had discovered there wasn't really any cure for it. But honestly,

Peyton had never felt left out or judged by any of these women. The opposite, in fact. They always made sure she was included. But it was just a fact of life that in this group of women, no matter how confident you were every other moment of your life, you would feel under-accomplished, unsophisticated and plain.

She also knew that if *any* of them knew she had those thoughts, they would be appalled.

She just thanked God that Tessa felt the same way.

"I heard that TJ is going nuts," Tess said, reaching for a cup of punch.

Peyton grinned. "It's hilarious. You know Hope, she's all into everything being natural and not getting worked up about things like due dates, but she's four days over now, and TJ is like a mother hen."

"What's Hope doing to deal with being overdue?" Tess asked. "She's huge."

Peyton nodded. She was. There was no way around the fact. "She's doing her yoga and lots of walking. But she's not worried or rushing things."

Hope was the most laid-back, Zen person Peyton knew. Or anyone around here knew. She was into herbs and natural remedies and natural, healthy living.

A little boy, holding a younger girl's hand, pushed in next to Peyton. "'Scuse me," he said. It was Carver, Adrianne and Mason's son. He was holding onto Kaelyn Spencer's hand, Phoebe and Joe Spencer's oldest, and reached for one of the banana pudding cups with animal crackers around the edge. Carver was a handful for his mother, but he was absolutely adorable. And he had a very obvious fondness for Kaelyn. It was probably the bright red curls that were just like her mom's.

"Thanks." Kaelyn beamed up at Carver as he handed her the pudding.

Peyton couldn't help her grin. It looked like there was a budding romance here.

"Have you tried the peanut butter cupcakes?" she asked.

"They're *super* good," Carver said with an emphatic nod. "I love peanuts."

His nickname was, actually, Peanut, since he'd been named after one of his father's agricultural scientist heroes.

"I love the circus!" Kaelyn chimed in.

Peyton laughed. "Me too." She watched as they ran off, feeling something achy in her chest.

"This really is amazing," Tess said, looking around. "It's perfect for Hope."

Peyton nodded as she looked over the food, decorations, and supplies for the games later on. "Well, we all know TJ's favorite saying is that it's not his circus or his monkeys. He doesn't even know how much more of a circus his life is about to be with a kid."

When Adrianne had said that Peyton could take the party over, she'd known what theme to use immediately. She'd envisioned chocolate-dipped bananas, in-the-shell peanuts, animal crackers, cotton candy, kettle corn and lemonade, and the cake had come to her within minutes. It was a circus tent, and Hope had teared up when she'd seen it. The entire theme for the party—circuses and monkeys—was a nod to TJ, because, in all actuality, he took on lots of "monkeys", and his life since meeting Hope and becoming Sapphire Falls' mayor had gone from a three-ring circus to about six rings. And it was clear that he loved every bit of it. Hope had made that happen for him. She'd made his life crazier, but she'd also made it bigger and more full of laughter and love.

Hope had been teasing him by referring to their baby as their little monkey since the pregnancy test had come back positive.

Tessa laughed. "Right? I can't wait to watch TJ with this baby."

Peyton couldn't either. TJ was going to be a great dad. He'd been keeping his three younger brothers in line for years, and he treated Hope like a princess. That yearning, tight feeling in her chest returned. Crap.

"I want some of that," Tessa said, sounding wistful.

Peyton looked over. "Yeah? Babies and stuff?"

Tessa nodded. "Definitely."

"Things are moving that direction for you and Bryan, right?"

Tess sighed happily. "Yes."

Peyton gave her a quick hug. "I'm so happy for you."

"And how are you doing with Scott gone?" Tess asked.

Peyton shook her head. "Not great. I miss him."

"Of course you do," Tess said with a little laugh. "You went from living with the guy to him being gone and totally cut off with no communication. I can't imagine not being able to talk to Bryan for a solid week."

Peyton looked at her friend. "You don't feel like that's kind of pathetic? That you can't even go a week without talking to him?"

Tess didn't seem offended at all. "It's called being in love, Peyton. If I didn't want to have Bryan around all the time and talk to him every day, then he wouldn't be the one."

Peyton thought about that. Yeah, she'd never known a guy that she wanted to see and talk to *every day*. Until Scott.

"And when was the last time you went this long without talking to Scott? Even before you guys were together, you saw him all the time."

She had. She hadn't really thought about it until he was gone, but running into him on a regular basis had been easy. And something she'd looked forward to. A lot.

"I just feel so...*dependent*." She gave a little shiver. "I hate that word."

"Dependent? Why? What are you not doing that you need him to do?"

Peyton focused on Lauren Bennett, who was holding her daughter Whitney and talking with her mother-in-law, Kathy. Lauren was one of the women Peyton admired most. She was taking care of her daughter, laughing with her mother-in-law, all while looking gorgeous and totally put-together. Peyton had no doubt that Lauren's email box was, at that very moment, full of messages from people in the White House, Outreach America— the aide organization her company IAS partnered with—along with a couple of naughty messages from her very hot husband, Travis.

Lauren was doing it all.

Peyton wanted to do it all.

But she was having a hard time even watching *Grey's Anatomy* by herself.

She'd done it. She'd stayed home every night since Scott had left a week ago. She'd cleaned her house, detailed her car, mowed her lawn, studied and watched TV. By herself. Because she thought it was important that she be able to do that. She hadn't even gone to the Come Again for the after-hours gathering that had become a regular thing now. She was...proving something to herself. Though she couldn't have really explained what that something was now seven days later.

So she could clean out her own gutters. Big deal. She'd never had Scott do it because she *couldn't*. And the only reason he'd wanted to was because she wouldn't let him do anything else for her—like make her laugh and make her feel safe and make her feel *wanted*. Gutters had been innocuous. Just like she'd called him when she'd had a flat tire and when she'd had too much to drink and when she'd almost been arrested in Vegas. Okay, that had been a bigger deal. But mostly she'd stuck with things that were straightforward. Things that would give her a Scott fix and that would make him feel like he was helping her out.

None of those things would ever be enough now.

No way could she be content to have him simply give her a ride home. Not even if he drove the long route to her house.

She wanted more than that from him. But the things she wanted were not innocuous. They were things like commitment and promises and a home and family. Things that would kill her if they went away or didn't measure up. If he didn't clean her gutters out adequately, it didn't matter. She'd do it herself. But if he didn't love her enough...

She kind of understood her mother now.

That was a scary thought, but if JoEllen really loved and wanted Dan, and she didn't know how else to hang on to him, Peyton could kind of see why she'd become so needy. Maybe losing that independent part of herself was better than losing *him*.

But that was where things were different with her and Scott. Scott wasn't tempted by anything else. He wanted to give all he had to Peyton. Had wanted to for a long time and had stuck with it for far longer than anyone else would have.

And, even more, she knew that he needed something from her too. He needed her to want him around even when her gutters were clean and her tires were perfect and her blood alcohol level was zero.

That was the biggest difference between her mom and dad and her and Scott. Her mom and dad *had* to be together. They were dependent on one another. Neither could really function without the other.

She and Scott just wanted each other.

They wanted to help each other out, fulfill the other one's needs, sure. But even when everything was perfectly fine and they were both perfectly content, they still wanted to be together.

And she'd realized all of this about three days in.

Seven days had never seemed so long in her life. He hadn't been able to call yet and had sent only one text two days ago that said *I'm thinking about you*. She'd read that one message over and over about twenty times.

And now, watching all of these women with their friends and sisters-in-law and kids, she was pretty sure she'd just decided that she also wanted to have babies with the guy.

Wow, if that happened every time he left for a week, they were going to need a bigger house.

P eyton had to clear her throat. "There's nothing I need him to do," she finally answered Tess. "I just want him here with me. And that's ridiculous. He's off doing important work and I'm fine."

"But you want him here," Tess said. "Yeah, that's being in love. And it's about time you fell into it with that guy." Tess gave her a grin. "Just enjoy it, babe."

"Peyton!" They were interrupted by Adrianne sweeping around the edge of the food table. "I hope you don't mind, but I said that yes of course you'd be willing to plan Tom Franklin's retirement party." Adrianne gave her a big grin. "Lori said you should just take it over."

"Really?" Mr. Franklin had been Peyton's high school math teacher, and his wife was here at the shower today.

"Really," Adrianne said. "Everyone loves this shower so much. And Emma has been telling everyone about what you did for her garden party. Lori said it would be a relief to turn the birthday party over to you. I swear, Peyton, you could throw a party for anyone in this town and get it exactly right."

Peyton almost immediately saw the party table in her mind, with cookies in the shape of plus signs and pencils and even a calculator. But then she instantly realized that no way could they do cookies...they had to do pie. She grinned. She didn't know if everyone would get the pie/ pi reference, but Mr. Franklin would.

They could also have math-problem races on a giant blackboard as a game. He'd always loved story problems, of course, so she could come up with a few funny ones that starred him as the guy who was buying one hundred watermelons and seventy-three oranges and twenty-five mangos.

"I'm going to take that smile as a yes?" Adrianne said.

Peyton focused on her again. "Well, I do like to party," she quipped with a big grin. "I've had lots of practice."

After the shower, Peyton went home and tried to study for a little bit. But her mind wouldn't focus. It kept wandering to the party for Mr. Franklin. To the point that she finally pulled out a notebook and jotted her ideas down. She sketched pictures, and wrote out some game ideas, and made a list of supplies.

And when she was done, she closed out of the website for the biology class and opened up her files from the classes she'd taken when she'd gone for an associate's degree in business management. She hadn't finished that program either. Because it hadn't really meant anything to her.

Now, it suddenly did. Or maybe it wasn't so sudden.

She found the file she was looking for, and an hour later, she had a business proposal written up. She e-mailed it to Adrianne. And then sat back with a smile.

Feeling what she could only describe as *good*, she headed out to her truck. She was in the mood to go for a drive. She ended up, as always, up on the hill overlooking the town.

It had been raining most of the last two days, but the sky was clear now as the sun began to sink. Peyton climbed up onto the hood of the truck, reclined back against the windshield and took a deep breath.

This place always calmed her. It helped her think. Gave her perspective.

But tonight, she didn't feel like she needed calming. She already felt content. Not as good as when she was sitting next to Scott on the couch in his living room, but definitely satisfied.

And she wondered how Scott would feel about getting married in this very spot. Eventually. In time. Or the week after he got back from North Dakota.

She laughed out loud. Yeah, she wanted to marry the guy. Without a doubt. All it took was him leaving town for her to realize that. She was sure he was going to cuss when she told him that. He would have probably left town a year ago if he'd known that's what she'd needed to see what he meant to her.

And that thought warmed her from a place inside that she hadn't even known existed. Scott wanted to be with her. He would do whatever it took to make that happen. She knew that. She trusted it. And it wasn't creepy or clingy or dependent. It was...exactly what she needed.

The idea of marrying him, of having everything they'd had for the past weeks forever, made butterflies swoop through her belly. She wasn't usually a butterfly kind of girl. But then she wasn't the wedding and babies and big goofy in-love grins and leaving-silly-sticky-notes-all-over-the-house kind of girl either. Until Scott had loved her.

She hugged her arms around herself and just let all of that sink in. Then she pulled her phone from her back pocket, suddenly missing him with an intensity that shocked her. *I miss you.* She had no idea when he'd see it or if he'd be able to respond, but she wanted him to know.

Her phone dinged with a return message almost immediately. *Ditto. So damned much. Home in two days.*

Her heart flipped in her chest. He was coming home early. She couldn't believe how excited she was about that.

Everything okay? she asked. She hoped it was a good thing he was leaving North Dakota more quickly than expected.

Will have to come back, but we have what we need for now. And I need you.

He'd have to go back. She swallowed. Okay. That was fine. The work mattered to him, and she could absolutely keep her shit together in order for him to go and do it.

But she was going to make his homecoming something special. Not a big party—she didn't want to share him—but this was definitely something she wanted to celebrate.

And she'd throw a party every time he came home to her. He'd need that after the ops, to remind him of all the things in life worth celebrating, and really, parties were her way of showing people she cared. Which she finally now fully understood.

I can't wait to see you, she told him.

I love you.

Those three words, in print, made her tear up. *I love you too.* She hoped it would do the same for him.

Oh, no, don't you think for one second that you're going to get away with saying that only over text.

Fine. I'll say it in person too. But you're probably going to have to take your clothes off right afterward.

Can do.

Yeah, she definitely missed him. Just him. And everything he made her feel.

With a stupid, in-love grin, she slid to the ground and got back in the truck. She had some plans to make.

She was ready to make him cookies. Because she definitely wanted to keep him, and while she was pretty sure she couldn't get rid of him even if she tried, she was pulling out all the stops.

But as she shifted into reverse and pressed the gas pedal, nothing happened. Well, the engine revved and the tires rotated, but the truck didn't move. She could feel that the back tires weren't grabbing onto anything. Dammit. It was muddy up here, but she hadn't thought she'd actually get stuck. She frowned and tried shifting into drive. But the tires were doing nothing but spinning in place.

Crap.

She took a breath and shifted into reverse again, trying to rock the truck as much as she could. But there was no way she could get the thing moving by herself.

Double crap.

Peyton thunked her forehead on the steering wheel twice and then took a deep breath and got out.

Yep, she was stuck in the mud. Deep in the mud.

Well, this was just great.

Her first thought, a reflex really, was to take her phone out and call Scott. She even got the usual little rush of yay-I-get-to-see-him with the thought. But then, of course, she remembered that he wasn't there.

And then she remembered, or *admitted*, that she knew how to handle this.

It just wasn't as fun as calling Scott and having him show up and flex all of his big muscles and be her hero, but she was a good country girl. She'd seen more than one truck unstuck from the mud down by the river after a party.

She still wished Scott was here.

Peyton climbed up into her truck bed and pulled out the shovel and the ax that she always had with her. Like a good country girl.

She hopped to the ground and began digging around the back tires, removing as much of the sticky mud as she could and widening the grooves under and around the tires. Then she headed toward the grove of trees about fifty yards away. She chopped at some of the smaller trees and bushes, cussing the scratches they gave her in return and the blister she was going to have on her right palm. But soon, she had enough branches and leaves to get some traction under the wheels. Trudging back to the truck, she also wished she'd changed into her boots and jeans instead of coming out here in flip-flops and shorts.

Finally, however, she had the leaves and branches behind her tires and was able to slowly ease the truck out of the muddy furrows and onto firm land.

She gave a triumphant shout and turned toward the road.

Damn right. She didn't need a man.

But she wanted one. One very particular one.

Her phone rang just as she pulled out onto the paved highway. She glanced down. Then frowned.

It was TJ.

Her heart kicked hard in her chest. Hope. The baby. *Oh my God, it's time.*

She pulled over on the side of the road, scattering gravel as she braked hard, grabbing her phone at the same time.

"Hello?"

"Peyton, it's TJ."

"I know," she said impatiently. "What's going on?"

"I need a favor." He followed it with a big sigh, as if this phone call was not one he wanted to make.

"Of course. Anything. What's up?"

"Travis needs some help at his place and I need someone to come stay with Hope."

Peyton frowned. "Is she okay?"

"She's taking her damned sweet time about having my baby is what she is," TJ said crossly.

Peyton rolled her eyes. "Is she okay though? Having contractions or something?" But surely TJ wouldn't go to Travis' place if Hope was actually in labor.

"No. She's completely fine. Says I'm being ridiculous and that she doesn't need anyone here with her. But I'm not leaving her alone. You're the only one we could agree on calling."

Peyton felt her eyes widen. "Really?"

"Well, she knows you're always willing to help out and I know that you'll chew her ass if she does something stupid."

Peyton grinned as warmth spread through her chest. They needed her and knew she'd be there for them.

"I'll be right over."

When TJ answered the door ten minutes later, he took one look at her and scowled. "What the hell happened to you?"

She looked down at her legs and feet covered in mud and grinned up at him. "My truck got stuck. Had to get it out."

"By yourself."

She shrugged. "Yeah."

His frown deepened. "Seriously? You could have called me for help."

It was a stupid thing to have hit her right in the heart, but yeah, of course she could have. She was just so programmed to turn to Scott that she never called TJ for stuff. But he would have been there for her. So would Kyle or Derek. Or any number of people.

"Well, *you're* the one needing *my* help right now," she said, with a very satisfied grin.

He ran a hand through his hair. "Apparently you and Hope both got your stubbornness from your father."

Peyton laughed.

TJ gestured down the hall toward the living room. "She's in there."

"I'll go clean up quick," Peyton said, starting for the bathroom.

"Borrow some of Hope's stuff," TJ called after her.

"Okay, thanks."

"And don't tell Scott that you dug yourself out," TJ said. "He'll kick all of our asses," he added with a mutter.

But Peyton just grinned at him over her shoulder.

She was definitely telling Scott. And yeah, he'd have a few words for her she was sure. But then she'd show him all the things she *did* need him for, and he'd forget about the truck and the mud.

She cleaned up and joined Hope in the living room. Her sister was positively glowing from where she rocked in the rocking chair near the front window.

"Hey," Peyton dropped onto the couch.

"Hi." Hope tipped her head, studying Peyton. "You look great."

Peyton laughed. "Do I have mud in my hair?"

Hope shook her head. "No, I mean it. You look great. What's going on?"

Peyton blushed. "Well..."

Hope's eyebrows rose. "Yes?"

"I'm in love."

Hope's face broke into a bright smile. "I know."

"You do?"

"Of course."

Hope was one of those people that had an innate ability to read people. It seemed that she was especially good at it with Peyton and TJ. Hope always said it was because of how much she loved them.

"And I've decided to get married," Peyton said. She fought a smile. She'd love to shock Hope for once. It seemed that her sister was always a step ahead of her even when it came to her own thoughts and feelings though.

Hope nodded. "Good." She didn't seem shocked at all.

"Really? Even considering my whole background and knowing nothing about marriage?" Peyton asked.

"Really. Because of your whole background," Hope said with a nod. "You'll be great at it."

Peyton sat up straighter. "You think so?" There was no person on the earth who had an opinion that mattered more to her than Hope's did. She felt her heartbeat stuttering in her chest.

"Of course. You have so much love pent up inside of you that you can barely keep it contained now," Hope told her. "Once you really set it free...well, Scott better be ready."

Peyton felt tears pricking her eyelids. "You think I have a lot of love pent up inside?"

"Growing up you didn't really have anywhere to put it," Hope said, absently stroking her hand over her belly. "Your mom and dad didn't seem to really want it and you got good at keeping it inside you so you wouldn't be disappointed. But it's evident every time you make a cake or do a party or pull someone out on the dancefloor."

Hope said it as if it was just a matter of fact. But Peyton felt her chest tightening.

"Really?" she asked softly.

Hope seemed to suddenly realize that Peyton was reeling. She stopped rocking and got awkwardly to her feet to join Peyton on the couch. Hope took her hand. "Really. Peyton, you are an incredibly loving person. And I see it in everything you do. No one could have put that shower together for me like that," she said. "Someone else might have been able to make the cake or make it circus themed if we'd asked, but you came up with that. And you put all the special touches on it. Because you did it with your heart, not just your head."

Peyton blinked rapidly, on the verge of tears.

Hope lifted her hand to Peyton's cheek. "I think Scott Hansen is the perfect guy to take all of that love you have to give."

S cott hit the city limits of Sapphire Falls just after ten p.m. two days later.

He was starving, he was exhausted, his mind was spinning with everything they needed to do to get ready to head back to North Dakota.

But most of all he needed to see Peyton.

He pulled into his driveway, his chest aching at the sight of his dark house. He'd lived alone for so long, how had one little brunette made it so normal to come home to a lit-up house full of life and laughter in just two weeks?

He sighed. Because it was Peyton.

His phone dinged on the seat beside him with a text. He let out a breath. Probably the task force leader again. Or maybe Kyle.

But it wasn't either one. It was Peyton.

I need you.

His heart slammed against his rib cage. He typed back. *Where?*

The sweet shop.

I'm on my way.

He pulled up in front of the shop three minutes later. He strode to the door and pulled on the handle. It was locked.

Well, she was being safe while she was here alone at night. But his entire body was aching with the need to see her, touch her...and tell her she was full of crap. He lifted a fist and banged on the door.

P eyton heard Scott's knock. She'd asked Ed to let her know when Scott got back to town tonight. Ed had parked his cruiser out by the Welcome to Sapphire Falls sign just for her. He'd texted a few minutes ago.

She pulled in a deep breath, smoothed her apron, and headed for the front of the shop.

Her knees actually wobbled when she saw Scott through the glass in the door. He had his hands in his jeans pockets, his white button-down shirt untucked, the sleeves rolled up, and he looked determined, and gorgeous, and her chest hurt just looking at him.

She pulled the door open.

"Hey."

The low, sexy rumble, the way he was looking at her as if he was starving and she was every one of his favorite things, made everything in her clench and strain toward him. But he hadn't called her Trouble. And she knew why. She'd told him she didn't want to be trouble for him. But she wanted to be *his* Trouble.

"Hey." Her voice sounded scratchy.

"So, I've been thinking about what you said about us needing time apart now that we did the two week thing and about me liking you because you have problems I can fix and well,...it's bullshit."

Okay, she hadn't expected him to do the talking. At least not at first. She'd called *him*. "I'm sorry? Bullshit?"

"Yeah," he told her with a nod. "It's crap. This whole thing about me needing someone who I could fix? No, Peyton. That's not it. If I just needed to clean gutters and fix cars to feel good about myself, there are about a dozen little old ladies in this town —and men for that matter, three or four divorcees, and a couple of single moms who I could have done that for. I wanted to do things for *you* because I love you. And as for me not going back to the task force because of you? Also bullshit. Yes, I wanted to be here instead. Because I wanted to have a relationship with you. I couldn't do that from another state. And honestly? I couldn't go back to the task force until I had you solidly and permanently in my life. You want to know why? Because you make me believe in the happy, Peyton. The happy that I *need* there to be in the world.

The happy I want to fight for. The happy that makes me get up in the morning, put on my badge, and go to places like North Dakota.

You not only found it, you grabbed onto it with both hands and squeezed every ounce of it out of every situation. You could have let all of the crap around you take over and mute your voice and hide your light. But that didn't happen. You made noise." He shook his head with a slight laugh. "Damn, did you make noise. And you shone. Was it always super positive and impressive? Maybe not. But you've been out there doing your thing all along. And your thing is being you—being bright and beautiful and finding fun and laughter and bringing it to others, *in spite of* all of the crap. And I need you to bring it to *me*. Every day.

And here's what I can give you in return, besides clean gutters. A place where you don't have to be loud and bright and crazy to be noticed. Because I notice everything. I *see* you, Peyton. You are everything that I want and need to believe in."

She felt the air whoosh out of her lungs. She swallowed hard and tried to blink the tears out of her eyes. "I had so many things I was going to say. I don't remember any of them right now."

"Well, here's the deal," he said, stepping closer to the threshold, but not yet coming inside. "I love you. That's not going to change. You can move back to your house, you can do whatever you want, however you want or need to do it, but I'm going to be here, loving you, picking you up when you need a ride, checking on you when you take a trip, hauling your pretty butt...hell, wherever it needs to go. And on the nights when you just want to watch TV or make a meatloaf or just need someone to hold you, you know where to find me."

She stared at him. "After everything, you'd go back to how it was before?"

"If that's all I can have. Will I like it? No. But damn, girl, I'm yours. What else am I going to do?"

Her heart hurt. But now it wasn't because of the loss or the fear. It was because there was so much love in it, it was filled far beyond its previous capacity. She wet her lips. "No matter what I do? No matter how long it's been? No matter anything?"

"Yep, just like always."

"Well, what if I don't want it to be like always?" she asked.

"Too damned bad," he told her firmly.

She smiled. "I mean, what if I want more? What if I want a relationship?"

He paused for a beat. "Wow, you said the R word without shuddering," he said, hope lighting his eyes.

She nodded. "Turns out, I'm only allergic to them when they're with people other than you."

"Well...that is excellent news," he said. He took a step over the threshold.

"And what if I quit nursing school? Or actually, never even officially started?"

He blinked. "Okay. If that's what you want."

"I wanted it because it was a way to take care of people, but turns out, I already do that." She spread her arms so he could really see the front of her apron. "I make cakes. And I throw kickass parties. And I want to be known as the area Party Girl."

He studied her apron. It was white with a huge caricature of her on the front with Party Girl underneath. Riley Ames had helped her with the logo last night at the Come Again after-hours.

He smiled, his expression partly amused and partly confused. "What's this?"

"My new business. Or my part of the business. Party Girl Party Planning is now an official part of Scott's Sweets. And I'm a partner."

He seemed to be thinking about that. Then he finally nodded. "That's perfect."

"You think so?" She really wanted him to think so.

"There are lots of ways to make people better," he said. He moved closer to her and completely into the shop. "You make people happy. You help them celebrate huge events in their lives. It's not just cake. Remember what we talked about? How it's important to celebrate things and make happiness a priority and work at being joyful in the face of all the bad stuff?"

She nodded.

He reached out and took her by the upper arms. "You're a part of that in this town. You're the one who gets people together and turns up the music and tells the jokes."

She felt her heart trip a little. "And I make the cakes."

"And you make the cakes," he said with a nod. "Do you remember what you told me on St. Patrick's Day?"

"That you were the best sex I'd ever had handcuffed on the hood of a police car?" she asked.

His eyes heated slightly but he shook his head. "You told me that your grandma had thrown you birthday parties when you were little—up until you were eight and she passed away."

Peyton swallowed hard. Yeah, she'd told him that. What the hell had been the deal on St. Patty's Day? She hadn't even been drunk. But she'd lain down on the backseat of his squad car, and spilled her guts.

"And you told me that you'd missed them after she was gone. You told me that having that special day, when someone went out of their way to make you feel important and surround you with all of your favorite things, is what made you love parties. And that when you were fourteen, you started throwing birthday parties for yourself." Scott pulled her closer. "And now you love throwing parties for other people and making them feel special."

She nodded.

"That's important stuff. How many times has someone asked you for something basic—a plate of cookies or a simple chocolate cake—and you've talked them into something bigger, something amazing that was absolutely perfect?"

"Well, that's just good salesmanship," Peyton told him. "Always try to upsell the customer."

Scott shook his head. "You do it because you want them to make it special. Even a good old garden club meeting," he said, reminding her of Emma and the club meeting that had tickled her so much that she'd sent Peyton flowers. "What else did you do besides the cookies for that?"

"The dirt cups with the gummy worms," Peyton said.

"And what else?"

"Nothing." But she focused on his chin instead of his eyes.

He squeezed her arms. "What else?"

She sighed. "She wasn't sure what all they were going to do, so I suggested they play a game where they had to guess the flower by its scent while they were blindfolded."

Scott's mouth curled at the corner. "What else?"

"And they met on her patio, so I just suggested she use watering cans for vases as centerpieces and she give them each a caterpillar kit as a gift."

"A caterpillar kit?"

Peyton felt her cheeks heat but she nodded. "You can buy these kits online. They ship you five caterpillars and everything you need to raise them into butterflies. So they can all raise them and then release them into their gardens."

Scott was quiet for a long moment. Peyton finally peeked up at him through her eyelashes. He was staring at her.

"What?" she asked. "They thought it was amazing."

"Because it *is* amazing," he said.

She felt her smile start. "Yeah?"

"Are you kidding? *Yes.*"

"But it's just butterflies. And cookies. And parties." She lifted a shoulder. "I just always thought I'd do something more...important."

Scott lifted a hand and brushed her hair back. "Peyton, making people happy is important. And you... God, you make people happy."

There was a sincerity in his eyes and his tone that made Peyton's heart thump.

"So, you'll still like me if I'm not a nurse?" she asked.

His grin was quick and full and a little naughty. "Well, since you won't be dressing up like a nurse, I might insist on you wearing an apron...and nothing else...around the house once in a while."

Relief and happiness and lust and a huge shot of bone-deep affection shot through her. Man, she liked this guy. And loved him. He got her. Well, he mostly got her. And even when he didn't, he still wanted her. She gave him a grin. "I think that can be arranged."

"Let's go home. With that apron. Right now," he said, grabbing her hand.

But she dug in her heels. "Hang on."

"There's more?"

She nodded. "Kind of a lot more." She took a breath. "I love you, Scott. More than I even knew it was possible to love someone. And I'm still kind of learning about loving someone like this. But it occurs to me that I have actually been loving people for a long time. I'm just more the baseball-bat-to-the-headlights-of-people-who-hurt-you kind of girl than a verbally *saying*-it kind of girl. So, I'm going to keep working on it, but, in the meantime, if anyone upsets you, just let me know. I know what everyone in town drives."

But he didn't smile. His eyes darkened and his voice was gruff when he said simply, "I love you too, Peyton. So damned much."

She blew out the breath she hadn't realized she'd been hold-ing. "I've never said that to a guy before."

"I've only said it to one girl before you," he said. "And it was when we were seven. And it involved a construction-paper heart, a melted chocolate bar, and some embarrassing hemming and hawing."

Peyton felt her heart expand. This man was...everything. He really was. Yes, she had the bakery and the cakes and the party planning. And she had her friends and maybe even an occasional lunch with her dad. All of that would keep her balanced. But at the end of the day, *Scott* was what mattered. And she was really, completely okay with that. "Well, you did a good job this time," she told him.

He tugged on her hand and drew her up against him. "So, Peyton Wells, will you be my girlfriend? And go out to movies with me? And hold my hand in the square?"

She looped her arms around his neck. "I will."

"And will you bring this apron home, to my house, and wear it, and only it, for the rest of the night?" he asked, skimming his hands down to her ass and pressing her forward.

Peyton wondered if her stomach would ever stop flipping when she felt how much he wanted her. "I will," she said. "But," she added as he started to turn toward the door again, "not until you come into the back with me. I...made you cookies."

"You did?" He lifted a brow.

"I did. And you can go ahead and read all kinds of things into that. As Adrianne said, I can come up with the perfect party for anybody in this town. And I came up with something special for you." She moved around him to shut and lock the bakery door, then she led him into the bakery's kitchen and swept her hand over the tray of cookies she'd just finished decorating.

Scott stopped and stared. Then he moved closer to the coun-tertop. And stared some more.

They were decorated sugar cookies, cut into a variety of shapes.

"A nurse's costume," he said, picking one up. "And a green high-heeled shoe." He looked up with a grin, then went back to studying the tray. "A jar of Booze. A pair of handcuffs. A pink pickup truck. A cookie that's shaped like pancakes?" he asked, glancing up again.

"All of the things that make me think of us," she said.

"There's even a pad of sticky notes," he said, almost like he was in awe.

She laughed. "That one was pretty easy. It's just a square." But she had used the icing to make it look like there were multiple sheets of paper. She was happy he could tell what it was.

He picked up a rectangular cookie. "Nice."

She'd decorated it to look like the front of the *Grey's Anatomy* DVD boxed set. She smiled.

There was also a cop car, a Band-Aid, a crutch, and a bottle of coffee creamer represented.

Finally, he got to the end of the tray. "Is this a vibrator?" he asked, picking up the hot-pink frosted cookie.

She grinned. "Things that make me think of you...and us."

Then he put that one down and picked up the last two.

"And is this supposed to be your breast?" he asked.

"Yep."

"And so this one is your..."

He trailed off suggestively as he held up the cookie that was oblong-shaped and tapered on both ends. She'd used a lot of pink frosting on that one. She gave him a big grin. "Yep."

His eyes locked on hers, he lifted the cookie to his mouth and gave it a long, firm lick, removing most of the frosting in the process. Peyton felt her smile die as heat shot through her body. Damn, she hadn't expected that.

"Delicious," he said. Then he crooked a finger at her. "Come here."

She took two steps forward and he pulled her the rest of the way in. He kissed her long and deep, tasting like frosting...and Scott...and her forever. She sighed happily and threaded her fingers through his hair.

When he lifted his head after several minutes, she said breathlessly, "You didn't see the very last cookie."

"I'm not sure I need to see any more cookies." He took another lick of pink frosting.

Her entire body was buzzing with desire, but he *had* to see the last cookie. "Just one more."

He turned toward the tray and scanned the various shapes. She knew the moment he saw the one she was talking about. He let go of her and reached for it, his expression stunned. He held it up. "What's this?"

"What's it look like?"

He swallowed hard. "It looks like you're giving me a diamond ring shaped cookie."

She pressed her lips together and nodded.

His expression changed almost instantly. His eyes went from surprised to hot and possessive. He wrapped his big arm around her again and pulled her up against his body. "Shouldn't *I* be giving you the diamond ring?"

Peyton felt tears pending as she shook her head. "I think this proposal should come from me."

"I'm going to look silly in a diamond ring," he said, his voice gruff in spite of the teasing words.

She gave him a smile, leaned in, and bit the diamond off the cookie, leaving only a band. "Will you marry me, Scott?"

A shudder went through his body and his arm tightened around her. He closed his eyes for a moment, then opened them and pinned her with an intense stare. "Yes. I will marry you, Peyton."

Emotions too numerous to name, flashed through her. She'd known he'd say yes, but *man*, she had not been prepared for what that would do to her. She took a deep breath and then gave him a smile. Possibly the most joyous, sincere smile of her life.

"Okay, let's go home where you can *really* lick frosting off of my cookie."

He huffed out a laugh. "Is that going to be a new euphemism?"

She nodded. "Definitely. And I'm going to be wearing this apron tonight while you do it. So whenever you see me in it, you'll think of this."

"Considering how much you talk about frosting and," he coughed, "cookies, that could make things...difficult. Often."

She grinned and stepped out of his arms. She started backing out of the kitchen, reaching under her apron and the skirt of her sundress for her panties. She slipped them off and tossed them to him.

"Well, after all, you don't call me Trouble for nothing."

MORE FROM SAPPHIRE FALLS!

Enjoy this excerpt from
After You
the next love story from Sapphire Falls!

Don't miss Kyle and Hannah's funny, sexy second-chance romance!

Only one thing has not gone according to Kyle Ames' grand life plan.

Hannah McIntire.

She was his first love, the woman he planned to make his wife, the one that got away—all that silly romantic crap that ended up biting him in the ass.

Two years ago, Hannah broke his heart and ruined all of his dreams... not necessarily in that order. Which has been, well, not exactly *fine*, but it's been something Kyle can, well, not exactly *forget*, but he's *handling* it because he doesn't have to see her every day.

In fact, Kyle had kind-of hoped to keep up with the not-seeing-Hannah thing for at least a couple more years. Or a couple more decades. Or forever.

But now she's back in town to help her grandmother, Kyle's patient and one of his favorite people, recover from hip surgery. Okay, so *two* things haven't gone according to Kyle's plans.

It's only for six weeks. Surely Hannah can survive living in her hometown, facing her family, and seeing Kyle again for six short weeks. But it won't hurt to have a pretend boyfriend, her best friend Michael, along. Everyone thinks he's the reason she's been gone for the past two years anyway. Having him there are a buffer will be good. Just in case her family won't talk to her. Or she feels the urge to spill all of her secrets. Or the urge to take her clothes off for Kyle. Little things like that.

But it quickly becomes apparent that she and Michael are never going to be able to convince the people who know Hannah best that they're madly in love. Which means she might just have to tell Kyle what really happened two years ago. And she's just not quite ready to confess all of the ways she majorly screwed up. And all the ways things can never go back to the way they were.

Kyle and Alice, Hannah's grandmother, are certainly not making anything easier by conspiring to constantly remind Hannah of everything she misses about Sapphire Falls.

And then there's the not-so-tiny complication of falling in love with Kyle all over again. And the fact that he's falling for her too. And that they're both realizing that maybe *this* time they're doing it right.

EXCERPT

He sighed. "Okay, so we need a plan."

A plan. Of course they did. "A plan for what?"

"You realize that Alice is planning on launching a whole campaign to convince you to come home, right?"

Hannah felt her heart thump. "She is?"

"Yes. She thinks that all you need is to be reminded of everything you left here. That after six weeks, there's no way you're going to want to leave."

Oh boy...

"So over the next six weeks, I'm going to try to win you back."

Hannah froze at that. She stared at Kyle. "Back?"

"Yes."

"You mean...romantically?"

"Yes."

"You want me back?"

"No."

Oh. Okay. Right. She blinked at him. That kind of hurt. But she was also completely confused. "I don't get it."

"Your grandmother wants you back. And she thinks *I'm* the key to getting you to come home."

Hannah blew out a breath. Wow. That was...not as easy as it sounded, but not as off base as it should be. If Kyle could adjust his plans, imagine a different life, forgive her for messing everything up, and love her in spite of her no longer checking all of the boxes on *his* Ms. Perfect List then...

But no, that wouldn't happen. One thing she had figured out while in Seattle and away from everything here was that she and Kyle had been drawn together more by practicality than by passion. Oh, things had been hot sexually between them. There was definite chemistry. But if she'd wanted to travel the world as a belly dancer or go into botany or open a winery, he would have never asked her out on that second date. Because yeah, they'd talked about their plans and aspirations on date one. That was how Kyle Ames rolled. He'd known what he was looking for, she'd answered all the questions correctly, so she'd gotten the job of girlfriend and future wife. Not that she'd ever doubted for one second that she wanted that job.

"I'll talk to her," Hannah promised. "I'll convince her that I'm happy in Seattle."

Kyle's jaw ticked again at that, but he just said, "Talking to her isn't enough. I've tried that. My grandma's tried that. Your mom and dad have tried that."

Ouch. Hannah didn't know that her parents had been telling her grandma that there was no way Hannah was coming home. She wasn't sure how she felt about them believing that. Especially since it was the truth. Or was supposed to be anyway.

"She thinks that she knows you best," Kyle continued. "And that you actually want to come home, but something is keeping you in Seattle. She also thinks that if I forgive you and show you that you can have everything you left behind again, you'll change your mind and move home."

Hannah's heart stuttered. "But you don't want to give me everything I left behind."

"No. You made your choice, and *I* understand that. I'm over it."

She nodded. "Got it."

"But I'm going to help Alice get over it too. She has this idea that we're fated to be together, and that it's only a matter of time before we're back together. I'm going to help you *show* her that you don't want Sapphire Falls, and that none of that is going to happen."

Hannah knew that the painful thump in her chest at the idea that she and Kyle were *not* fated to be together was ridiculous. Her grandmother had always talked about fate, had loved fairy tales, and believed in soul mates. Hannah, on the other hand, knew that things happened and people made choices—and mistakes. Hannah crossed her arms. "How?"

"I'm going to do exactly what she wants me to do—give you a second chance."

There's more to it, don't overreact, she told herself, but she still felt her heart flutter. Stupidly.

Kyle frowned. "And you're going to turn it all down."

Return to Sapphire Falls with After You!

ABOUT THE AUTHOR

Erin Nicholas is the New York Times and USA Today bestselling author of over thirty sexy contemporary romances. Her stories have been described as toe-curling, enchanting, steamy and fun. She loves to write about reluctant heroes, imperfect heroines and happily ever afters. She lives in the Midwest with her husband who only wants to read the sex scenes in her books, her kids who will never read the sex scenes in her books, and family and friends who say they're shocked by the sex scenes in her books (yeah, right!).

Sign up for Erin's newsletter and never miss any news!

Find ALL of her books right here!
http://www.erinnicholas.com

And find Erin at
www.ErinNicholas.com,
on Twitter and on Facebook

<u>Join her SUPER FAN page on Facebook</u> for insider peeks, exclusive giveaways, chats and more!

MORE FROM ERIN NICHOLAS

More sexy, contemporary romance...

Now Available at all book retailers!
Sapphire Falls

Welcome to Sapphire Falls
Getting Out of Hand
Getting Worked Up
Getting Dirty

Naughty and Nice in Sapphire Falls
Getting In the Spirit, Christmas novella
Getting In the Mood, Valentine's Day novella
Getting to the Church On Time, wedding novella

Ferris Wheels & Fireflies in Sapphire Falls
Getting It All

Getting Lucky
Getting Over It
Getting to Her (companion novella)
Getting His Way

Ever After in Sapphire Falls
After All
After You
After Tonight (coming spring 2018)

Lots more from Sapphire Falls at
www.SapphireFalls.net

If you love Sapphire Falls,
you'll love

Billionaires in Blue Jeans
Diamonds and Dirt Roads
High Heels and Haystacks
Cashmere and Camo

CPSIA information can be obtained
at www.ICGtesting.com
Printed in the USA
LVHW04s1640260618
581952LV00004B/872/P